CLOISTERS
ARTHUR AVENUE
T0357251
BOTANICAL GARDEN
TAXI
YANKEE
STADIUM
THE BRONX
QUEENS

SUMMER IN THE CITY

WILLIAM MORROW
An Imprint of HarperCollins*Publishers*

SUMMER IN THE CITY

A NOVEL

ALEX ASTER

This is a work of fiction. Names, characters, places, and incidents are products of the author's imagination or are used fictitiously and are not to be construed as real. Any resemblance to actual events, locales, organizations, or persons, living or dead, is entirely coincidental.

FIRST EDITION

Designed by Nancy Singer

Endpaper illustrations by Ruby Taylor/Central Illustration Agency

Art credits: pp. ii–iii: New York City skyline ©chuck/stock.adobe.com; pp. 1, 268: cinema clapperboard ©Bulgakova Kristina/stock.adobe.com; pp. 9, 222, 265: airplane ©Vectors Point/stock.adobe.com; pp. 13, 85, 198, 248: New York skylines ©phant/stock.adobe.com; p. 20: milkshake and sandwich ©Artlana/stock.adobe.com; pp. 26, 179: computer ©olllikeballoon/stock.adobe.com; pp. 32, 78, 141: coffee cup ©dimagroshev/stock.adobe.com; pp. 37, 54, 71, 92, 99, 206, 216, 254: clock, Empire State Building, Flat Iron, tenement ©redchocolatte/stock.adobe.com; p. 62: fountain ©B.inna/stock.adobe.com; pp. 123, 193: gems ©Alina Pear/stock.adobe.com; p. 151 pizza ©StanMikov/stock.adobe.com; pp. 166, 232: flowers ©FourLeafLover /stock.adobe.com; p. 210: ice cream tub ©josepperianes/stock.adobe.com; p. 210: spoon ©Visual Generation/stock.adobe.com; p. 257: taxi ©Софи Веснина/stock.adobe.com; p. 243: Eiffel Tower ©saint_antonio/stock.adobe.com.

Library of Congress Cataloging-in-Publication Data has been applied for.

ISBN 978-0-06-344580-2

ISBN 978-0-06-341166-1 (hardcover deluxe limited edition)

25 26 27 28 29 RTLO 10 9 8 7 6 5 4 3 2 1

For my love—you make every day feel like summer

SUMMER IN THE CITY

1

IN NEW YORK CITY, EVERY WEEKEND IS A CHANCE TO LIVE IN A MOVIE. DRINKS on a rooftop in the shadow of a skyline cut like it was custom-made for you, glittering just for that highly saturated and Facetuned-within-an-inch-of-itself picture you're about to post. Dinner seated next to a celebrity who doesn't touch any of their food and loudly discusses gossip about a movie star that might make you choke on your gin and tonic. A party with drugs that look like pieces of candy, spread across a marble table in a penthouse that has back rooms for the staff and a Pilates studio as big as your studio apartment.

Unless, of course, you're like me, and a perfect Friday night looks less like mooching your way into the periphery of a table at Marquee, and more like watching Netflix in some ratty shirt that once belonged to your college roommate's ex-boyfriend. A shirt you might have stolen in one of your weaker moments, because you kind of pined for him as much as you pine for that weekly pint of Ben & Jerry's you *swear* you're only going to have a few scoops of, truly believing in your self-control, right up until the spoon bluntly hits the cardboard at the bottom.

"Sorry!"

I suck in my breath like I've been sucker punched, because some girl wearing stilettos with heels the size of knitting needles just stepped on my toe.

I had my wisdom teeth taken out without anesthetic by a dental student my mother really shouldn't have trusted.

This hurts more.

Just as I'm considering an intelligible string of profanities and wondering if it's possible to press charges against a heel, a gentle hand comes down on my shoulder.

Penelope, my best friend and former college roommate with the great taste in guys but not so great taste in the idea of a good night, sighs, looking down at me with the pitying look of a near-professional partier staring down a newbie. "That's why you don't wear open-toed heels to a club, Elle."

Taking a deep breath, my toe throbbing like a heart going into cardiac arrest, I say, "I don't *have* other heels. And I've never been to a club."

Penelope stares at me for a solid ten seconds before frowning. "You know, I can't decide which of those statements is more tragic."

I give her a look. "We've been here nearly two hours. Soon, I'll turn into a pumpkin. You have fifteen more minutes."

The only way I let Penelope drag me away from the comfort of my foams-like-a-cappuccino comforter was the promise that we would be here an hour, tops, and that we would get fries at the place around the corner that sells them only after midnight. Also, because tonight was supposed to be tamer. Some important business magazine rented the club out to celebrate the companies that made its list of Next Big Exits. Penelope's trying to network with a legendary VC who funds the company at the top of the list, Atomic.

It's technically a work outing.

"Fine, fine." She takes my hand and latches it to the corner of the bar, a captain tying a boat to a dock. The marble is as sticky as you would imagine. "Stay here," she orders. Then she seamlessly braids herself within the crowd with the ease of someone who has memorized the mazes of New York City's dark, sweaty, sticky underground.

I don't listen. There's a couple next to me that's grinding so hard, I wonder if their clothes will just burn away from the friction, escalating into full-on intercourse. And if that would be considered strange in a place like this. I try to make myself as small as I can, while shielding my body, elbows tucked in tight, before diving headfirst into the mess in a desperate attempt to find the bathroom to inspect the damage done to my foot.

As quickly as I'm sucked in, I'm spit out of the crowd, deposited into a far quieter corner of the club.

Quieter—but not much emptier.

There's a line snaking out of the single bathroom.

Single. I frown. Surely a club of this size has more than *one.*

I find a bouncer standing against the wall, scanning the club with the diligence of a Secret Service agent.

"Um, excuse me?" I poke an arm wider than my head. It takes three pokes for the giant to even register my presence. When he does, his eyes narrow, inspecting me like I might be in violation of some club rule.

Do clubs have rules?

Have I broken one in speaking to him?

I swallow. "Is—is there just one?" I ask, pointing toward the bathroom.

He grunts and nods, and I know how to take a hint to get out of a person's general vicinity, so I back away, back toward the line.

After five minutes, when it hasn't moved in the slightest, I decide to use my phone's light to study my toe.

It's fine. Which really is just a testament to my toe, because I was expecting a hole in it, or at least a broken nail.

Satisfied that I still have all my digits, I sigh and look at the time. Eight minutes. Penelope has eight minutes.

"Having fun?"

The voice comes from so far above me, I'm forced to look up—and up and up—to see the source. Another bouncer. Taller than the other one, decked out in the same all black.

I blink.

Is having fun a rule?

I internally roll my eyes at myself. *Don't be stupid, Elle.*

Though . . . maybe not so stupid. I can imagine exclusive clubs like these, the ones with a block-long line of gorgeous people in packs waiting in the rain to get in, would kick someone out just for *looking* like they weren't having fun. Wouldn't want a sourpuss ruining the mood, right? Maybe the magazine has strict orders to keep the ambience pleasant for all the entrepreneurs in their forties and fifties littering the dance floor, hiding their wedding bands in their pockets?

I shrug inwardly. Who cares? I'm leaving anyway—I glance down at my phone—in seven minutes.

So, I tell the truth. "No."

He raises an eyebrow. He glances around at the club, then at me, looking genuinely confused. "No?"

Do I look like the type of person who thinks all of this—the floor sticky with alcohol, my long dark hair wet with someone's drink it accidentally dipped into, sweat sliding down the middle of my chest from all the proximity—is *fun*?

Interesting. The idea I managed to blend into this crowd is a little . . . thrilling? This completely foreign, wild—

The bouncer is still frowning down at me.

I sigh. "Look, if you're going to kick me out, just do it already. Save the judgment."

His frown deepens. "Kick you out?"

"Yeah." I wave him up and down. "Aren't you, like, a bouncer?"

"You think I work here?"

Now, it's my turn to frown. "You don't?"

His eyes glisten with something. Excitement, maybe. He bends down, so close I can smell the mint in his breath. "What gave me away?"

What, is he a secret type of security? Meant to blend in?

Wow, clubs are weird.

I shrug a bit haughtily, slinking further into my role of a New York party person, the type of twenty-five-year-old who talks to guys in dark corners of clubs. "Well, you're huge, for starters."

He seems to balk at the word "huge." I roll my eyes.

"You're, like, a foot taller than me. In *heels*. And . . ." I motion to his arms and find myself staring. His shoulders are so wide, they look like cliffs. And his arms, his *arms* bulging in his—I clear my throat. "And your outfit. The all black."

He nods slowly, considering.

"If you're supposed to be discreet, you should try to blend in more," I say, high on my own confidence. Now I'm truly playing someone else. Someone who tells total strangers how to do their jobs.

His lips curl into a smile. He dips even lower, until his mouth is nearly at my ear. "Well, between you and me, this is my last night."

"It is?"

He nods. "And *you* could be more discreet as well."

My eyebrows come together. "With what?"

He raises a shoulder. "Everyone knows the types of people who come here, to this club, on nights like these. Who mill around the bathroom, where it's quiet . . . Who come to party with naive tech millionaires."

I'm genuinely confused now. And strangely intrigued. What kind of person does he think I am?

He continues. "Who wear heels like those"—his gaze travels up my legs—"and a skirt like that." His eyes trail up my body, and it's like they're casting flames. Heat pools in my stomach. I've had a couple of drinks—which might as well have been five, considering the strongest thing I usually drink is Penelope's kombucha—and the attention is even more intoxicating. How long has it been since someone has looked at me like this? How long since I've worn a skirt so short, I'm one wrong move away from showing my underwear?

There's another reason I agreed to go out with Penelope. This is my last night in New York City. Tomorrow, I'll be across the country. For good.

That's why I agreed to wear this outfit, to be out past midnight, to have a last chance at my own movie moment.

His eyes linger on my chest before finally finding mine. And I'm nearly knocked off my precarious heels at the intensity there. Pure want.

Like he's looking for his final chance at a movie moment too.

I'm not sure who moves first—but before I know it, we're in a stairwell. And I'm pressed against a wall. We're both breathing too quickly, my neck is craned up, his down.

And this isn't *me,* and this is a *stranger,* but it's the closest thing to a movie moment I've ever had, so I grasp it and his face, and suddenly, his lips are on mine.

It's a frenzy.

His mouth is hot against my mouth, my neck, my chest, and then he's lifting me, with an ease that makes me breathless, and my legs are wrapped around his middle. His giant hands are gripping my ass, and he's driving his hips into mine, and I'm seeing stars.

One of his hands is beneath my shirt. His rough fingertips gently trace the lace of my bra, then his thumb slips under it, right across—

I pull back, and it's like I've sobered up a bit in the last few moments. Or maybe it's the fact that the light here is brighter than in the club.

Because I can actually see him now, and he's *perfect.* Piercing green eyes. Dark hair that's a little too long, so it curls around his ears. Cheekbones like the panes of an emerald-cut diamond. Probably one of those models who work at clubs to pay their rent. Maybe it's his last night because he's finally booked something good.

"What do you want?" he demands, deep voice knocking me out of my thoughts.

Still breathless, I manage to say, "What?"

He's breathless too, but his eyes are surprisingly clear as they pin me in place. His hand trails back down my stomach, calluses scraping, making me shiver. "I want to take you home," he says very carefully, like he's making sure I understand every word coming out of his mouth. "What can I do to make that happen?"

He studies my body again, like he can't help himself. I stare too and see that my skirt is just a bundle of fabric around my middle. I gasp and meet his eyes again. He's waiting for my answer, looking at me so closely it's like he's trying to see through me.

"What. Do. You. Want?"

My heels clank as I unlock my legs, landing back on my own two feet, nearly falling over in the process. He steadies me, but I shove away his help. "What do you mean, *what do I want*?"

He shrugs a shoulder. "Everyone wants something." He looks unfazed by the anger building in my expression. "I want you." He motions toward himself. "Am I enough for you? Or . . . is there something else?"

For a moment I'm shocked by his words. I almost want to laugh.

Then I'm furious.

"You want to *pay* me?"

He gives me a look. "No. I don't pay for sex. But"—he sighs—"would you like me to take you to dinner? Or a helicopter ride over the city?" He looks completely serious when he says, "That's what you want, right? Why you're here?"

I blink. Though he's basically describing dating, I don't like what he's insinuating. I don't like that he's painting me as wanting anything from him beyond a good time.

I remember his words from before. About what *kind of person I am*.

A person who could be enticed into someone's bed because of their money.

"So that's what this is? You think you can buy someone's affection? Take them on a fancy date and woo them into your bed?"

He lifts a shoulder. "I can buy anything I want."

I'm seeing red. *Who does this guy think he is?* "Clearly not," I say, before ripping the door open and walking back into the club.

Movie moment officially over.

The sudden blaring of music is temporarily disarming. I nearly trip in these stupid, *stupid* heels before a hand shoots out and steadies me. Penelope.

"I was looking everywhere for you!" she says, face panicked in a two-minutes-away-from-calling-*Dateline* kind of way. "What were you doing in the *stairwell*—"

The door behind us opens again, and the guy every single part of me was just completely pressed against walks through it.

Her eyebrows travel almost all the way to her hairline. "—with the CEO of Atomic . . . ?"

I blink. Turn slowly in the direction of the towering figure who I can still taste in my mouth. "The *what*?"

He looks unfazed. Raises an eyebrow. "Does that change anything?"

I almost do something I would certainly regret later. Would have, but Penelope takes both of my hands in hers, and all I manage to do is get really close to his face and say, "I hope this tech bubble pops and your stupid start-up dies a slow, *painful* death."

We leave before we're escorted out of the party by *actual* bouncers. And it's only outside, under the lights of New York City at 2:00 a.m., a block away from the French fry place, and far enough from where I left my dignity, that I turn to Penelope and say, "I think that jerk called me a gold digger."

2

TWO YEARS LATER

"YOU KNOW, IT'S PRETTY EASY NOWADAYS TO SELL A COMPANY FOR BILLIONS of dollars. It's really not that impressive."

I'm pressing my phone so tightly against my ear that I can hear Penelope sigh, even past the intercom voice telling me that *baggage and other personal items should not be left unattended,* the kid riding their robot suitcase into the bookshelf a few feet away, and the flight attendant at the closest gate berating passengers for flooding the boarding area before their group has been called.

"Keep telling yourself that, Elle," Penelope finally says.

It's been years, and the sight of those green eyes, looking at me from that same business magazine that had hosted that party—on the *cover* this time—still fills me with rage. He didn't even attempt to look pleasant in the picture, staring down the photographer, and now *me,* with an apathy that hints at having been forced into doing the photo shoot.

Below sits a headline that makes me want to break my phone into tiny shards and completely discredits my ability to curse others into oblivion:

"Atomic Sells to Virion for $10 Billion."

"They're calling him the Billionaire Bachelor," Penelope continues, while I shove another magazine in front of the whole row of them, erasing him, and walk out of the Hudson News toward my gate. Because apparently, she didn't get the memo that she's supposed to hate him as much as I do.

When I tell her so, she scoffs. "We both agree, he's a jerk. But you'll never see him again, who cares?"

I care, I want to say, but I already sound pathetic enough for keeping this grudge for so long. So he lied about his identity and made out with me in a stairwell for a few minutes, basically accusing me of being some sort of money-grubber. Big deal.

Yes.

Big. Deal.

"Can we talk about something else?" I snap. "Like, maybe, how much you'll miss me? How you won't know what to do with yourself in LA while your best friend is forced back into the perpetual flash mob that is New York City?"

Penelope laughs. "First of all, *you* brought him up. Again," she mutters, before smartly moving on. "And yes, Elle, I don't know how I'll survive these next three months without you. I'm definitely not going to do things you refuse to do, like go to the beach or the boardwalk, or on a hike, or literally anything that involves changing out of sweats."

I wish we were on FaceTime so she could see the depths of my glare.

"Or . . . hang out with that hot surgeon who wears the scrubs with the drawstrings . . ."

I stop right in the middle of the terminal, earning myself a splash of burning hot coffee on my sleeve, from the person who just ran into me. "He called?"

I can almost see Penelope's grin, can picture her sitting with her knees to her chest, making a shelf for her chin to rest on. "He didn't just call . . . he showed up at my house. Said it took him hours to find my address."

My head rearing back, I blink. "And . . ."

"Yes, Elle, I liked it. You know better than anyone that disturbing behavior is only really disturbing—"

"If you don't think the guy is attractive. I know, I know. Like Edward watching Bella sleep in *Twilight*."

Someone at the gate I've finally arrived at shoots me a strange look, and I stare them down until they look away.

"Okay, *then* what happened?"

Penelope sighs. "He brought prosciutto and prosecco from the same region of Italy my family is from—he found that information online somewhere too—and used his own set of expensive knives to slice the meat himself!"

I wince. "Okay, don't take this the wrong way, but are you *sure* he's not a serial killer?"

"He's not a serial killer. He's just committed."

"Um . . ."

She clicks her tongue. "Don't worry. I already did a full internet sweep of him. Followed all his past girlfriends with my shadow account. Put a Google Alert for his name. Verified his identity back to middle school—he went to a *really* good one, by the way. You know. All the normal stuff."

I tilt my head and shift the phone to my other ear. "Okay, are you sure *you're* not a serial killer?"

The guy is almost certainly not a serial killer, and not just because statistically, there are only about twelve active serial killers at one time (thank you, true crime podcasts that help me fall asleep).

No, I can pretty much guarantee he's a *truly good guy,* which in LA is to be treated with the care and reverence of encountering an endangered species. Penelope has a habit of attracting the best men. It's almost uncanny. She says it's her freckles, they make her seem friendlier. I don't know what the science on that is.

Whereas most people would have happily run off into the sunset with any of the men Penelope has been with, she allows each only a handful of months before calling it off. She leaves heartbroken men in her wake and never brings them up again.

She's awful. She once broke up with a guy by Postmating him a giant cookie cake with a sad face on it and RSVP'ing no to his sister's wedding.

She's my best friend and I would protect her to the ends of the earth.

"Funny," Penelope says. "They're calling your boarding group, Elle. Wishing you a hot seatmate and minimal turbulence!"

Then she's gone.

And I'm on a plane back to the city I swore I would never return to.

3

SUMMER IN NEW YORK CITY IS A HELLSCAPE.

It's hotter than my hometown in Southern California, and that heat is reflected off two-hundred-feet-tall glorified mirrors that shoot the sun right into your face. All the rich people flee to the Hamptons Friday afternoon like clockwork, and the *really* rich ones don't come back until September, when the heat has fizzled away and it's a comfortable, balmy, practically fall situation.

June is not that.

By the time I haul my suitcases into the building lobby, I'm drenched in sweat. My hair is stringy and stuck to my face, and my light gray lounge set is now dark gray with perspiration.

The doorman does his best not to wince.

"Oh, yes. *Elle*. We've been expecting you. Let me get those."

Before I can half-heartedly insist on carrying them myself, all my things are loaded onto a luggage cart and deposited, with me, into an elevator that's more spacious than the bathroom in my place in LA.

One of the top buttons is pressed.

There are just two units on this entire floor, and I'm about to spend my summer in one of them.

I unlock the door with my phone, already knowing with near certainty that I will get locked out one day because I'm terrible at keeping anything charged, and almost trip over the threshold.

The ceilings are twenty feet tall. Windows eat up the entire back of the room and show the city in a wider crop than I've ever seen it in. There's so *much* of it, unobstructed, and so high above buildings that would normally block the bulk of the skyline from view.

This is insanity.

Everything is relative. We think of things compared with other things. I learned that in a marketing class Penelope roped me into in college. Twenty-five dollars is expensive for lunch, but not for a dress. Two hundred thousand dollars is a lot of money for a wedding, but not for a house.

This apartment is big for an office, for a restaurant.

This is huge for a house *period,* let alone one right in the middle of Manhattan.

My luggage filled up a hefty fraction of the apartment I just left. It's a pathetic heap in this huge living room now.

Who needs this much space? I ask myself as I walk farther inside, feeling smaller and smaller with each step.

It's just not practical. This room alone would need an army of Roombas to keep it clean. I hope that's not a responsibility I'm meant to take on.

House-sitting during renovations. That's it. That's all I signed up for.

Rolling my shoulders and bending over with an impressive—and concerning for twenty-seven—crack, I go straight for my laptop, sticking out of my tote the way a baguette might if I were in some Netflix movie set in Paris. But I'm not in Paris.

Or in a movie.

I'm just writing one.

There's a blank page before me, and I struggle to fill it, flight-tired fingers working overtime to get the words out: small observations, little ideas, kernels I hope will pop into some movie-worthy popcorn. All about a city I hate. A city that smells way worse than I remember.

Right on cue, my phone rings, and I take a deep breath before smoothing my annoyance into a semi-agreeable "Hey, Sarah."

"Elle! Big summer in the city. How's it going so far?"

I stare at the time on the oven. "Um . . . I've been here two hours." And one of those hours was spent in an Uber that smelled like a sandwich was decomposing under the seat.

She laughs, then sighs wistfully. "Still, the city slips on like a sweater, doesn't it? So comforting, so fitting."

"It's ninety-two degrees right now."

Sarah laughs again, like I'm the funniest client she has, and not a screenwriter who has a strict no-comedy policy. Then she gets right to business. "So . . . any ideas yet?"

I blink and am very close to repeating that *I've only been here two hours,* but Sarah is one of the top agents at CAA, and just like my rule for comedy, I also have a strict no-starving-artist policy.

"Not yet," I say, turning to look at the city in question through the giant windows. "But . . . something will come to me. It always does."

"*Always,*" Sarah emphasizes, and it makes my stomach sink.

Because I haven't written anything meaningful in almost a year, and she has no idea.

Because I have only three more months to write a screenplay that could change my life.

Because I'm supposed to set it in a city I hate. A city I thought I had escaped.

She hangs up, and coffee—I need coffee. For the exact opposite reason people normally need it.

I need it to relax.

I force myself to take my laptop, thinking inspiration might strike between here and the closest Blue Bottle, then make my way out of the apartment, even though I know I look like garbage.

Honestly, in New York City, I *prefer* looking like garbage. Never have I once walked the streets of the city in sweats and been catcalled, or had my ear talked off by a barista, or even been *looked* at. And that's how I like it. The few times I had to stop by a bodega dressed up after a dinner or meeting, you would have thought I was a dignitary or reality star or Instagram model. The seas of New York parted for me: suddenly, doors were being held open. The guy at the deli counter, who had been certifiably rude to me on every other occasion, didn't even *recognize* me in a skirt, and I had to keep popping my earphones out and saying "Huh?" because he was trying to make conversation. It's not even about looks, I've decided, because there are thousands of girls more attractive than me in New York. It's almost as if men see a woman who has decided to dress up and immediately think she's dressed up for *them*.

The city's changed in two years. Some stores have been replaced by social media–friendly, pastel-painted cafés. Outdoor seating is apparently a thing now. I don't recognize the names of any of the healthy fast-casual places that will likely be replaced by another concept in six months, then another, and then another, like some endless trendy reincarnation.

I'm picky with my coffee shops.

It's not about the coffee in most cases (though a smooth espresso certainly helps). It's about the stuff people probably don't care about.

The cups: I like a firm sleeve. I like the lids that have the transformer part that covers the drink spout and looks substantial, like a suitable hat for my drink. One that won't crinkle beneath my mouth or fall off.

The space: I like tables tiny enough that no one will try to share one with me, but big enough to fit my laptop and drink and inevitable pastry.

The pastries: I like baked goods that get sourced from bakeries that don't also supply Panera. I like variety. A single cream-filled doughnut. A flavor-ambiguous muffin. A big, flaky croissant that kind of looks like a crab.

The extras: Throw in toast. Bagels. Granola and yogurt.

I could spend my entire life in a good coffee shop, with just my wallet and laptop. Working in one feels like an indulgence, a college experience I got to keep. One of the best parts of my job is that a revolving door of coffee shops can always be my office.

I don't recognize any of these coffee shop names, so I judge the essence of the shops by the people I see inside them.

The ballet-pink one that has the word "matcha" in the name and has a line of aspiring influencers waiting to take pictures in front of a tiny mural that somehow incorporates both coffee *and* wings? Pass.

The hole-in-the-wall with suited-up Wall Street types and to-go cups I've seen at Costco? No thanks.

Finally, I end up in front of a rickety-looking wooden door. The windows are slightly glazed. I would have thought it was a bar if I hadn't seen a woman who looks a lot like me right now—messy bun, sweats, earphones in, laptop under her armpit—walk out eating the crème de la crème of coffee shop croissants: an almond one, dusted with sugar.

It's been the kind of day I'm going to try very hard to forget, but the moment I walk inside this place, I feel . . . at peace. It smells like coffee, cream, and sugar and perfectly steeped tea. There are a dozen tables sprinkled throughout a space with high ceilings and a *skylight,* and there are even couches and a pastry display.

I'm home. I've officially found the coffee shop I'm about to haunt for the next three months and hope they don't post a picture of me on the door with an X for how much I'm going to monopolize one of their tables.

For a few hours, I start to think maybe being back in New York isn't so bad. It *does* have an endless array of coffee shops.

I don't write while I'm at my new favorite table, but I go through all my emails and my to-dos—basically everything *except* for writing. And things start to seem genuinely okay.

Until I leave, filled with coffee and baked goods, feeling kind of like a latte myself, and it begins to rain.

At first, it's just a drizzle. I start to hurry. It's not so bad, just some dampening of my bun, some sprinkles on my hoodie.

Then, without warning, the skies break open, and I'm unceremoniously drenched.

Like a mother whose thoughts go immediately to her child, mine go to my beloved laptop, and I don't waste a moment before slipping it beneath my clothing and protecting it with my life.

I run, nearly losing an eye in a sea of umbrellas, rain pummeling my head so thoroughly that my fancy silk hair tie becomes a victim to the storm and falls away, leaving me with long wet hair clinging to the side of my face.

I'm so drenched that by the time I reach the lobby, I'm almost turned away. Just as I'm about to start banging on the glass, the doorman recognizes me, and this time he *does* wince as I make my way across the marble floor, making squeaking and slopping sounds with every step.

My hair is in my face, my laptop is stuck to my stomach, and I don't even process that there's someone else in the elevator with me—perfectly dry—until we reach to press the same floor number at the same time and our fingers collide.

We turn to look at each other, and I nearly complete the process of becoming a puddle.

It's him.

The guy on the magazine. The guy on the news.

The guy I made out with in a stairwell not too far away from this very elevator.

The Billionaire Bachelor.

Parker Warren.

I look away so quickly, I'm positive he hasn't seen my face. Not that he would recognize me if he did. He's probably hooked up with hundreds of girls since that night, if the press is to be believed. He practically lives on *Daily Mail*'s homepage with the number of stories on him and his dating habits.

He presses our button, and the floor starts moving. Or maybe that's me, maybe I'm about to pass out.

What is he doing here, in this building?

Going to *my* floor?

More often than I would care to admit, I would daydream about seeing him again one day. Shoving in his face that he was completely wrong about everything he thought I was, maybe with an Academy Award for Best Original Screenplay in my hand.

Not looking like a full-on *mop*.

The elevator stops, and I bolt out of it, head down, in the direction of my unit, so quickly that I'm inside before he even takes a step into the hallway.

It's pressed against the other side of the door, breathing too hard, dripping onto the imported hardwood floor, that I hear the only other unit on this floor's door open . . . then close.

He's my floor-mate.

Talk about a movie moment, I think.

Only this time, it's horror.

4

"I MUST HAVE FLIPPED OFF AN EVIL EYE IN A PAST LIFE," I TELL PENELOPE ON THE phone.

She's too busy laughing to string together an intelligible sentence. She keeps starting, then bursting out into a sound that alternates between drowning on dry land and impersonating a witch, and I stay on the line only because I don't want to experience this brand of panic alone.

"You—

"He was—

"The same *floor*—"

When she's finally settled down, she sighs. "Wow, Elle. Karma is so not your boyfriend."

"Did you just quote Taylor Swift?"

"Of course I did." She hums. "So, is he still ridiculously hot?"

Yes. He still looks like a model or professional athlete, not a twenty-nine-year-old tech genius who disrupted an industry and just had a multibillion-dollar exit. It's no wonder the media is so fascinated with him, from a cover piece in *Forbes* to a deep dive in *Cosmo* about why he's never had a serious relationship.

"Not really," I say, hoping that maybe the next time I see him karma *will* have become my boyfriend—nay, my fiancé—and he'll have aged forty years and lost all his hair.

Penelope tsks. "If I didn't know you for almost a decade, I might believe you."

"If I didn't know you for almost a decade, I would have hung up after thirty seconds of your suffocating witch laughing."

That makes her laugh even more. And she really does sound like a suffocating witch.

Penelope is the best thing I got from Columbia and likely the only reason I graduated. After taking a semester off for personal reasons, I thought about just . . . not returning to New York. She's the one who flew across the country to California, packed up my stuff, and forced me to come back with her.

So, I put up with the laugh. No, I *love* the laugh—though you couldn't waterboard me into admitting it to her face.

It's interesting how love colors things I would normally hate into my absolute favorite shade.

"Penelope," I say evenly. She stops laughing, knowing very well that the use of her full name, all four syllables, means a shift to the serious. "What am I going to do?"

She sighs. "Nothing, babe. You live on the same floor, but we both know you're a hermit. You'll only leave to single-handedly keep the nearest coffee shop in business, so you probably won't interact with him again. And if you do . . . pretend you don't remember him." There's a moment of silence. "Can I be honest?"

"You always are." *Sometimes brutally.*

"Elle, he probably doesn't remember you."

There it is: a needle puncturing my lungs, making me feel even more ridiculous for harboring this strange hatred for a practical stranger.

If I dig into it—which I have with my therapist, multiple times—I know it's because he represents everything I hate. He judged me by my appearance, as if I couldn't possibly be successful on my own. As if I *needed* to rely on a guy, as if I were some lecherous gold digger.

Did it cross his mind that I could be a successful screenwriter, who, the very night before he met me, signed a deal to write a movie that ended up grossing over half a billion dollars?

No. He saw me and assumed I was after someone else's money.

Maybe it wouldn't have bothered me so much if my mother hadn't raised me to be fiercely independent. If she hadn't worked two jobs while getting her master's to keep me and my younger sister in a good school after my dad left. If she hadn't told me, since I was a little girl, to never rely on anyone else or let anyone else control me, especially a man.

We are strong, she used to say. *We can get through anything. We don't need anyone else.*

So where does that leave me, now that she's gone?

Thinking of her makes my throat go tight. I reach up to rub my thumb across my necklace, the charm that used to sit along her pulse, the only thing I have left of her other than her lessons.

Since that day in the stairwell, I pinned all my hatred on him. I would look him up every few weeks, like some sort of addiction. Like we were in some sort of one-sided competition. Seeing his face, being reminded of that night, kept me focused. Inspired me to work harder. To be better. To prove to myself—and *him,* if I ever saw him again—that I was the woman my mother had raised. Because that kept her alive, in some way.

"You're right," I say, and she is. Though I've used him as a mental target for two years, he probably doesn't remember me at all. Our encounter lasted all of five minutes. Most people have lots of memories with lots of strangers. Most people don't *remember* strangers.

Penelope shifts the conversation, her voice entirely too casual. "So! In other news, have you . . ."

Written. She abandons her sentence midway through because that word has been banned from our apartment for the last few months while I dealt with . . . whatever this mental block is.

"No. But I've only been here a day. I'm sure inspiration will strike soon."

Penelope agrees. And if I hadn't known her for almost a decade, I might believe her.

PROCRASTINATING HAS MADE ME SURPRISINGLY PRODUCTIVE. I make every excuse not to sit in front of a blank page—cursor mocking me from the sprawling comfort of its home, blinking as if to say, *I'm supposed to move, remember?*—and right now, that means unpacking.

The couple I'm house-sitting for has never actually lived in this apartment before. It's currently in the final stages of renovations—which I'm meant to lightly supervise in exchange for free rent—so most of it is livable. The only unfinished sections include the second powder room—what a thing to have—the master bedroom, and a soon-to-be office bigger than my bedroom at home. My room is the only one currently furnished, and it has a view of a ticking clock tower, the Empire State Building, and about a dozen fire escapes and water towers. The floor is so high up, I see the city through its rooftops, like a giant craning my head down, clouds at my ears, sun on the back of my neck.

When Penelope helped me pack she said, "Elle, you're going to New York for the *summer*."

I said, "Penelope, are you having a stroke?"

She took the sides of my suitcases and shook the contents. "These are all sweaters and sweatpants!" She sighed. "We've lived in LA for years and I haven't seen you wear a dress once, or anything that is remotely flattering on you. Are you allergic to the sun? Are you afraid I'll hate you for having a daily intake of saltine crackers, ice cream, bagels, and lattes and somehow still having a Pilates body?"

My face scrunched. "Pilates body?"

"You know what I mean!"

I really didn't, but now I kind of see her point about the clothes. They're all either faded Columbia merch—because they are soft as pajamas but semi-acceptable to wear outside of my writing cave—or cashmere sweaters that have pilled enough to make an entirely new sweater out of their collective pieces, yoga pants that have never seen a yoga studio, and fuzzy socks. Working at home, on my laptop, for my entire adult life has led me to making clothing choices purely based on comfort and not at all on aesthetics.

There's only one dress in the pile, and it's Penelope's. It's also so short and tight, it could only ever make sense inside the walls of a nightclub. She must have snuck it in, along with her smallest pair of red bottoms.

I roll my eyes and stick them both in the closet, knowing with complete certainty that they will never see New York beyond this custom California Closets shelving.

I take a shower, using three types of my favorite soaps to scrub away the New York City rain and any remaining recollection of the person living just on the other side of the wall. When I get out, it's still slightly drizzling, storm clouds peppering the sky. From this high up, they're waist-level, as if I could open my window and army crawl across them.

Comfort food. That's what I need. Nothing solves a bad day better than a cookies-and-cream milkshake and fried chicken sandwich for dinner. I eat my feast on the floor, in the exact place a Cloud couch will one day reside, with *90 Day Fiancé* set up on my laptop in front of me.

Even I can see it's a sad picture.

First night back in New York City, and this is how I spend it. If I were Penelope, I would be at the most exclusive club, dancing in shoes suction cupped to the bottoms of my feet. If I were my little sister, I'd be at an art gallery opening, using terms like "postmodernism" and eating small squares of food. If I were the main character of my last screenplay,

I would be standing in the middle of a storming Times Square, face up to the sky, smiling, not a care in the world.

But I'm me, and this is what a perfect night has looked like for years.

I go to bed wondering how I let my life get so boring—and when I started noticing.

5

I'M AWOKEN BY BLARING. FLASHING LIGHTS. I POP ONE EYE OPEN AND WONder if I'm in some sort of fever dream, before being told by a sleek, modern robot voice to *make your way to the nearest exit. Do not take the elevators. This is a fire alarm.*

I'm instantly on my feet, and my stomach cramps. Maybe that milkshake and fried chicken sandwich weren't such a great idea. I panic, because I have anxiety and this is about the worst possible situation I can imagine, then inexplicably start feeling myself up to see what I'm wearing instead of just looking down. A tank top and sleep shorts. That's fine. It's probably a million degrees outside.

The robot tells me to get out of my unit, and I do, before rushing back.

My baby!

I grab my laptop off the kitchen counter, shove my phone under my armpit, slide my feet into worn tennis shoes, and throw myself into the hallway.

The robot is louder out here, and so is the blaring. I find the emergency exit stair entrance, then shoulder it. The door slams into something solid—

A person.

Not just any person.

I stand frozen in the doorway, clutching my laptop to my chest, my face illuminated by the no doubt unflattering flashing emergency lights.

It's him. Parker.

And we're back in a stairwell.

Elle, he probably doesn't remember you. Penelope's low, no-bullshit voice is in my head, and she's right. Even now, not soaking wet from the rain, his eyes don't widen with recognition. He doesn't ask me if we've met.

He just glances at my laptop and frowns.

"You're going to carry that down sixty flights of stairs?"

Sixty? I managed to completely forget how high up we were. I let out a laugh that sounds half crazed, especially echoed through the stairwell.

"Nope," I say, shouldering the door back open. "I'll take my chances with the fire."

His arm juts out and catches the door. "You can't just go back to your apartment."

"It's probably a false alarm."

"And if it isn't?"

I cross my arms around my laptop, annoyed. "You were just standing here. You clearly were weighing your options before I came along."

He glares at me, and I would be a liar if I didn't admit that it makes my stomach sort of flip. His eyes are unfairly green, a color I can't imagine being able to have on my face. "Now that you're here, I can't in good conscience let you go back inside. In case this is a real fire."

"How heroic. Are you going to carry me down sixty flights of stairs too? Because I haven't done a moment of exercise since tenth grade PE, so chances are the stairs would take me out before the fire did."

His gaze slides down my body for just a moment before meeting mine again. And for that *just a moment,* it feels like he might be . . . checking me out? "Really?" he says, half bored, half unbelieving.

I think about what Penelope said about the Pilates body, then shake it off. No, he's not admiring my nonexceptional body in this tank top that now seems way too scandalous to be wearing outside and these shorts I've had since freshman year of college. He probably flirts with anything with a pulse, if all those paparazzi photos outside of clubs are any indication. He's never been photographed with the same woman twice.

Not that I read those articles.

I force myself to form the biggest scowl imaginable and sigh. "You know what? I warned you," I say, and push past him down the stairs.

I wasn't lying. My physical exercise for the last few years has mainly consisted of me walking seven steps to my Breville coffee machine, five steps to the bathroom, or four steps to my bed to take a midafternoon nap. Penelope once checked my phone's health app and said, "Elle! You averaged *nine steps* this week? Apple probably thinks you're dead!"

It's descending. It can't be that bad.

After three flights, I'm bent over, heaving like I've run a marathon. I'm convinced he has passed me and climbed down by himself, but when I finally open my eyes, I see him standing there, leaning casually against the wall, like there isn't a blaring fire alarm still going off. "You weren't kidding."

I shake my head, breathless. "Why would I joke about having a body completely devoid of muscle?"

All he does is stare down at me, two piercing green eyes taking me in like I'm a line of code waiting to be deciphered. Then he stretches out his hand.

For a moment I think he's offering to hold my hand, or give me a piggyback ride, or something equally and completely unappealing, but then he scowls at my horrified expression and says, "Your laptop."

I clutch it to my chest and turn away from him, like he's some sort of thief. "No."

He frowns. "No?"

"No. I can carry it." I absolutely cannot. The extra weight is making this descent unbearable.

He looks at me, incredulous. "Do you think I'm going to *steal it*?"

I shrug. "I don't know you."

He lets out a startled laugh. A moment later, his face is back to its favorite stormy expression. "I have plenty of laptops. So as nice as those stickers are—"

I immediately regret the dozen different illustrations of coffee that decorate my laptop's entire top.

"—I don't need yours." He stretches out his hand again.

"Fine." I hand it over and add, "It has a bunch of encryptions and stuff, so even if you wanted to, you couldn't use it."

My laptop has no such thing. Though, honestly, it probably should.

The laptop looks laughably small against his side when it took up almost my entire torso. "Does it now," he says slowly, as if he couldn't break all my imaginary encryptions in five seconds if they truly existed. He graduated top of his class at Stanford and was so good at coding that the US government hired him when he was in high school.

Not that I've looked at his Wikipedia page or anything.

We walk in silence, and I'm impressed that I make it ten more flights of stairs before I lean against the wall, gripping my side. "Go without me," I say, really meaning it. "Save my laptop. There's important stuff on there."

He tilts his head at me. "Then I guess you should probably make it out of the stairwell, since no one will be able to crack your *bunch of encryptions*."

I glare at him and his tone. Then I groan. "Ishouldn'thaveeatenthatmilkshakeandfriedchickensandwich."

"Was that English?"

"I said," I say, wincing, "I shouldn't have eaten that milkshake and fried chicken sandwich."

There's a pause. Then: "I'm pretty sure you *drink* a milkshake, not eat it."

I shake my head, still folded over. "Nope. I eat mine with a spoon. It's ten times more enjoyable and lasts way longer."

I almost feel his eyes on me, but mine are scrunched closed in pain. The cramp in my side feels like being stabbed by an entire knife block.

"Go," I groan. "Seriously. It would be a shame for the world's billionaire count to go from 2,668 to 2,667."

A moment of silence. Two. "You know who I am?"

"Of course I do," I say, my tone grating, reminded again of the fact that he doesn't remember meeting me. "Your face is on every magazine right now." I peer at him over my shoulder. "Sorry, was I supposed to bow in your presence? Congratulate you on your exit? Pitch you my start-up? I don't know the rules."

I think I see the sides of his mouth twitch, but no, that must be an illusion, because a moment later, he's frowning again. "What's your name?" he demands.

"Why?"

"You know mine. It only seems fair I know the name of the person I'm going to die in a stairwell with."

I roll my eyes. "We're not going to die."

There isn't a whiff of smoke, and there are only a few people in the stairwell below, meaning most residents have decided to stay in their units. They're probably smart enough to call the doorman downstairs and ask if it's a false alarm.

"It's Elle."

"Like the magazine?"

I raise an eyebrow. "You know what *Elle* is?"

"They put me on some ridiculous list."

I remember the list now, because I actually read *Elle* and because, *yes, I've read every article that mentions him.* They'd put him on a list of Most Eligible Billionaire Bachelors. It's probably how he got his nickname.

"Come on, Elle," he says, and my traitorous body seems to curl at the way he says my name. "Do it for your child—I mean laptop," he adds, holding it up in one hand. The other, he reaches out to me.

For a few moments, I just glare at it. I remember the words he said to me that one night; I think about the fact that he doesn't even *remember* that night, when it's haunted me for years.

I can buy anything I want.

He implied I would go home with him because of his money, that I would be impressed, instead of repulsed by his utter arrogance and presumption.

You hate him, you hate him, you hate him—

Just then, the blaring comes to an end.

"Thank you, universe," I say, before making my way to the closest door. I shove it open and am happy to be out of the stairwell, away from him.

"Forgetting something?"

I turn around to see him offering me my laptop. I take it, probably more forcefully than I need to, before mumbling a half-baked "Thank you."

We take the elevator back up to our floor, and I don't even look in his direction before rushing into my unit and slipping back into the comfort of my bed.

6

SUMMER IS SUPPOSED TO BE WARM AND REJUVENATING AND INVITING, BUT there is nothing warm and rejuvenating and inviting about me.

I hold grudges like security blankets. I treat everyone I meet like a thief, someone who will inevitably betray me if I'm dumb enough to let them inside my house. I resist change, like if I sit solidly in place and keep everything around me very still, nothing new will come through the net I've cast around my little life, and that means nothing can hurt me. Not anymore.

Not ever again.

Because I am also weak. I have these rules and no desire to grow past them, because the truth is I am a gaping Jenga tower, and I have a sneaking suspicion that I'm just one move away from crumbling.

Last night was a mistake. I shouldn't have spoken a word to him, let alone allowed him to cradle my most valuable possession. His words from years ago *hurt* me; he made me question my sense of self, he made assumptions. I *hate* him.

The hatred is so sharp, so saturated, that I just start writing. I don't know what I'm typing or if it makes any sense. I have no outline or plan, but this is catharsis, this is therapy, this is me turning my nebulous and stinging thoughts into physical shapes on a page, like pinning an emotion down and spreading it open, giving it an autopsy, studying its inner workings, stealing its color, draining it of its hurt and essence, until it is harmless and dead.

When I'm done, I have ten pages, and I'm exhausted, my feelings wrung right out of me and spread onto the page. It's unusable, but at least it's something. At least I'm writing.

And I don't think too hard about the fact that, after months of being stuck in a creative drought, he is the one who finally got me out of it.

THE COFFEE SHOP IS CLAMORING. I USUALLY PREFER A QUIETER environment—no one close enough to look over my shoulder at what I'm writing, no conversation so loud it drowns out my thoughts—but unless I plan on buying the coffee shop and becoming its only patron, I have to deal with it.

For the last few days, I've come here early in the morning and left midafternoon without getting anything done. That is, if you don't count online shopping, checking my horoscope on every site until I find one I like, or looking at photos from college just to make myself feel something.

Today, in addition to my laptop, I have a notebook. This coffee shop has wi-fi, and I'm apparently incapable of resisting the internet and all its various black holes of distractions, so I popped into a place that sells fifteen-dollar notebooks with silk-soft pages and pens with fancy names. I bought one of each and expensed it to CAA.

As a kid, every year, when I was the top of my class (because it meant getting the scholarship we needed), my mom would take me and my sister to the Hello Kitty store. It was all stationery and plush toys and characters with somewhat disturbing anatomy, but I especially loved the notebooks: puffy with pages of sticker sheets and rainbow-colored notebook lines. We got to pick out one thing each, so one year I got a notebook, and the next I got one of those pens with a half dozen different colors inside, and I never used either. To take one of the stickers was to waste it. To draw on any of those colorful pages was to ruin it. I've made rules to live by since childhood, it seems.

For a moment, as my pen hovers over this luxury notebook's page, I think about just keeping it as it is. Spotless. Perfect. Unchanged.

Then I think about how that Hello Kitty notebook I refused to ruin is probably sitting at the bottom of a landfill, pages yellowed, stickers having long lost their stick, and I draw a big X on the first page.

"There. Ruined," I say to myself, and then I start to write.

Not a screenplay, no. I write the list.

"The studio's movie fell through," Sarah said on that phone call, two months ago. "They've already invested millions in setting up the permits and logistics for filming in New York City. They want to hire you to write a story around these six locations."

Originally, I said no. No way I was writing a screenplay set in a place I hate.

Then Sarah told me the fee. It's enough money for me to have the kind of freedom my mom always wanted for me. The kind that would ensure I'd never have to rely on anyone else. The kind that would make me feel like if something unpredictable—like hundreds of thousands of dollars in medical care—came at me again, I could handle it.

The kind of money I wished I'd had when my mom didn't go to the doctor for years, because she didn't have good insurance. The kind that would have paid for any treatment she needed when she finally did—and the medicines that cost more than mortgages.

We were able to get that kind of money, in the end. My mother lived her last year under the best care. But only because I was desperate enough to make the biggest mistake of my life to get it.

Never again.

So, I said yes. The studio offered to rent me an apartment in the city to help *inspire me*. I refused, thinking I could write the screenplay from LA, and I tried, up until Penelope kindly suggested that maybe going back would be a good idea.

The cards all fell together when I agreed to house-sit, because the apartment's owner is someone I am apparently physically incapable of saying no to.

So now I'm here, spending the summer in a city I despise.

I take my time writing the list of movie locations, making my normally questionable handwriting as legible as possible, because, again, I will do absolutely anything but actually write this screenplay. When I'm done, I sit back and stare at the list. I wait for the name of the first location to shake something free in my brain and for a bunch of words to fall out behind it.

I stare so long that my eyes glaze over, and my list becomes a bunch of jumbled shapes.

"What's that?" a voice says, and I startle so much, I almost spill my latte on my closed laptop.

Forget horror. My life is a series of unfortunate events, leading to a no doubt tragic ending.

Parker Warren is standing there with an espresso in a to-go cup, wearing a button-down shirt and slacks far too formal for a Saturday afternoon.

I use my hands to wall off my list like it's the damn nuclear codes. "What are you doing here?" I demand.

He raises an eyebrow. "It's a coffee shop, Elle. What do you think I'm doing here?"

I eye his espresso cup with disdain, and he notices.

"Is there something wrong with my choice in coffee?"

"Yes."

He takes a seat that I certainly did not offer, and I close the notebook. "Explain."

"It's the worst thing you could have possibly ordered."

He frowns. "Is it?"

I nod. "You might as well drink a 5-hour Energy or something. There's no milk, no foam. What's the point?" I say, then open my laptop, pretending like I'm actually going to start writing.

He slowly pushes my screen down so he can meet my eyes, and my chest feels unexplainably tight. "Elle," he says, very slowly, callused fingers still curled around the top of my laptop. "You are a complete snob."

I bristle. "And you are a complete *menace*. What do you want?"

"Who are you?" His eyes are clear. Sincere.

"I'm Elle, your neighbor," I grumble, "unfortunately."

He presses his hands upon the table, and they're big hands. I'm staring. I'm unbelievable. He nods. "That, I know. What else?"

"What do you mean, what else?"

He shrugs. "What do you do? Why are you here? Why do you have three beverages in front of you?"

Through gritted teeth, I say, "I write. I'm house-sitting for the summer. And the latte is for energy, the water is for hydration, and the hot chocolate is for fun."

He nods. "Interesting. Tell me more."

"No."

"Why not?"

I answer with complete honesty, because what do I care what this person I spent hours hate-writing about a few nights ago thinks of me? "Because I don't know you, and I'm almost certain I don't want to."

He sits back in his chair. Nods. Doesn't look deterred in the slightest. "You know, I could find out everything about you with a few strokes of my keyboard. I'm being polite by asking."

"Because you're a stalker?"

"Because I have access to basic internet."

A slow smile forms on my face. What he doesn't know is he's talking to someone who lives her life under an alias. Someone who has scrubbed the internet clean of her presence. Someone who doesn't have social media.

"Is that so?" I say. "Good. Google away. Find out everything about me."

I force my laptop back up, erasing his face, and pretend to start writing. It's only when I hear the scrape of a chair and footsteps that I know he's finally left me alone.

7

SIX DAYS LATER, I HAVE WRITTEN A TOTAL OF TEN WORDS. WHICH I THEN DEleted. Wrote again. And promptly deleted.

Then I briefly considered flinging my laptop across the apartment, before cradling it in my arms, stroking its silver exterior in near tears, and whispering, “I’m so sorry for even thinking that,” to an inanimate object.

This is why writers can’t live alone, I reason. I’ve gone full writing goblin mode, with no Penelope to remind me to eat vegetables or hydrate or seek out sunlight. That would be completely fine if any writing *was actually taking place.*

A knock on my door startles me from my incredible focus on the third page of reviews for a pair of joggers that I plan to wear from the comfort of my couch.

True crime podcasters would tell me I basically deserve to be murdered and they can’t wait to cover my case, because I swing the door open without looking through the peephole. That’s how I end up standing in front of Parker Warren while wearing a shirt so oversized it could be a moderately conservative dress, SoulCycle sweats I stole from Penelope, and a lopsided bun like melted ice cream on the cone that is my head.

He looks me up and down in a way that can only be described as appraising. "Casual Friday?" he asks.

I glare at him. He's wearing a suit. Of course he is. It's not like we're in the middle of summer, and, as far as I know, he doesn't have a job right now.

"This is, happily, how I look every day of my life," I say, with a smile so sweet it can only be construed as poisonous. "Did you come to mock my clothing choices, or ask for my opinion on whether you should wear a suit in ninety-five-degree weather? I would say no, because you would die of heatstroke by the time you got down to the subway, but you know what?" I purse my lips. "That outcome wouldn't really bother me, and we both know you're not taking the train."

He ignores everything that just came out of my mouth and says, "What is your name?"

I frown. "I already told you."

"Your full name."

"Why? Couldn't find it on *Google*?"

"What is your full name, Elle?" he says.

"Who are you, Rumpelstiltskin?"

Now, it's his turn to frown. "Rumpelstiltskin asks the miller's daughter to guess his *own* name."

Is that true? "I had no idea you were so familiar with Germanic fairy tales," I say, halfway closing the door. "They should add that to your next *Fortune* feature. Goodbye."

"Wait."

I pause, if only at surprise at the sliver of desperation in his voice. Against my better judgment, I open the door again.

"I need you," he says.

My head empties out. "You need me?"

"To be my date."

I almost fall to the floor. Is he this shameless? "Excuse me?" My voice is treacherous and brittle.

He leans against the doorframe, and it's a big frame, and he's making it look diminutive. "Is that such a horrifying prospect?"

Yes. "Yes."

He sighs. "I need a date I can *trust*."

I laugh. "You don't even know me."

"Would you sell a story about me to Page Six or *Daily Mail*?"

My eyes widen, my fingers curl, and my mouth opens, ready to launch a tirade of *How dare you?* Does he really think I need to *sell stories about him—*

He laughs, and it is an annoyingly deep and pleasant sound, scraping against my bones. "Exactly. You're perfect."

I glare at him. "Seriously, Parker. You probably have hundreds of willing women within a twenty-block radius. I would rather streak in the lobby than go on a date with you."

He stares me down with an intensity that makes me understand why those hundreds of women would be so willing. "Exactly," he says again. "You're perfect."

Something unexplainable bubbles up inside me, champagne in my bloodstream. I frown. "Unfortunately, I have nothing to wear, no desire to go anywhere with you, and a plethora of things to do."

Then I slam the door in his face.

"PENELOPE. THERE IS A DRESS IN THE HALLWAY."

An hour later, I'm still wearing the *casual Friday* outfit, phone wedged between my ear and shoulder, staring down at a dress draped across the decorative couch right outside my door, on a hanger covered in silk that looks like it cost a lot of money, with a brand that is French and couture, and—

"And there's heels."

When I tell her the brand, Penelope lets out a low whistle. "Your hallway has expensive taste."

"Tell me about it."

Penelope sighs. "Don't kill me."

"I would never. We both know DNA testing is too good nowadays, I'd never get away with it." Thank you, true crime podcast.

"I think you should go."

I shift my phone to my other ear. "On second thought, no body, no crime, right?"

"I'm serious," she says. "Elle, he might be the worst, but getting out of the apartment wouldn't be the worst idea."

Leaving the comfort of my bed sounds like the *absolute worst idea.*

And maybe that's the issue.

"Look, I know you like to be independent. I know you like to be alone. But it's gone too far. You have become an island, Elle. Like, a deserted one."

I bristle. Maybe I like being an island.

"When was the last time you went on a date? A year ago?"

And it was disastrous. "This isn't a date," I whisper, only now realizing I'm speaking in a shared hallway. I dart back inside. "It's a fake date."

"Exactly. Even more reason to go. You know, maybe living next to him turned out to be a good thing, if he's getting you to do something that requires leaving your emotional support five-block radius."

I sigh. "You want to know the worst part?"

"Always."

"I'm writing again." Well . . . it's not exactly the screenplay. But at least I'm writing *something.* "Kind of."

Penelope sucks in breath like a vortex. "Elle!" she exclaims. "I was really starting to worry." Then she says, "How is that a bad thing?"

"Because *he's the one who prompted it,*" I say, walking circles around the kitchen.

"Oh my god. The guy you hate . . . is *your muse.*"

I make a disgusted sound. "Don't call him that."

"No, no, wait," she says, and I can tell that she's pacing. "He's *always been your muse.* Hear me out! After that night in the staircase, you were so angry, you wrote that screenplay. The one that won all those awards. Every time some news would come out about him, you would lock yourself in your room for days and just write."

"I did that before," I argue.

"Sure, you wrote a *lot*—and are the reason I have to listen to computer key ASMR to fall asleep years after we stopped sharing a room—but never with this much passion. You must admit, you wrote your best work after that night. He has, in this weird way, pushed you to be better."

"Of course I wrote my best work after that night!" I exclaim. "I grew up! My writing improved! Are you really going to attribute every single success I've had from twenty-five onward to *him*?"

"No," Penelope says calmly. "But you used your hatred of him as fuel. He was your twisted muse."

Twisted muse. I make a disgruntled sound.

"You wouldn't be getting this angry if it wasn't sort of true."

That is the bad part of being friends with someone so long. They start to become family, and family is allowed to talk to you plainly without fearing that you will leave them forever.

"Listen, babe," she says. "Who cares? Whatever gets you writing, right? Honestly, I wouldn't be surprised if CAA found out that he was your sort-of muse and arranged for him to be your neighbor."

I laugh without humor and say, "Honestly? I wouldn't be surprised either."

THERE WAS A NOTE IN THE HANGER BAG, PINNED TO THE DRESS. *See you at 8:00.* I'm looking down at my phone, so I know he knocks the moment the clock changes.

Part of me doesn't want to open the door. This is all so very unlike me. I want to cancel, and hide under my covers, and only leave my apartment at odd hours like four o'clock in the morning so that we never run into each other again.

Another part says this is a good thing. Penelope's right. Parker is my *twisted muse*. Maybe tonight will inspire something. Maybe I'll even have fun.

I open the door.

He's wearing a different suit. This one is fancier, and sleeker, and tailored to perfection, like it was made for him—which, in this case, I don't think is a figure of speech.

For the last hour, I debated whether to actually get dressed up. A dress is one thing, but doing my hair? My makeup? That's another. I have my mother's dark brown shiny hair and high cheekbones, but I didn't get her red lips, thick eyebrows, or permanent glow, or much color whatsoever on my face, so without any makeup, I'm plain. With makeup, I look like a different person. Maybe that's why I hate it so much. If you like me only when I don't look like myself, what's the point?

In the end, I decided to put it on, if only to do something with my hands. Because, though I don't like wearing it, I like *doing* it. For some reason, I was gifted with the ability to do a near-perfect cat eye, which I've practiced hundreds of times on Penelope. *She* apparently gifted me a full set of makeup—which I had the pleasure of discovering tucked into my second suitcase—so I played with the different colors. Before I knew it, I'd done myself up, and it was time to go.

The dress is short but elegant, with long sleeves and a modest neckline. The heels are not short, but they're not the tallest I've worn either.

When I open the door, Parker Warren looks at me like I'm wearing far less clothing. His gaze is intense, like it was that night in the stairwell, as he takes me in, inch by inch. "Perfect," he says, for the third time that day, then offers his hand. "Don't be alarmed, but we're about to go into a lion's den."

"A *lion's den*?"

His eyes are glittering mischievously. "Only the worst of society. Social climbers. Social tearer-downers. Heiresses with nothing better to do than meddle in private affairs."

I pale. "What?"

"Relax," he says, looking down at me. His deep voice is making me do the exact opposite. "I know you can take it."

My face goes inexplicably hot, even though I keep any space I'm in for more than a few hours at a crisp sixty-eight degrees.

He offers his hand again.

And, this time, I take it.

WE'RE IN THE BACK OF AN ESCALADE WITH WINDOWS SO TINTED, I can only see the faint twinkling of New York City lights outside of them. Something tells me Parker didn't call an Uber. The man at the wheel has an earpiece and looks like he could kill someone with a shoelace.

My last Uber driver had a toupee two shades lighter than the rest of his hair and a penchant for scream-singing along to pop songs from the '70s.

"So, do you normally take your neighbors on dates?" I ask, casually looking over at Parker. We're in each of the window seats—there are several feet between us—but the space still feels too small. He takes up far too much of it.

He nods, expression completely serious. "I took Ms. Andrews out last weekend."

Ms. Andrews is eighty-four and pushes her cats around in strollers.

I smile despite trying not to and turn toward the window so he doesn't see. It doesn't work.

"You smiled," he says, with the awe of discovering a new product to patent.

"I did not."

"You did. And now I'm going to have to find it within myself to be funnier, because I want you to do it again."

I glare at him because I'm convinced he must be making fun of me somehow. "So, where are we going? And why couldn't you have just showed up dateless?"

His eyes lose some of their previous light. "Have you heard of Edith Adelaide?"

"The heiress?"

He nods. "She has a Park Avenue apartment with the largest terrace in New York City, overlooking Central Park."

My eyebrows scrunch together. "And you really want to see it?"

He barks out a laugh. "No," he says, eyes twinkling again. "I wish it were that simple. Edith Adelaide knows everyone in the investing world and is why I was able to get funding with a prototype I built as a college freshman. She was one of the first people to believe in me." A shrug. "Every few months, she hosts an important gathering, and this time, she said I couldn't come without a date."

"I don't understand. Why is this so important? Didn't you just sell your company?"

"The acquisition hasn't been as straightforward as expected. There are a few . . . loose ends I need to deal with. Tonight."

So, the dinner is critical, for some secret business reason. He needs a date, and preferably one who won't spill all his secrets—or anyone else's—to the nearest tabloid. It makes sense.

I'm a date of convenience. Maybe that should make me feel small, but I don't care. Because tonight could be just the inspiration I need for my screenplay.

We pull up to a building with a long green canopy. A doorman helps me out. He's wearing a hat and suit like he works at the Plaza. Parker gives his name, and we're whisked into a lobby that is gold and ornate and old New York. To my surprise, the doorman walks right into the elevator with us and begins pushing on an old crank, like we've gone back in time. We rise and rise, until a bell rings, and the doors open like curtains, right into an apartment that dwarfs even the one I'm staying at.

I'm greeted by a Picasso sitting above a Steinway piano.

Then by a teacup poodle, who jumps up and greets Parker like he's his most favorite person. Parker kneels and plays with the puppy, and part of me aches in a strange way. Another part kicks that part in the shins and reminds it that we are supposed to hate this man. This man who plays with puppies, and fills suits like he was the model for them, and says things like *Relax, I know you can take it.*

He stands once the poodle has zipped away and leans down to whisper, "She has five of them. Cloned. They live in each of her houses."

Then, before I can recover from that fact, he takes my hand.

My first reaction is to pull my hand away, but Parker seems to sense that, because he holds it tighter, and his thumb smooths down my knuckles, and for some reason that simple gesture sends chills raining down my spine.

Penelope's right. I really need to get out more.

"Parker!" a booming voice says. It belongs to a frail woman who is shorter than even me. She's wearing clothes that have no logos, no names, but by quality alone I can tell they cost a fortune. Pants fitted to perfection. A silk shirt without a single wrinkle present. She's barefoot. Her hair is an elegant white halo around her head. Eighty-seven, and she has more energy than I do.

Her smile is as radiant as the emeralds in the mines her family used to own in South America. My googling in the clearly-not-an-Uber revealed that her mother married an American, John Adelaide, who had enough scandalous affairs and bad business savvy to nearly bankrupt them. When her parents died in a plane crash above the Amazon—spawning at least a thousand conspiracy theories—Edith took over the remaining funds and began investing in people she believed in. She single-handedly made another fortune out of her nearly gone inherited one, though she is forever labeled an *heiress*. I wonder about her life, about the stories in it that I could stretch out and explore and perhaps translate to the screen.

Edith's eyes widen when she sees me. "And you really brought a date!"

"You said you wouldn't let me in without one."

Edith laughs, the sound hearty and not at all eighty-seven years old. "You know very well I would have let you in regardless."

I turn to look at Parker, incredulous, but someone has already come up to him, a man in his late thirties or early forties. Is this the person he really needed to meet?

Edith turns to me and says, "Welcome to my home. I'm Edith."

"I'm Elle."

She shakes my hand. "Would you like to see my wonders?"

"Wonders?"

She gives me a conspiratorial smile, then motions for me to follow. "I collect things," she says. "Things that make me happy, that make *me wonder.*"

She points out a bowl from 500 BC that's sitting simply on a table, no glass case in sight. I spot an impressionist painting I studied in an art history class. An entire room in this apartment was taken from a castle in France.

Edith looks at me. "Before you judge me too harshly, I have no heirs and willed my entire fortune—all of this art included—to ten charities I know and trust." She shrugs. "I figure I have five more years on this earth, give or take. Is it too selfish to enjoy my money so frivolously in that time before I give it all away?"

I'm glad she doesn't look like she expects an answer, because I have no idea what to say to that.

Just as Edith shows me to another room—a library filled with books that look like they should be touched exclusively with gloves—a hand finds my lower back. "You're not trying to add Elle to your wonders, are you, Edith?" Parker asks casually.

There is nothing casual about the erratic beating in my chest at the heat of his hand on me. I could move away. I could pretend to really want to inspect the illuminated manuscript in the corner. But I don't. Because as much as I hate to admit it, I *like* the feeling of him touching me.

I must be losing my mind.

Edith laughs. "I wouldn't dare. You've already tried to buy this place from me enough times. Getting your girlfriend involved would just make your obsession worse."

I open my mouth to tell Edith that I am *not in this or any Marvel cinematic universe Parker Warren's girlfriend,* but Parker starts to make slow, low circles on the bottom of my spine, and what am I doing? Why am I letting him?

Why do I lean into his touch just the slightest bit?

I look up, only to find he's already looking down at me, studying me like he really does think I'm a wonder, and—

"So, how did you two meet?"

The heat thrumming beneath my skin turns to anger as I remember that night in the stairwell. How it ended.

Parker opens his mouth to answer, but I beat him to it. "We're neighbors."

"In San Francisco?" Wait—does Parker even live in New York? Is he here for only a short while, like me?

"No. Here, in the city," Parker says.

Edith looks at me expectantly, like I'm supposed to gush about this great man I despise, so I smile my sweetest smile and say, "He was just so neighborly. And welcoming. Not at all intrusive."

He mirrors my expression. "And she was just so easygoing. And friendly. Not at all obsessed with her laptop."

Edith's gaze travels between us, looking just the slightest bit too interested, but then the elevator dings somewhere in the gilded maze that is her apartment. "That will be the rest of them," she says. "If you'll excuse me."

I turn to look at Parker and say through my still-plastered-on smile, because there are guests milling around us, "I am not obsessed with my laptop."

"Right. That's why you treat it like a small child or treasured pet.

You should get a stroller for it and walk it around Gramercy Park like Ms. Andrews."

I stare at him, wide-eyed, anger temporarily forgotten. "Ms. Andrews has a key to Gramercy Park?"

It's the only private park in New York City. There are only just over a hundred keys in existence, and they go to those who live directly on the park—which we do not—or members of the exclusive clubs that circle it. I've always wanted to go inside, just once, but it's strictly closed to the public, except for on Christmas Eve. The town house of my dreams is located on its perimeter. I used to tutor a kid who lived there when I was at Columbia.

"*I* have a key to the park," he says.

Immediately, I'm plotting to steal his key to Gramercy Park.

Just as I'm about to ask how he possibly came to possess one, a woman walks up to us. Well, not really *us*. She seems to be operating under the assumption that I am incorporeal, because she shamelessly steps right in front of me and starts talking to Parker.

Her hair is so blond it's almost silver. She's tall and slim and wearing a dress that seems to defy physics, since it's backless, there is no strap in sight, and there is very little fabric to speak of, yet it's somehow kept upright. When she turns slightly, I see that it's her impressive chest that is keeping her decent.

I look down and frown at my own chest. Definitely not enough there to act as a hanger.

Half a second has passed, and every anxiety is already playing out in my mind. I'm going to stand here like an idiot. No one is going to say anything. The woman will keep talking to Parker, and I will either keep waiting here, a doormat in heels, or wander off to pretend to study the wonders and wonder why I'm even at this gathering, and maybe I should just leave, because I really don't belong here, and—

"Carissa. This is Elle," Parker says. He sidesteps the silver blonde and places his hand back on the base of my spine.

Her gaze darts between us, and she doesn't even attempt to hide her disdain. Her eyes are large and blue, like gemstones set in her face. Her skin tone is slightly pink. "Elle," she says flatly. "Would I know you from anywhere?"

I blink. "I—no, we've never met."

She rolls her eyes. "Who's your family? What's your Instagram? Where do you summer?"

I have a habit of categorizing people I meet as tropes. She's playing her role of out-of-touch socialite far too well. Maybe I should put one of those in my screenplay?

Part of me admires her for being so to-the-point. What was it that Parker said? We were entering the lion's den? Full of social climbers and social tearer-downers (a term I'm 99 percent sure he made up)?

"I don't have social media," I say, "or use 'summer' as a verb."

Carissa is clearly done with this conversation. She just looks at Parker and says, "Nice seeing you, as always," the bottom of her Eighth Wonder of the World dress swishing as she walks away toward a woman I'm relatively sure has starred in one of my movies.

Parker looks at me, green eyes glimmering with humor. "I did warn you."

"She wasn't that bad." Even a hermit like me has encountered a thousand people just like that in LA.

His hand on my back stills. "You're right. Here comes the worst."

This time, it's the exact opposite. The man who comes over to us completely overlooks Parker—which is hard, considering Parker towers over him—and comes up to me.

"I thought I'd met all of the most beautiful women in New York," he says, staring far too long at a place that is not my face. "Turns out I was wrong." He extends his hand. "Walter Dresden." Walter looks to be in his forties. His forehead is a seascape of deep lines. His appetite for women seems to have frozen in time, while he certainly has not.

I give him the most cursory of handshakes. "Elle."

"Elle," he says, dragging out my name like he's tasting it. Gross. "Why have I never seen you before?"

"I only got to the city about a week ago."

"Do you work?" he asks, and I have to physically stop myself from letting the disgust reach my face.

"I do."

Walter smiles, and it's as grimy as his overly gelled hair. "Wonderful," he says, like I'm a ten-year-old who just declared she wants to become an astronaut when she grows up. "What do you do?"

"I'm a writer."

He nods solemnly. "Well, there's no money in that, is there? But it's certainly a commendable pursuit. A nice hobby."

"There are plenty of successful writers," I say through my teeth. *And you're standing right in front of one.*

He laughs like I've told the world's funniest joke. "There's no such thing as a successful writer," he says. Then he finally acknowledges Parker's presence with a frown. "I suppose it doesn't matter, though, when you have a Parker Warren."

That's it. I'm seething. I've never wanted to use my in-depth *How to Get Away with Murder* knowledge more in my life. I've never wanted to pull up my Wikipedia page or scream out my accomplishments in a long monologue until this very moment, just to prove him wrong.

Parker's looking at Walter like he's gum he's discovered on the bottom of his shoe, but he doesn't say a word. I'm glad. Walter Dresden already thinks not-my-boyfriend-in-any-space-time-continuum Parker supports my entire life. I don't need him also coming to my rescue.

Before I can say something I'll probably end up regretting, Edith comes into the room and announces that dinner has been served.

Edith's private chef serves course after course of the best dishes I've ever tasted. Wine pairings are offered.

Parker is seated on my right side. The moment we sit down, he whispers, "If you want to see something even better than any of Edith's wonders, look at Walter in about five minutes."

I never want to look at that man again for the rest of my life, but exactly five minutes later, I watch Walter Dresden glance at his phone and drop it into his soup. The color drains from his face. He makes some garbled sound, napkins off his phone, then bolts out of the room.

"What did you do?" I whisper to Parker, who's leaning back in his chair, expression showing nothing.

He takes his wineglass and turns it a bit. "I just made his divorce proceedings a little more interesting."

"I don't understand."

He looks at me. Leans over. "At some level, information becomes more important than money. I was able to get some that is going to make it a lot easier for his ex-wife, Portia, to enact the infidelity clause in their prenup."

I blink. "Do I even want to know how you did that?"

"Probably not," he says, then takes a sip of his drink.

The woman on my other side is lovely. She's an art curator at the Met, and I've picked up enough from my little sister, who once dreamed of being a curator, to make conversation. She animatedly tells me about the last exhibits she's worked on and the current trends.

Between dinner and dessert, Edith announces that she would like to engage in a healthy debate about the future of internet currency. While most follow her into one of the many living rooms, I break away to use the bathroom. The faucets look like fountains, and the toilet tries to talk to me.

On my way back, I see an open door leading outside. There's a rush of laughter, and some voices rising above others, coming from the other direction.

I step onto the terrace.

It has the square footage of a sprawling apartment. There's furniture everywhere and a railing that isn't as tall as I would like, but I test its strength, then lean forward to look at the park below.

It all looks so geometrical: the rectangle of never-ending park, the jutting buildings like a frame made of Jenga towers. One of them is alone, far taller than anything around it. It looks like the city is sticking its middle finger up at me.

"I bet the stars hate us."

I freeze. I'm still facing the park. I might as well be a mannequin in a Fifth Avenue storefront, because I don't move a muscle.

The voice behind me continues. "I bet they're angry about that time I said that the universe looks dull, now that I've seen you."

My bones have suddenly revealed themselves to be Play-Doh, and I feel like I'm about to melt right onto this balcony. After the longest moment of my life, I turn around and whisper-yell, "What are you doing?"

Parker Warren is leaning against the opposite wall without a care in the world. He lifts a shoulder. "Just quoting my favorite movie."

I swallow. "Your favorite movie is an alien love story?"

His eyes are glittering. "Only if you've written it."

I close mine. No. This can't be happening. "How?" I finally ask, forcing myself to look at him.

He reaches into his suit jacket and pulls out two envelopes. He tries to hand one to me, but I don't take it, so he shrugs and keeps them both. "We were both invited to the 30 Under 30 party. Our mail must have gotten stuck together," he calmly explains.

My world turns into a keyhole. Anxiety and panic close in all around me.

"As you know, only under thirties are invited. That narrowed down my search significantly." He tilts his head. "You're a writer, which shrunk the pool. None looked remotely like you, but then I figured you must write under a pen name or be anonymous altogether. And there are only so many honorees without a picture." His smile creeps slowly across his face. "Who knew my neighbor was one of the world's most successful screenwriters?"

He knows. He's known this entire night.

Hearing him say those words should make me feel triumphant. *One of the world's most successful screenwriters* is a far cry from the gold digger he accused me of being. It's a far cry from Walter Dresden's view of a writing career.

But I don't feel any of that. I just feel anger. And fear.

My voice shakes as I say, "Who knew *my neighbor* was one of the world's richest stalkers?"

He laughs at that. "You told me to figure it out, Elle," he said. "In fact, you encouraged it."

I did, didn't I? It was only because I truly believed he would never find out. Without the 30 Under 30 connection, I'm not sure he would have. Nothing besides that list connects me to my screenwriting career. I get paid through an S Corp. The studios don't even know my identity.

I was cocky, and I'm an idiot.

My hands are trembling. "Please don't tell anyone."

He frowns. "I don't know why you insist on keeping your genius a secret, but it's your choice. I would never."

"Good," I say, shrugging off the warm feeling that goes through my chest at him calling me a genius. I am no such thing, but it is the greatest compliment I've ever received, and I hate that it comes from him.

8

WE DON'T SPEAK DURING THE CAR RIDE HOME. MY ANXIETY IS WORKING overtime. He found out. Who else could find out?

No one cares, I try to tell myself. Even if someone else somehow made the connection, I'm not exactly Hannah Montana. The overall population doesn't really care about the identities of screenwriters.

Still . . . I've kept this secret for so long. It's been like a security blanket around me, shielding me from things like meeting studio executives in person, or having to maintain a social media presence, or receiving angry mail from fans who hated the ending of their favorite franchise, or cyberbullying because of the end of said favorite franchise.

It's kept me from growing up. My lifestyle is almost the same as it was in college when I wrote and sold my first screenplay. Exactly how I like it. Nothing has had to change.

When we get to our hallway, I give him the best of my fake smiles, anxiety turning my stomach into a storm, then turn toward my door. Before I can unlock it, Parker stops me.

"Be my date again," he says.

I turn back around. Squint. "For the next dinner?"

He shrugs a shoulder. "I was going to say for the entire summer."

I sigh. "Good night, Parker." I pull my phone out. The stupid app to open the door is frozen. Of course it is.

"Why?" he asks, while I angrily press my screen over and over.

"Why what?"

"Why do you hate me?"

That makes me look up from my screen. I don't try to deny it. Especially not now, not when I'm still seething because he knows who I am.

I want to tell him. I want to rub what he said in the nightclub in his face.

But that would mean revealing that we've met before and that he doesn't even *remember,* and that's a shame I'm not willing to bear tonight.

Instead, I say, "Because you're clearly some entitled jerk who thinks he can get whatever and whoever he wants because of his money."

He rears back a little, like he wasn't expecting me to be so blunt. He recovers quickly. His smile is pure malice as he says, "You really think you know me, don't you?"

"I know everything I need to."

I go very still when he shrugs off his suit jacket, puts it on the decorative hallway couch, and that white button-down beneath it . . . looks way too good on him. He starts to roll his sleeves up, and when did forearms become so attractive? He motions to himself. "Give it to me."

I swallow. "Excuse me?"

His smile is entirely too wicked. "Throw all your assumptions at me. Everything you think you know about me."

I stand up straighter. This will be fun. I like to think of myself as a good judge of character, given the fact that I literally write characters for a living. "You went to Stanford. You were a computer science major. You started your company while you were a freshman."

"Tell me things you can't find in my LinkedIn profile."

My cheeks heat. Fine. "You grew up rich, or at least upper middle class. You went to a fancy high school. You started a company because you wanted to be a tech bro with a bunch of money. You sleep with models every weekend. You get anything you want when you want it."

He smiles. His green eyes are pinning me in place. "Wrong."

"Which one?"

"All of them."

I laugh without humor. I don't believe that for a second. "Fine. Throw your assumptions at me."

He looks at me. Takes a step forward. This hallway, I think, is far too narrow for the prices of these units. "You went to arts school. Your parents sent you to creative writing camps and told you to follow your dreams. You don't date anyone because you don't think they're good enough for you."

I almost choke on my laughter. "Wrong," I say. He's so wrong, it's almost absurd.

"Which one?"

"All of them."

I don't know when we got so close, but we're only inches away, glaring at each other. I'm breathing a little too quickly. His eyes drop to my mouth. I swallow, and then he's looking at my throat with far too much interest. I take a step back, right against the wall. I can't think straight when he's this close, and I don't trust myself not to do something stupid again, like repeat what happened that night in the stairwell against this very wall.

"Look," I say. "I know you're probably used to women throwing themselves at you, but I'm not one of them. I'll save you the trouble of pretending to be interested in me, because I am not, under any circumstances, going to sleep with you." I say it with a straight face, even though, inexplicably, that is all my body wants right now.

I wonder if this attraction is one-sided. Maybe he doesn't want to sleep with me at all. Maybe that night in the stairwell was just a fluke, one that was clearly unmemorable.

I fully expect him to walk away, to decide I'm not worth this trouble.

But Parker only looks down at me with an expression that is far too amused. "Date me," he says. "Just for the summer."

I stare at him, incredulous.

"Please."

I blink, wondering when he last had to use that word. "Did you not hear a word I just said?"

"I said date. Not fuck."

My mouth is suddenly too dry. "Why?"

"Is it so hard to believe someone wants to spend time with you?"

Yes. "It's hard to believe you want to spend time with any one person at all, given your track record."

His eyes narrow. "I don't usually have time to date, that's true. I don't have time for a relationship. Especially after this sale goes through."

Not that I have any interest whatsoever in being Parker Warren's girlfriend, but his statement doesn't make any sense. "Your company will belong to someone else. Won't you have all the time in the world?"

He shakes his head. "A condition of the acquisition is that I become Virion's CEO."

Oh. I'm not even sure that's public knowledge. I don't know why he's telling me.

"I'll have even less time than I had before. But this summer, while the deal is still going through, I have time—for the first time in my adult life. I want to spend it with someone who doesn't care about my money. I want to spend it with someone I actually *like*."

I say absolutely nothing, so he keeps going.

"You're right. I'm an asshole. I've lost touch with how to act like a decent human being. Did you know, for the last five years, I've had four security guards with me at all times?"

I frown. "Are you really that important?"

He gives a rueful grin. "The board made me. The company had insurance on me. I invented the technology. My life was a commodity.

The only reason I don't have security now is because I negotiated it into the purchase agreement. I wanted a break. One summer of freedom." He looks at me again. "Date me, Elle."

I shake my head. I despise him. I shouldn't even have gone with him to the dinner tonight. All he's brought me is trouble.

"Give me one good reason not to."

I have a million, but instead of listing them, I say, "Give me one good reason why *you* want to."

"I've already given you two."

"I said a *good* reason. A *real* reason."

He looks at me for a long while before saying, "These next few months are going to be rocky for the acquisition. A relationship would drown out any negative press, to make sure it goes through."

I laugh without humor. There. There is the real reason. "So that's what this is? A PR thing?"

"It's not, but if you want a reason you might actually believe, since apparently you're incapable of trusting someone might just like spending time with you, there it is."

His words sting. Penelope's own words come back to me: *You wouldn't be getting this angry if it wasn't sort of true.* Is he right? Am I that untrusting? I guess I am, because I say, "No thanks," and turn to unlock my door. Thankfully, the screen has decided to unfreeze. I'm one foot inside, when he says something I would never in a million years expect.

"You're not writing, are you? You have . . . writer's block?"

I stop. Turn, slowly. He lingers at my door, keeping it open but not crossing the threshold. "I don't know what you're talking about. I'm writing fine. I'm writing *a lot,* actually." I drive the point home with the unfortunate phrase "I'm completely . . . unblocked."

"Yeah?" he says, leaning against my doorframe, still far taller than me, and the sight is unfortunately attractive.

"*Yeah,*" I say, many shades less casually than he did.

"Right. Because pacing at four o'clock in the morning is a key sign of productivity." He shrugs at the incredulous look I give him. "As expensive as these units are, the walls are thinner than you might think."

We stare at each other so long, I start to see the golden flecks in his green eyes. His eyebrows are naturally straight, no arch to be seen. I start to wonder where he got the small scar on his right one, which cuts it in half. I'm pretty sure that scar has a fan-created social media account.

"Fine. I'm not writing," I admit. "Why do you care?"

He grins, and I hate it, because it is also unfortunately attractive. "Because, Elle, you've just given us the other half of our rom-com agreement."

I'm baffled the word "rom-com" has exited his mouth. "Excuse me?"

He gives me a look. "Elle. You're the screenwriter. Tell me you know what I mean."

"*Of course I know what you mean,*" I whisper-yell, because the last thing we need is for another resident to file a noise complaint and for Richard the doorman to think any less of me than he already does. I wave him into my apartment, and the door closes behind us. I watch him study the place quickly for the first time, eyes snagging on the three different types of cacti on my kitchen counter. I bought them a few days ago, at the Union Square Greenmarket. I love plants but hate when they die (why gift flowers when they don't last more than a few days?). Cacti with little red spiky tops that looked flower-esque were my solution.

I snap my fingers to bring his attention back to me. "But we're not in a rom-com, *Parker Warren*. There is nothing romantic or *funny* about this," I say, waving frantically between us.

"I would say it's pretty amusing I ended up living on the same floor as a woman who hates me. And I wouldn't necessarily call myself a romantic, but if you ever change your mind about not sleeping with me, I—"

"Stop," I say. "I get it. You need a date for the summer, for the press. You need someone to hang out with who isn't falling over themselves to get your money. What could I possibly get out of this arrangement?"

"I saw your list, at the coffee shop. Locations in New York. You're writing a screenplay based on them? Based in the city?"

"Among other places," I say through my teeth, angry at myself for not doing a better job at guarding my writing.

"I'll help you. I'll go with you to all the locations. Talk through ideas with you. Help you act out anything you're having trouble with . . ."

Ordinarily, the idea that this billionaire playboy could possibly help me with my screenplay would be laughable. Ludicrous.

But Penelope is right. He's my twisted muse. Every time I'm with him, I start to *feel*—even if most of the time that feeling is hatred—and it's the only thing that has gotten me writing.

I need to write this screenplay, fast.

He might be the only person who can help me get the words out.

"*If* we do this," I say, and I can't believe that just came out of my mouth. "It would only be for the summer. Come September . . . it would all be over."

"Come September, I'll be back in San Francisco," he says, confirming my previous suspicions. He doesn't live in New York.

"And I'll be back in LA," I say.

He nods.

I'm really going to do this, aren't I? "So . . . how exactly is this going to work?"

Parker blinks. He looks almost surprised. Excited? It makes me realize the gravity of what I've just agreed to, but before I can think better of it, he says, "I have a few work and social engagements to attend. The last one is Labor Day weekend in the Hamptons. That can mark the end of this . . . agreement."

Normally, my blood would drain at the thought of spending an entire weekend together in close quarters. But chances are I'll have finished my screenplay by then, and we'll probably have already called this whole thing off early anyway.

He keeps going. "Between now and then, we'll make our way through your list of locations. What's the first one?"

"Central Park. Near the big fountain."

"Perfect. We can go for a run there tomorrow morning. Does seven work for you?"

"What? Parker, I don't run, I—"

He shrugs. "We'll take it slow."

Before I can protest, he's out of my apartment.

And I'm officially fake-dating the Billionaire Bachelor for the summer.

9

"I THINK I'M GOING TO THROW UP."

Penelope inhales deeply. "Did you eat five red velvet cupcakes in a row again?"

I temporarily thank whatever god that will have me that I don't have speaker on, considering Parker is right, these walls are obnoxiously thin. "No," I whisper-yell into the phone. "You know I can't look at any red foods the same way again." I sigh, then tell her about the deal I made with Parker.

Witch laughing ensues.

I deserve it, I really do.

She shouldn't even be awake right now, but I was the lucky beneficiary of an emoji-laden text a few minutes ago that, after much deciphering, means she just got back from her date with the doctor.

She tells me the details, promises she locked all the latches in our apartment, and then I say, "I have to go. He's going to be here in five minutes."

"Don't sound so dour, Elle," she says in a singsong way. "After today, who knows? Maybe your screenplay will be in its first trimester."

I made the mistake of comparing writing a screenplay to giving birth once, and Penelope has never let me forget it. "Ew, Penelope."

"I wonder if the script will have its father's green eyes? Or a tech trust fund?"

"I'm hanging up now."

I do, and there's a knock on my door, and I really hope it isn't thin enough or Penelope isn't loud enough for him to have heard any of that.

"Last chance" is what I say in greeting when I throw the door open.

He just raises an eyebrow at me. He's wearing a short-sleeved shirt, and I immediately make eye contact with his arms.

"You can back out," I say, shrugging a shoulder like I haven't spent the last fifteen minutes trying to get the top of my hair to lie flat. "It's your last chance."

He narrows his eyes at me. "You would like that, wouldn't you?"

I would, I think, which I think is the problem. I'm the type of person who gets *happy* when someone cancels plans with me.

More time with my bed!

Doing that a thousand times in a row equals years spent inside, when all of life is decidedly happening outside of my apartment.

His eyes trace my body. "Tough."

"What?"

"Tough luck. You made a deal. So did I. And I intend on keeping it."

I glare at him. "I don't recall consulting my lawyer or drafting a contract."

He looks surprised. "You have a lawyer?"

"I've sold eight screenplays to studios, asshole. Of course I have a lawyer."

His face lights up when I call him an asshole, which I'm pretty sure is the exact opposite reaction that word is supposed to elicit.

"Well, I can have one drafted if that would make you feel better," Parker says smoothly, and his eyes are wicked. He's mocking me. "I'll have my lawyers contact yours. I'll make sure that one provision you had is included. What was it? No sex?"

I give him one last glare, then sigh to myself, because I can't believe I'm actually about to step across the comfort of my door's threshold.

Parker looks at my shoes of choice and frowns. "Those won't be that comfortable for running."

I had hoped he had forgotten about the running part.

"Look, you saw me in the stairwell. I'm not exactly a cardio person."

He's leaning against the doorway again. He needs to stop doing that. I need to stop watching so intently. "Which is exactly why we should go running," he says. "In case there's another building fire and I'm not around to cradle your laptop."

I roll my eyes. "It wasn't even a real fire."

"Put the running shoes on, Elle." He's peering inside the apartment. A pair of running shoes that have been exclusively used for walking to places within a three-block radius are sitting against the wall. Great.

"Fine," I say, and he keeps the door propped open while I do just that. "But I'm warning you. I'm even worse at running than I am climbing down stairs."

"I can be patient," he says.

"Good," I reply, meeting him at the door. "Because I'm working before we run."

PARKER WARREN IS TRYING TO READ OVER MY SHOULDER, AND I want to stab him in the eye with my pen.

"Can you not?" I say, pressing my page against my chest. He backs up a few steps.

"Sorry," he says. "I didn't know you were so precious with your words."

"No. Just my personal space."

Prickly. That's how I've been described, most of my life, by men, at least. Probably because my first instinct when being romantically approached is usually to put my barbs up. Penelope—lovingly?—calls me a cactus, when she's not calling me an island.

I blame it on having a beautiful mom. I still remember how men would leer at her at the grocery store, at the bank, at the post office. I remember being disgusted. I remember being so outraged when one once tried to speak to her, in front of me, when I was eight, that I exclaimed, "She's a mom!" even though my dad was long gone at that point, as if that one fact automatically precluded her from all romantic attention.

It didn't help my case that my mother despised the male notice too. Once, I asked her why she got dressed up and wore heels if she hated when people looked, and she said, "This is for me. No one else."

My overall presence can be summed up as *unapproachable,* which is why I'm so surprised Parker approached me in that club in the first place. And why he hasn't already ended our tenuous agreement.

Instead, I'm sitting sidesaddle on the edge of a fountain where the characters in my screenplay are supposed to meet, and he's still hovering over me.

"Bethesda," Parker says, and I squint up at him.

"What?"

"That's the name of this fountain." He frowns. "Who names a fountain Bethesda? What kind of name even is that?"

I blink at him. "Your name's derivative is literally 'park,' Parker," I say. "I wouldn't go around criticizing people's names."

I go back to my notes.

Parker already asked me what I was doing, and I managed to ignore him long enough to not have to explain that I like to visit locations that will be in my screenplays, if possible. I'm not an author, I don't have to worry much about setting the scene beyond a few small descriptions, but I always feel like a place speaks to me, in a way. No matter what I think I'll write, seeing the place in person always inspires something else.

I know the characters must meet here. But how?

I look around for a hint of inspiration.

Parker is staring at me.

"Yes?"

"What's *your* name a derivative of?"

I laugh. "Why, do you want to find my Social Security number too?"

He frowns at me. "I can't even know your full name?"

"No."

"You're my girlfriend."

My skin inexplicably prickles. "*Fake* girlfriend," I say.

"We share a wall."

I shrug a shoulder. "For a summer."

"I've seen you soaking wet from the rain, in a sweatshirt with clearly nothing but a laptop beneath it, and—"

I stop him with a crazed look. I look around—a bored-looking baby in a stroller looks back at me—then stand very slowly in a sad attempt to reach anywhere close to his height. "Have you lost your mind?" I whisper-yell through my teeth.

"Maybe"—he seems to consider me—"if I'm standing in a park right now in eighty-five-degree weather, watching you doodle in your notebook, when I don't even know your full name."

My eyes narrow. "I am not *doodling*. I'm writing observations, if you're so curious. I'm trying to set the scene in my mind."

"You're letting the setting dictate the plot," he says.

"Exactly. Kind of."

He nods. He sits down next to the place I have just vacated, and I convince myself I have no choice but to join him.

He finally goes quiet. He's just looking at the people around the park, same way I was, only without a tiny pink flower-covered notebook.

We watch a family take a photo with a tripod that then defies physics to fold up and fit into a purse. We watch the strained smile of a bride posing in front of the fountain. A professional photographer is going into yoga poses to get the best shot. A few feet away from them, a man is taking a picture of his black Lab with his iPhone.

"She looks miserable," I say. It's the type of thought I usually keep in my head.

"What?"

"The bride. Look at her. She looks like she wants to run."

A few seconds while he looks.

He nods. "She does."

I'm staring. I'm wondering why she would go through with this. She's not even touching her new husband. Her eyes are glazed over, she's—

"If you're not going to write down what you're thinking, you could at least tell me," Parker says.

Fine. "I'm just thinking to myself why she would go through with marrying someone she clearly doesn't even like."

He shrugs a shoulder. "Maybe she does like him. Maybe she just doesn't like"—he waves a hand around—"all of this."

Their families are making wild motions behind the cameraman. Someone is holding up a light that looks extraterrestrial. Tourists are stopping to take their own photos of the couple.

"Yeah, I mean, this seems like my own personal hell," I admit. "But . . . they're not even looking at each other. Not even in solidarity in this chaotic moment."

I ask myself *why* a lot. That's where the best story ideas come from.

Bride who looks miserable, I scrawl across my notebook. *Why get married?*

"Money, maybe," Parker says. He mumbles it. It's a casual statement.

I look at him. "That's what you're going to think, isn't it? Whoever you marry. You're going to think it's because of your money."

Parker's gaze slides to mine for just a moment before he looks back at the bride. "Yeah," he says. He sounds sad. "I guess I am."

It *is* sad, but I don't say any helpful words or try to tell him that isn't true. Unless he goes on one of those telenovela shows my grandma used to watch when I was little, where women date a secret prince, his money is going to always be a factor in his relationships, whether he wants it to be or not.

"Do you want to get married?" he asks.

I shoot him an annoyed look.

"Not to me."

"Obviously," I say far too quickly. Then I take a moment to actually consider the question. "The idea is nice. But, in practice, no. I don't think I want to. I like being alone too much. My independence is important to me."

My mother treated having been married as a personal failing. *The only good thing I got out of it was you and your sister,* she used to say.

When my little sister used to wrap her Barbies in tissues, around and around, to make some sort of wedding dress, my mom would remind us that our great-grandma had an arranged marriage, and that *her* great-grandma had a husband who literally locked her in a house and forbade her from speaking to anyone except for him.

It was kind of depressing.

The best gift I can give either of you is the freedom to live your life exactly the way you want to. Don't let anyone ever take that away from you. She was speaking from experience.

Parker nods, as if in understanding. "You?" I ask.

"Never," he says. He laughs. "Marriage has to be the least beneficial contract imaginable."

Contract. I wonder if spending his entire adult life building one of the world's biggest technology brands has made him think of everything in business terms. I suppose he has to think that way, when marrying someone could mean giving them half of his company in a divorce.

We watch the bridal party for a few more minutes, until the equipment is packed up, the bride shuffles away, fabric fisted in her hands, and their spots are happily taken by a group of silver-painted street performers. A toddler has tried to hand her stuffed dog to a silver-painted corpse bride in lieu of payment, and she has taken it.

"There's a couple in your screenplay?" Parker asks.

"There's supposed to be. It's . . . it's a love story."

He considers this. "And you want them to meet in Central Park? That's . . . their meet-cute?"

I slowly turn to face him. "Did those words actually just leave your mouth?"

He glares at me. "I have a mother who loves rom-coms."

"Right."

He shakes his head. "What if they're strangers?" he says. "What if they're both here for different reasons, but they end up watching a wedding photo shoot together?"

I give him a look. "You mean like we were just doing?"

He shrugs. "But they're in a movie. So they agree that if they don't find anyone in five years, they'll just marry each other. In Central Park."

My head tilts. "You know, I'm starting to think that mom of yours doesn't exist."

"You're right. You figured it out. I don't have a mom."

I roll my eyes. "So the love story continues years later, when they don't find anyone?"

He seems to think about that. "No. I don't like movies that pick up years later."

"Me neither."

"So maybe they keep running into each other."

"How? New York is giant. They've never even met before that moment."

"True. But in these movies, there's always something that has changed that makes sure they're constantly seeing each other. Like he's the new guy at her work. Or he's her friend's brother she's never met."

Or he's her neighbor, I think, then immediately shove that thought away.

My first reaction is to tell him that I'm the writer, not him, and some tech guy isn't going to write my screenplay for me, but his ideas have unlocked new ones.

I don't like his idea about the marriage vow, but I do like the fact that they bond over seeing a wedding.

Maybe she hates weddings?

Why?

Maybe she doesn't believe in love?

Why? What in her past made her that way? What do the relationships around her look like?

What does he think? Does he agree? Or is *he* the secret hopeless romantic in this situation?

I also begrudgingly agree that forced proximity *is* usually a necessary trope in these types of movies. They must have a reason to keep bumping into each other. I also need a reason to use all these locations the studio already got licenses for . . .

Maybe she's the head costume designer for a movie, and he's the star of it? Maybe she was talking bad about the actor she has to work with, after hearing he's a huge jerk, and then *he* ends up being the actor?

Damn it. Penelope was right.

Parker Warren is my twisted muse.

I shrug a shoulder like I haven't figured out a huge part of my movie. "It's an idea."

"Come on, Arielle," he says. "You can admit it's a good idea."

I give him a look. "My full name is *not* Arielle."

He shrugs. "If you say so." Then he gets up. He takes the miniature notebook and just-as-tiny pen from my hand and puts them into the pocket of his joggers. "Time to run."

It's as horrible as I imagined.

10

THERE IS A SIX-FOOT-FOUR MAN WITH PIERCING EYES AND A DIMPLED SMILE standing at my doorway. And it's not Parker Warren.

How many of these are allowed to exist in a single Manhattan block anyway? Is there a quota or something?

I swung the door open without looking through the peephole, because I figured it would be Parker, ready for our next excursion. Reason #207 that I wouldn't survive an encounter with a serial killer, according to my favorite true crime podcast.

Maybe I look like I'm about to spray him with my nonexistent Mace (reason #208 I wouldn't survive an encounter with a serial killer), because he puts his hands up and smiles. "I'm Luke, the contractor," he says. When my brow knits together, he clarifies: "For the unit renovations."

Right. The main reason I'm house-sitting in the first place.

"I just need a few more photos of the interior, if that's okay," he says. His hands are still up.

And I'm pretty sure the true crime podcast hosts are screaming at me from wherever they record, because I just shrug and let him in, no identification or other reasoning required.

He's doing more than I am to protect myself from hypothetical murder, because he leaves the door propped completely open, with a doorstop he apparently keeps with him.

"The photos I need are of the master bathroom. Is it okay with the other person here if I access it?"

I frown. "I'm the only person here."

I really am serial killer candy.

He squints at me. "I thought I heard you speaking to someone."

I swallow. I've been talking to myself for half an hour, trying to hype myself up for another run that I am so not ready for, because, according to Parker, that's the best way to visit the High Line, the second location on my list. Apparently, I talk to myself a lot louder than I thought. The excuse blurts out of me: "Oh, you must have heard the TV."

We both do a slow turn to the television, which is still in its box.

"That I stream on my laptop."

Both of our eyes drop to my computer, which is sitting closed on the counter.

"Right," he says.

I gesture for him to feel free to go get the photos he needs, while I linger by the door and wonder if there's a chance the floors weren't installed correctly and they might do me the favor of swallowing me up.

I blink, and there he is. The hot contractor.

I watch a lot of home improvement shows. I know hot contractors exist. But I always kind of guessed they were basically actors, and other people did the actual work.

"I bet you're overcharging them, right?" I say as he finishes up and goes to leave. "You know, you could honestly probably charge them more. They likely wouldn't even notice. I hear they have a *lot* of money."

He just looks at me, says, "Nice to meet you," and turns around.

Only to almost run into a man who is just a hair taller.

Parker is scowling.

"Sorry about that," the contractor says, smile bright. Parker just looks at him, not saying anything, until the contractor bends down, collects his doorstop, and leaves.

Parker turns to me. "Who was that?"

"The contractor," I say. "The people who own this place are doing renovations."

He nods. He's still frowning when he says, "Are you ready?"

"Absolutely not."

OUR LAST RUN, I LASTED ALL OF THREE MINUTES BEFORE MY LEGS felt like they were going to give out.

"Let's try five minutes today," Parker says.

I shake my head. "I don't mean to be dramatic, but that would kill me."

We walk through the lobby, and nosy Richard the doorman looks up from his phone behind the desk, then double takes. The idea of two residents hanging out together is no doubt very interesting to him.

"Four minutes?" Parker says, while we walk down the block.

"I honestly think three minutes was beginner's luck," I say. "And my legs are still really sore." His frown deepens, but I wave off his concern. "It's okay. I have a massage tomorrow."

"Is it that painful?"

I shake my head. "No, I get one every month. CAA pays for it." When I'm on deadline, at least. Sarah swears by massages and thinks a stress-free writer is a productive one.

Parker glances over at me. He echoes my words from a few days ago. "Are you really that important?"

I almost laugh. "No. The movie is." My voice is light, but the tension in my shoulders isn't. "No pressure."

We run in spurts. One block jogging, one block walking. Parker is surprisingly patient. I'm clearly slowing him down. If he wanted to exercise, he would be better off running without me.

He doesn't, though. He actually looks at the buildings on the block, whereas I've never studied them very closely. We pass a movie theater.

"Do you ever see your own movies?" he asks.

I think he's trying to distract me from the fact that I already have a cramp in my side. I shake my head. "No. I never go to the premieres. Well, because I'm anonymous, for starters. But even if I wasn't, I wouldn't."

"Why?"

"I prefer to watch them alone. It feels . . . too personal to watch with other people."

That seems to interest him. "Are your movies usually personal?"

I feel the defensiveness surge, with the predictability of the tide. Part of me wants to ignore him. Another part realizes that if we're going to spend the summer together, conversation is a given. We're going to talk. I'm going to have to learn how to stop acting like every question is some sort of personal attack.

"In a way," I say. "Writing . . . is how I make sense of the world. How I make sense of *myself*." I glance over at him, bracing for some sort of retort. Some way he's going to make me feel small or make me regret sharing anything at all.

But he doesn't. He just looks intrigued. "Do you have a journal?"

His question surprises me. I shake my head. "No. I can't . . . I can't write anything in first person."

"Really? Why not?"

I feel the prickliness returning, like a second skin. Too many questions. My voice comes out a little more irritated than I mean it to. "Writing other characters is the closest I can get to expressing my own emotions. I see myself through others. It's the only way I can bear to look at the ugly parts, without flinching. Like staring at the sun with sunglasses."

He nods. He seems to understand, though I have no idea how he possibly could. "We should watch a movie together," he finally says. "Not one of yours," he adds, in response to my look.

Yeah, that's never happening. Our agreement is clear. It does not involve watching movies, unless one of Parker's vague appearances takes place at a theater. "You wouldn't want to watch a movie with me," I say. "My best friend, Penelope, stopped about three years ago."

"Why?" He shoots me a look. "You don't use subtitles, do you?"

"Worse. I get the script and have it in front of me while I watch. I take notes. I pause and rewind liberally."

He winces.

"And, also, I use subtitles."

I don't think I have to fear Parker Warren asking me to watch a movie with him ever again.

The sun is blazing in full force by the time we reach the High Line, and I am soaked in sweat. Parker is annoyingly *not*. He hands me my small notebook from his pocket, and this time he leaves me alone while I take my notes.

The High Line used to be a train track. Now, it's like an endless bridge, an enchanted elevated road running through the west side of Manhattan, in between silver skyscrapers and over traffic.

Technically, it's a public park. Nature has been planted everywhere but the walkway. There's something almost dystopian about it, grass growing through abandoned train tracks.

Every few minutes, I stop, scribbling some notes. Parker stays by my side but doesn't try to read over my shoulder. We walk through old terminals with stands selling ice cream and iced coffee in plastic bags that look like the juice pouches my sister and I used to beg my mom to get us from the supermarket.

We have the filming permit for a few days. That means this could be a night scene. At this point in my screenplay, the protagonist is still denying her attraction to the guy. He's trying to win her over, but she's not budging. She needs to fold a little. She needs to relax and have some fun.

Maybe there's a movie premiere party on the High Line?

Maybe the actor invites her, so she can meet her costume designer idol, but things go wrong?

Parker doesn't approach until I put the pen down, and, frustratingly, something in my marrow sings at the fact that he has learned a part of me, like I am some sort of board game with strict and confusing rules.

My marrow needs to raise its standards. It needs to remember that this man thought he could *buy* my affection.

He holds his hand out, and I hand him my notebook and pen. He slips them into his pocket.

"Run home?" he says.

"I would rather die."

SOMEHOW, OVER THE NEXT FEW DAYS, A ROUTINE TAKES SHAPE without my permission. Parker shows up almost every morning for a run. More often than not, he's holding a latte from my new favorite coffee shop, so I don't immediately slam the door in his face.

No . . . little by little, I start getting up earlier. Getting ready. Slipping my running shoes on just before I hear the two solid knocks against my door.

Forget witch laughing. Penelope would need CPR from the hot doctor she's dating if she found out I was regularly exercising.

Afterward, we usually part ways, and I'm *thinking in the shower again*. I'm rushing to my computer to write, still wrapped in my towel.

It feels like college when I couldn't get the words out fast enough. Within a week, I have more than enough ideas.

Now, I need to shape them into the Skims shapewear of screenwriting: Save the Cat plot structure.

There are sticky notes coating my floor, like a neon carpet. I look like I'm trying to solve a cold case on cold hardwood.

I'm a visual person, and putting scenes on note cards usually helps me see the story. The CVS on the corner ran out, so here I am with a Frankenstein's monster mix of what it did have: neon-pink and -green sticky notes and faded yellow legal pads.

Of course, that's the moment the contractor decides to make his second visit. His eyes immediately go to the mosaic of paper across the living room, and his joyful smile strains. Between this and me talking to myself, he must think I've lost my mind.

It's a good thing, I tell myself. Maybe he'll think I'm too crazy to murder.

Maybe he thinks *I'm* going to murder him.

I continue to work, sitting regally on the floor, while he and two of his employees start painting what will one day be an office. I'm crawling toward the inciting incident of my screenplay when my phone rings.

It's my sister.

"Ellie!" she squeals—she's the only person who calls me that. "How's my apartment?"

11

MY SISTER IS CURRENTLY AT AN UNDISCLOSED HOTEL ON THE AMALFI COAST. Undisclosed, because she doesn't know where she is, since she didn't book it. She tries and fails to find the name in her room, but it's the type with a butler, so there isn't anything as pedestrian as a room service menu or branded notepad. There's just a sleek phone without any buttons that magically summons anything she needs. Even me. I'm flattered she remembered my phone number so our call could be connected.

"You sound stressed, Ellie," she says. "You should take the summer off."

For my sister, summer is not a season or a verb—summer is her life. She bops around from location to location, taking so many vacations that it doesn't make sense to have a home base. She didn't until this apartment, which was only purchased in February, right after she found out she was pregnant. It was her version of settling down, even though she, physically, was settling into a first-class cabin on her way to Europe just days after closing. *Staying in one place makes me anxious,* she'd said. *Anxiety is bad for the baby.*

Months after that came the tearful phone call. *The house manager quit. The renovation is stressing me out. Stress is bad for the baby. Would you stay there while it's being completed? You're the only person I trust to make sure it goes smoothly. I want it to be perfect.*

I'd like to think it took more than a single phone call for me to cave, but I turn into the plushiest of doormats when it comes to my sister. By the time the call ended, her tears had mysteriously turned into a chirping *Yay, I knew I could count on you!* And I was booking a one-way plane ticket to the city I hate.

Penelope says I need to start creating healthy boundaries, but I promised my mom I would take care of my sister. No matter what.

When I'm gone, all you'll have is each other.

I remind myself of that promise as my teeth grind. "I can't take the summer off. I have a job, remember?"

I can imagine her frowning, tiny lines forming wherever the premature Botox hasn't settled. "Can't they find someone else to do the movie reviews?"

My sister thinks I write *about* movies. It was the easiest way to explain why I was always reading scripts and typing away at my laptop. Not that she ever cared enough to do a quick Google search to find out that I, Elle Leon, am not, in fact, a movie critic.

It's not that I want to lie to my sister about my career, or that she would care at all really, unless I wrote a movie incorporating all Real Housewives universes. It's the fact that she has an unfortunate habit of not being able to keep her mouth shut, mixed with regularly speaking to the one person who made me want to be anonymous to begin with.

"Nope!" I say cheerfully, smiling broadly at the wall like a horror movie character, because the psych class I took freshman year of college said it would trick me into improving my mood. Then, before she can say anything else, I cut in with "How's Pierre?"

"Ask him yourself," she says. "You're on speaker."

My smile strains. Great. It's only been five hundred times that I've asked her not to do that. "Hi, Pierre," I say, trying to summon an iota of excitement.

He mumbles a reply with about the same level of enthusiasm. It's not that there's anything *that* wrong with him. It's just that before my sister met him—on a vacation, of course—she was weeks away from starting her master's degree in art history. She dreamed of becoming a curator. All that changed when Pierre entered the picture. In some ways, their vacation never ended.

Sometimes I wonder if that's why they travel all the time. Maybe they're afraid that if they ever stay in one place long enough, they'll realize they only really work in paradise and not in the real world. Like the contestants from *The Bachelor* who are absolutely shocked to discover that the love that blossomed during weeks on a beach with endless cocktails doesn't hold up when taxes, kids, jobs, and distance come into play.

Mom would have hated Pierre. She would have hated the nonstop fun-and-games playtime that my sister's life has become.

Isabella Leon valued hard work and independence, never relying on someone else for financial stability. She had found that out the hard way and had made sure both of her daughters would learn from her mistakes.

I love my sister more than anyone—but sometimes, I wonder how we could both be raised by the same woman and have turned out so differently.

I ask Pierre if he knows which hotel they're at. He does not. I would insist on my sister sharing her location with me, but she left her phone at the last resort, when she decided social media and texts were toxic. And toxicity is bad for the baby.

"Don't worry, Ellie," she says in a singsong voice. "You worry too much."

Of course I worry. I worry so much it feels like there's a permanent knot in my gut.

"Besides, we're on to the next location in the morning."

"Which is?"

"Sicily."

"I don't assume you know the hotel . . . ?"

They don't.

"I think it's a villa," Pierre says unhelpfully.

I ask for the name of the travel company they used to book everything, but he doesn't know that either.

"Ask Paola," he says. Paola is their assistant. I'm not sure what, exactly, she assists with, because neither of them has a job. Also, I'm pretty sure Paola has my number blocked.

"Are you sure this much travel is okay?" I ask, trying to keep my voice light, because negativity is, you guessed it, bad for the baby.

"Yep! Dr. Connors says it's fine as long as I avoid boats."

I wince. They are traveling every few days, up through her delivery date. She says it's like a roulette to see where their child will be born in the world. She thinks that's funny.

It gives me hives whenever I think about it.

"So," she says. "How's the contractor?"

"Luke's fine," I say. "I already told you that the renovations are going—"

"No," she says, and I know her well enough to hear the smile shaped around the word. "I mean how is *he*?"

And, because I truly know my sister, I close my eyes tightly and whisper-yell into the phone: "Cali. You didn't hire him and ask me to move here to supervise to try to set us up. *Right?*"

"No! Of course not!"

Relief floods through my bones. "Good, because—"

"Though, you know, Pierre and I were talking . . . and we just thought it would be so romantic and so *good for you* if—"

"Oh my god, Cali!" I say, then look around to make sure Luke is not right behind me. "That's so *presumptuous,* so *invasive,* so *unprofessional*—" I pause. "Do you even *need* renovations done?" I wouldn't put it past my sister to literally rip the wallpaper down and floors up just for an excuse to manufacture a love story for me.

I am almost certain she's rolling her eyes right now. "*Yes,* Elle," she says in a voice that makes my blood boil. "The entire apartment was entirely too gauche. It would have clashed with the Calder we got in Amsterdam."

You made a promise to your mother on her deathbed, you made a promise to your mother on her deathbed, you made a promise—

"I'm hanging up now. Please have Paola send me the rest of your itinerary. Love you."

Deep breaths. I'm in the middle of doing a child's pose over my first act, when I hear a throat clear in front of me.

Of course Luke is standing there, studying me as though I might be about to contort like a ghost and crawl up the wall. "We're taking lunch," he says.

I just nod and watch the three men walk out of the apartment.

My sister really tried to create a forced proximity situation with me and the contractor she hired to renovate her apartment. Of course. Her life is a never-ending summer, a continuous Ferris wheel joyride; she does things only because they're *fun,* without thinking about the consequences or about anyone other than herself. She really thinks of me and everyone else around her like board game figurines she can move around anywhere she wants for her own enjoyment.

I go back down into child's pose and sigh against my thighs. I can't even be upset at her.

Cali used to have ambitions. She used to care about other people. She used to follow my mother's lead. We used to be *close.* She never would have changed if it wasn't for me and my own bad decisions.

It all went downhill when I went against my mother's wishes.

"SO, HOW'S OUR COUPLE DOING?"

I'm at my favorite table at my favorite coffee shop and have almost dropped a blueberry scone I would sell an organ for on the floor.

"Lucky for you I caught this," I say, waving the teardrop-shaped pastry at him. Then I take another small nibble and thank celestial forces for butter and sugary crust.

"I would have gotten you another one," he says, staring at the pastry as if trying to figure out what about it is so special.

I delicately place it back onto its plate, next to the fork and knife the barista gave me but that I decided not to use because I'm a goblin and don't want to lose any crumbs from cutting.

"This was the last one," I say slowly. "They only ever make them on the weekends. They're always gone by eight fifteen, so I wait in front of the door before they open to make sure I get one."

He blinks. Stares at the pastry, then back at me. "It's that good?"

"It's better than you could possibly imagine. And no, I'm not letting you try it. Show up at seven forty-five tomorrow if you want one."

With that, he gets up and leaves me alone with my pastry.

Happily, I pick it back up and take another bite. I close my eyes and focus on the crunchy sugar on top and buttery crust and crumbly inside. The taste elicits a moan I would be embarrassed by if the shop wasn't empty and I wasn't sitting in the corner, in my favorite chair by the window and outlet.

"So that's what that sounds like."

I startle, and this time I do drop my pastry. It lands on my plate and breaks into a puzzle.

Parker Warren is sitting in front of me, his eyes darkened in a way that makes my throat feel tight.

"You—you *left,*" I say, feeling my face go red.

"To order the *worst of coffees,*" he says. He reaches over and takes one of the small pieces my scone has broken into.

He doesn't break eye contact as he slowly puts it into his mouth. Chews.

"It is good," he says.

I'm still frozen in mortification when I hear the barista call his name and watch him casually walk over, get his drink, and sit back down.

"So." He takes a sip. "How's our couple doing?"

I finally find my voice. "*Our* couple isn't doing anything."

"Fine. *Your* couple."

They've just been introduced on set and are about to go to their first filming location, but I don't tell him that. Instead, I say, "Don't you have a job or something?"

"You're up."

"Excuse me?"

"I frolicked in Central Park and went to the High Line. Tonight, I need my girlfriend."

I raise an eyebrow at him.

"*Fake* girlfriend."

"For what?"

"Me and some friends have a monthly basketball game when we're all in town. Their girlfriends usually join."

"You have friends?" I deadpan.

"Surprising, I know." He takes another piece of my pastry, and I almost stab him with my fork. "They're not my closest friends," he admits. "I suspect one or more of them are selling stories about me to the press, actually."

My jaw goes slack. "And you still hang out with them?"

He shrugs a shoulder. "I've had friends do worse," he says, and for some reason that makes me sad.

Then I mentally berate myself. Poor little billionaire? I don't think so.

"If the press is going to believe this"—he motions between us—"the people around me need to believe it too." It makes sense.

A basketball game? I can handle a basketball game.

He gives me the time and address, then finally leaves me alone with my pastry.

12

IMMEDIATELY, I REALIZE I'VE MADE A MISTAKE.

It's too late. They've all seen me. And I've seen them.

A woman comes up to me, beaming. She has short blond hair immune to frizz, is wearing a nylon dress that can't possibly be comfortable, and is towering over me in heels covered in crystals.

I'm wearing my beat-up running shoes, shorts I somehow still have from middle school, and a T-shirt that has been washed into sandpaper consistency and is currently rug burning my armpits. My face has a visible sheen from the sunscreen that wouldn't blend in after ten minutes of trying. Not that the sunscreen was necessary, apparently.

We're in an apartment. One of Parker's friends has a basketball court *in the middle of his apartment.* I must have gone lovers to enemies with karma, because the walls of the court are glass, so the moment I see Parker and his friends, they see me too.

One starts laughing.

The woman is still smiling at me, though her eyes widen. Her pale cheeks go pink. "Oh! They—we don't usually play. They're pretty competitive . . . they've never asked us to . . ."

There's a woman wearing jeans and a cropped T-shirt on the couch in front of us. She has dark skin and box braids and is wearing bright purple eyeshadow. "I would play if they let us." She shrugs a shoulder. "They're not that great anyway."

Parker and his friends have left the basketball court. They're walking toward me, and I'm contemplating taking a few steps back and flinging myself down the elevator shaft.

"Elle," Parker says, and for some reason, just the sound of my name from his mouth makes a chill crawl up my spine. He looks happy to see me. And a little confused by my outfit. At least he's not laughing at me, like the guy next to him with way too much gel in his hair. "Do you want to play?"

"She can't play," Over-Gel says before I can decline and pretend that I forgot that I need to be somewhere else entirely. Maybe another country. "The teams would be uneven."

"Then maybe you can do everyone a favor and sit this one out, Charles," the woman on the couch drawls, without even looking up from her phone.

There's another woman seated on a kitchen barstool. She has black hair, light skin, and long legs. She looks like she walks down runways for a living, and hasn't looked at any of us once.

"Funny, Taryn," Charles says, then looks back at me. "Yeah, she can't play."

Parker doesn't even acknowledge him. He just looks at me expectantly, waiting for my answer.

Charles has more acid in his expression now. He's staring at my shoes as though I've sullied what I can only assume is his apartment. His lip curls in disgust.

"You know what?" I say, surprising myself and apparently also everyone around me. "I would love to play."

"We'll be uneven," Charles repeats.

The woman on the couch—Taryn—hops up. "I'll play," she says. "Em, you have some shoes I can borrow, right?"

The woman on the stool nods in the direction of what must be her room.

The blond woman who greeted me looks excited. She races after Taryn, heels clanking.

Charles is seething. "They're on your team," he grumbles to Parker, before sulking back to the court.

"Elle," Parker says when we're alone, "we don't have to play. We can leave."

"No," I say, eyes on Charles's back as he walks into the glass enclosure. I meet Parker's gaze. "I'm . . . weirdly good at basketball."

Now he looks confused. He must be remembering when I told him I hadn't exercised since tenth grade PE, which is true. "You . . . played in school?"

"Kind of. My mom had a bunch of jobs when I was in elementary and middle school, so she was always late picking me up. The teachers would put us in the gym to wait . . . and we would play. I got pretty good."

That was about fifteen years ago, but Penelope and I volunteer at community centers with gyms, and every once in a while, we'll play afterward. I'm still, weirdly, good.

Parker looks at me for a second too long, and I realize I let something about my mom slip out. And my childhood.

Taryn returns. She has her braids tied back out of her face and is wearing a pair of designer athletic shoes that look brand-new. "Ready?" she asks. She leans in close to me. "I'm terrible, by the way. I hope you're not."

I smile back at her. I wonder if it expresses any of the enormous gratitude I feel. She doesn't even *know* me, and she stood up for me. "I'm not."

"Then this is going to be very fun."

Taryn was right. They really are bad. *Especially* Charles. Parker is, annoyingly, the best of the bunch, but even he misses a few baskets.

I don't. Maybe it's the sheer willpower to beat Charles that does it, but it's like I'm twelve again, back in front of the hoop, weirdly just knowing I'm going to make the shot before I do.

Parker's friends are better at defense, but Taryn's more skilled than she let on. We form a sort of routine with our teammates, a rhythm. They pass it to me last, and I never miss.

Parker is beaming with pride when we win.

Charles is glaring at me. I give him my best smile and he sneers at me. "It's a basketball game. It's not that big of a deal. I don't even play much."

"You literally have a court in the middle of your apartment," I say.

"I could probably fit your apartment inside of it," he says back through his teeth.

Honestly, he's right. My apartment in LA is not large by any stretch of the imagination.

"Careful, Charles," Parker says. His tone is casual, but it has an edge. "You rent. I'll buy this place straight out from under you."

Charles goes quiet, but in his eyes there's a simmering hatred. It doesn't take a detective to realize he's the one selling stories about his friend.

That's why I loop my arms around Parker's neck and say, "Let Charles keep his apartment. Most of his self-worth is clearly attached to it."

Taryn laughs. I smile.

Parker goes rigid beneath me. At first, I think I might have taken it too far, blatantly insulting his friend, but he's staring at my mouth, and I'm pretty sure he didn't hear anything that just came out of it. I give him a look. If he doesn't stop seeming so surprised or affected, everyone around us is going to know this is a sham. He swallows.

Finally, he says, "How thoughtful of you."

Any additional retorts I had planned eddy out of my head when Parker's hands slowly slide down my spine. I try to ignore the heat that races to meet every place he touches. I'm sweaty. We just played. That's all this is.

His fingers curl around my waist, and I never really noticed how long they are until now. His thumbs strum down my stomach, making my skin prickle. Suddenly, my breathing hikes more than it ever did during the game.

One of his other friends clears his throat, and Parker steps away. I feel my face flush as I turn toward Taryn. We exchange numbers, and on my way out, I say bye to the blond woman (who I now know as Gwen) and Emily (who congratulates me, before calmly asking Charles if he's going to let this loss ruin his day like last month).

Parker stares at me in the elevator. He's standing as far away from me as possible. "That . . . was convincing," he finally says.

"Good." I lean against the opposite wall, fighting the red I can feel heating my cheeks. "If computers start writing screenplays, I'm glad I can add 'amazing fake girlfriend' to my résumé."

He doesn't look so amused. "Charles is an ass," he says, his voice a shade darker than I've ever heard it.

"Yeah. He is."

"I'm pretty sure he's the one selling stories about me."

I nod. "He is basically a cartoon villain with a really nice apartment and a girlfriend who only seems to semi-tolerate him."

Parker makes a noise resembling a laugh, but he's still frowning, like he can't get over how Charles treated me. I'm glad he didn't say anything else. I can handle myself.

"Why do you hang out with them?" I ask, wondering if I'm overstepping.

The doors to the elevator open, and he waits for me to walk through first, something I didn't really realize I appreciated until he did it. "We all met in college," he says.

"At Stanford?"

He nods. "My better friends are all still in the San Francisco area. These are just the ones who ended up in the city. Charles has always sucked, but the rest are good guys." He shrugs a shoulder. "They knew me before I started my company."

"So what?" I ask. "Anyone you meet after, you'll always secretly suspect they just want to be your friend because of your success?"

"Probably." He looks faintly amused. "Everyone except for you. You're the only person I've ever met who would probably like me more without it."

"No," I say. "I don't like you either way."

He smiles. "Right. Stupid of me to forget."

We're in front of the building now. Parker's SUV is waiting by the curb. He opens the door for me, but I shake my head. "I have a call with my agent. I'm going to take it while I walk home."

Sarah's been calling me every day for the last week. It's only now that I've decided I have the mental strength to call her back and give her an update.

It's only now that there *is* an actual update.

What I don't say is that right now, distance would do me good. My skin is still heated where he touched me. My chest has started to do this strange little dip in his presence.

It's unnerving. My treacherous body is forgetting *who* it's feeling this way toward.

Parker nods and makes to get in the car, but I blurt out, "My next location."

He looks over his shoulder. "You're ready to go?"

I nod. I have my first act hammered out. The second act is where I've planned most of the locations to be used.

This is all professional. It's practically a business agreement.

"Where is it?"

I tell him, and his eyes narrow just the slightest bit. It's such a small motion, something I would never notice in anyone else's face. But, I realize with a touch of unease, I'm starting to know him. "Is that a problem?"

He's quick to shake his head. "When does it open?"

"Nine." I looked up the hours the night before.

"Does that work for you?"

I shrug a shoulder. Normally, I would be having a very important meeting with my pillow, but runs with Parker before the sun gets too hot on weekdays and staking out the coffee shop for the pastry of my dreams on weekends have cleared those from my calendar. "Sure. See you then."

I can feel his eyes on me as I turn off the side street, around the block, and out of the shade. Then I'm back on Fifth Avenue, walking with the crowds again, all of us toasting beneath the skyscrapers.

13

"WHAT IS WRONG WITH YOU?" I ASK, EYEING PARKER. HE'S BEEN QUIETER THAN usual. On the way here, he wouldn't stop fidgeting. As we walked into the building, he looked almost wistfully back at the entrance. "Beyond the obvious," I say, just to see if I can get him to glare at me.

He doesn't. He just swallows. His hands are now pointedly rigid by his sides.

We're one of the first ones in line, and then we're in an elevator. Parker stares at the air above my head for the forty-something seconds it takes to get to the ninety-something floor. I'm not sure he's breathing.

We're at Summit One Vanderbilt, a newer NYC attraction. It was a real score for the studio, according to Sarah, who was so happy that I had finished outlining a third of the screenplay that she told me to take a spa day on the agency's dime. She also asked me for my New York address, and a celebratory champagne bottle with a box of chocolates showed up an hour later. I ate all of them while on the phone with Penelope. Now, as we are whisked away into the sky, my stomach flips, and I start to regret my life choices.

The first stop is called Transcendence. It's a floor that makes me feel like I've somehow crawled inside an emerald-cut diamond. Endless panes cut the world into geometrical shatters. I squint after a few minutes, wishing I'd brought sunglasses—the sun is reflected everywhere, just like us. I look up, and there we are, upside down.

I lightly hit Parker's arm with the back of my hand, so he can see too, and watch his eyes slowly slide up to the ceiling. He grunts in response, then goes back to a state that seems to be *pretending to be anywhere but here.*

Whatever. Notebook in hand, I start scribbling furiously.

Sometimes, locations in movies are ways to subtly show the progression of a relationship. If the characters are standing in here, they would be reflected everywhere, laid bare, nothing hidden between them. Maybe the actor can tell the protagonist how he feels here? Maybe she rejects him? Maybe this place becomes his own version of a horror house of mirrors?

We enter Affinity, an exhibit of dozens of silver balloons floating everywhere.

"I feel like I'm in a magical bubble bath," I tell Parker, kicking the balloons around us. One hits the side of his head by accident, but he doesn't even seem to register it. He clearly hates it here. I wonder why he agreed to come to this location to begin with. "You know, you could have said you were busy."

He takes that opportunity to gently push one of the balloons toward my head. It's moving about 0.2 miles an hour, so I duck in time. He smiles a bit, but it doesn't reach his eyes. My chest tightens, from annoyance to concern. Did something happen? Is it something with the acquisition?

Why do I even care?

I want to ask him, but I don't. If he wanted to tell me, he would. Maybe nothing's wrong. Maybe he really *would* just rather be anywhere but in a skyscraper with me, for my screenplay, at nine in the morning. Maybe he's regretting this entire agreement.

That's fine. It's not like it's been a complete and utter pleasure spending so much time with him for me either. If there was any indication that I could keep writing without him, I would be the first one to call all of this off.

The reflective glass multiplies the balloons tenfold. It's like we could drown in them. My excitement has withered, however. "Let's go to the last part," I mumble.

Levitation—the closest I'll ever feel to flying. It's a glass observation deck, a shard of transparent floor hanging off the side of the building. Even with Parker's bad mood, I can't help but grin. I'm walking right over New York City. Taxis look like toys; people are as small as pinpricks. Buildings look like Lego sets.

I turn, only to see Parker pressed against the wall. His posture is rigid. His face has turned paler than usual. That's when it all makes sense.

"Oh my god. You're afraid of heights."

He doesn't even try to deny it. He just continues to stand there, like he is physically incapable of moving even an inch in any direction. His head tilts back, his eyes on the ceiling.

I shake my head in disbelief. "But . . . you're so *tall*."

At that, he gives me an incredulous look. "Elle, I'm six four. Not a thousand feet tall."

His eyes refocus, gaze shifting somewhere past me. Mistake. He shuts them. Swallows. He's seen past my face, down into the depths of New York City.

"We can leave," I say immediately, even though I want to spend more time on the glass strip. It could be the perfect place for my main characters to have their first big fight.

My words surprise me. I should be relishing in his discomfort. Right?

I'm not. His hands are in fists, veins visible, and I have the strange urge to uncurl every finger, to see him cocky and relaxed again.

What is wrong with me?

He shakes his head. "I'm fine."

"You're not."

"I will be."

He makes to take a step, as if to prove it, his eyes cracking open just a little. The moment his foot connects with the glass again, every bit of him tenses, as if bracing for impact. He shudders.

I don't know what makes me take his hand, but I do. I take one, then the other.

He stiffens again, like me touching him is worse than even his fear of heights. But a moment later, his fingers are folding over my own. His hands are enormous, almost swallowing mine.

"Don't look down," I say. "Look at me. We'll do it together."

His gaze meets mine.

Green. His eyes are like a maze I want to get lost in. He follows my order, staring intently, and my heart inexplicably begins to hammer.

I open my mouth, and his gaze slips to my lips. His thumb grazes the center of my palm, and I inhale too quickly.

It's an effort to move backward, away from him, but I do.

And eyes never leaving mine, he steps forward.

"See? We're fine. It's solid."

I take another step. His gaze slips down my body, then to a thousand feet below. He tenses again, but he doesn't go still. He keeps moving.

"I've got you," I say, and something in his expression changes. Loosens, just a little. The Parker Warren on the magazine melts away, and I see a glimpse of vulnerability. Trust.

He nods. Takes another step.

My back hits the wall, and I jump, scaring myself for a moment, but his hands grip mine. *I've got you too,* he seems to say, as he squeezes my fingers.

I'm dying to get my notebook, to put all these thoughts down, but I don't. I tuck them in the back of my mind and hope I remember later.

I'm not dropping Parker's hands, not when his chest is still moving as quickly as it does when we're running.

He's not looking down anymore, though. He's only looking at me.

"I've got what I need. Let's go," I say.

"Are you sure?"

I nod.

Hand in hand, we make it back the way we came.

"WHY WOULD SOMEONE AFRAID OF HEIGHTS LIVE ON THE SIXTIETH floor?" I ask. We're sitting in a diner around the corner. Parker looked a little like he was going to pass out, and my first thought: *Milkshakes*. For his blood sugar.

I'm not actually sure if that's a thing, but when are milkshakes ever a bad idea? I was ready to silently judge him as he looked at the flavor options, but then he chose cookies and cream, and I had no choice but to respect it.

"Did I pass your test?" he said. "Or did I choose the worst of milkshake flavors?"

It unnerves me that he's starting to know me.

"Obviously not," I said. "I ordered the same thing."

He takes a sip of his milkshake before answering my question. "I figured it was one of the best ways to overcome it."

I reach toward a fry on his plate because I finished mine. Fries also seemed like a good idea. For the nausea. "You don't like having weaknesses, do you?"

Parker pushes the plate of fries toward me. "No. I try my best to conquer them." He glances at me. "Not usually with an audience."

It seems very unlike Parker to put himself in a situation where a weakness would be on full display. It's the first time I've ever seen him not be completely in control.

"You could have canceled," I say.

"You would have been alone," he says back.

I don't have anything to say to that.

He watches as I dip a stolen fry into my milkshake before popping it into my mouth. "Is that how you *eat* your milkshake?" he asks. "With a fry as a vessel?"

The fact that he remembers that small fact from our conversation in the stairwell during the fire alarm surprises me. "Sometimes. I usually use the straw if I don't have a spoon, but it didn't seem polite to suck on it in front of you."

Parker blinks at my choice of words. I wonder when the universe will allow me a delete key for real-life conversations. He's looking at my mouth again. My lips part.

His phone rings.

He doesn't reach for it until its fourth ring. Then he says, "I'll be right back," before sliding out of the booth.

Parker is outside for no more than a minute before returning. He frowns at the receipt on the table.

"You got the check?"

I give him a poisonous smile. "I can, surprisingly, swing two milkshakes and fries."

His frown deepens. "I didn't mean—"

"Is everything okay?"

He looks confused.

"The call."

In the weeks I've known him, his phone hasn't rung once. I get the sense that he's told everyone to leave him alone during the summer.

"Just a snag," he says. "I have to go back to San Francisco."

"When?"

"Now."

My emotions must be as transparent as the walkway we just conquered, because he seems to know I'm upset.

"Do you need me? I can see if—"

I shake my head quickly. "No, don't worry. I don't need you."

I wonder who I'm trying to convince: him or myself.

"Right." His eyes have lost some of their warmth. He straightens, and he's back to the guy on the magazine: the aloof tech CEO. "I'll see you when I'm back, then."

We go our separate ways—him home, me to get more sticky notes for my plot monster—and I try not to examine the tug in my chest that withers in his absence.

14

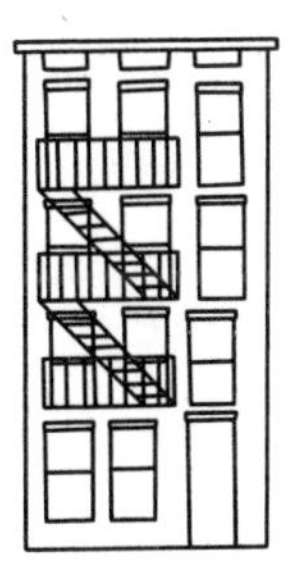

I'M IN A CLOSET WITH LUKE THE CONTRACTOR. I'VE JUST ACCIDENTALLY stepped on his foot. The bulb in here hasn't been installed, and the nearest window is covered for painting. We're using a flashlight he apparently always keeps on his person.

"All these colors look the same to me," I say to the samples on the wall.

His laughter is worn but polite. This man is tired of me. "I can assure you they're very different. This one has a hint of silver. The other is more green toned, see? This one is bluer."

They are literally all gray.

Normally, I would be FaceTiming Cali and telling her to choose her own damn closet color, but she doesn't have a phone and hasn't called from her latest location. I wouldn't be able to reach her if I tried (and *I've tried*), which sends dread sinking through my stomach.

"I see now." I absolutely do not. "This one," I say, pointing to the second swatch color. "The bluer one."

Luke frowns. "That's the—"

I step out of the closet. "Amazing work. Thank you. I'll be on the floor of the living room if you need me again."

I'm moving around the sticky notes that encompass my second act when Penelope calls.

"Your boyfriend is on the news."

I roll my eyes. "He's *not* my—" Then I sit up straight. "Wait. Which channel?"

I say that as if I have cable, or a plugged-in television, and plan to flip through channels with a remote. Luckily, Penelope sends me a link to a livestream. I click it open on my laptop, phone balanced between my ear and shoulder.

Parker fills the screen. It's a photo of him in a suit, his face unreadable. His green eyes are as intense as ever.

The text at the bottom of the screen says "Atomic Acquisition in Trouble. Virion Stock Drops Ten Points."

"Wait, does this mean the sale isn't happening?"

"No," Penelope says. "It's just a leak. There's probably some sort of snag, but neither company has confirmed it."

I don't understand. "Who would leak something that could hurt the acquisition?"

"Competitors, maybe," she says. "Media about it isn't good, especially when anything surrounding him always goes viral."

I find myself feeling oddly defensive of him. Angry at anyone who would try to hurt him. Part of me hopes Charles will leak the news of our "relationship" to offset this press, just like Parker intended.

Which doesn't make any sense. We barely know each other. All of this is very much pretend.

The news anchor plays a video of him speaking in front of a congressional committee a few months ago, advocating against selling customer data. Parker's voice is clear, his argument sound.

"This is kind of sexy," Penelope says.

My cheeks heat. "Penelope."

"What? He's not your real boyfriend, right?" she says the last word like she's hoping I'll admit he secretly is.

But that's not the truth. "Right," I say sharply, then hush her so I can hear the rest.

MY COMPUTER KEYS ARE LOUDER THAN USUAL, SOUNDING LIKE A horse clomping on the street in the middle of this coffee shop. A few people look over at me, but I ignore them. I'm currently at the second act of my screenplay, but I'm typing the words as though I'm writing a scathing letter to the building's board about the neighbor downstairs who won't stop having piano recitals in the middle of the night.

The sound of my keys drowns out the world. I don't even notice someone's in front of me until they say, "Only one drink? Is there a latte shortage I should be aware of?"

Electricity races through my chest.

I give my keys a break and sit back in my chair. Parker's leaning against the wall in front of me.

"You're back," I say quietly. He's been gone a week. I didn't realize how much I had come to anticipate our morning runs and run-ins in the hallway, until I was the only one on our floor.

"I'm back," he says, just as hushed.

A few people are looking at us. No, not at us. At *him*. He sits down like he doesn't notice.

"I saw the news," I whisper. "Is there something wrong with the acquisition?"

He looks around. Leans in. I lean in too. "Virion wants to sell our data," he says into my ear. "Their plans came out in the middle of due diligence. I refused."

It makes sense. I shamelessly spent the night watching his entire presentation in front of that congressional committee, rewatching certain sections.

"I've never sold my customers' data, even when the VCs wanted me to. We would be far more valuable if I did."

I turn to meet his eyes, only to find our faces just inches apart. I swallow, then lean toward his ear. My bottom lip touches his warm skin as I say, very quietly, "Do you think that will be the end of it then?"

He shakes his head. "No," he says, his breath against my temple, making my spine curl. "They're still interested. We'll see how it shakes out."

We turn to look at each other at the same time, and nearly collide. He stops just short of my lips. We're far too close, both leaning over the coffee shop table. Sharing breath. Eyes locked, like we're back on the glass floor. One second passes. Two.

I'm the first to sit back. He does the same.

Then his gaze narrows. Either Parker knows me better than I thought or my feelings really are as transparent as that walkway we conquered, because he says, "Elle, what's wrong?"

"What?"

"You look upset. I could see it the minute I walked into the shop."

I wonder how long he was watching me before I noticed him.

"Also, I'm surprised none of your keys have fallen off."

No use in denying it, even though I know he's about to think I'm the most ridiculous person who has ever lived. Especially when he's currently going through real problems. "They stopped making the scone."

He frowns. "The blueberry one?"

I nod, invigorated by his outrage on my behalf. "I showed up this morning, and there were none in the case. When I asked, they said they weren't making them anymore. Something about the cost of the ingredients or something."

Parker nods. "Ah. And you didn't get a latte in solidarity with the discontinued pastry?"

That's exactly what I did. "How did you know?"

He lifts a shoulder. "It seems like something you would do."

Maybe I am a transparent walkway.

I sink deeper into my chair.

"I don't mean to be dramatic," I say, preparing to be the most dramatic I've ever been in my life. "But that pastry got me out of bed on the weekends. I looked forward to them all week. It was my joie de vivre. I know that's stupid."

"It's not stupid," he says. And I can see he means it.

Which is really just kind, because it is objectively stupid.

I stretch my fingers against the semi-sticky table edge. Taking out my feelings on my keys has led to stiffness.

"So, are you going to find another coffee shop?" he asks. "One with scones?"

I shake my head. "No. Even though they don't reciprocate, I'm loyal to a fault when it comes to coffee shops. And this one was perfect . . ."

My phone makes a noise and I frown. The only person who ever texts me is Penelope, and she's supposed to be on another date with the doctor.

The confusion only deepens when I read it.

"Something wrong?" Parker asks. "Besides the scone?"

"No . . ." I say. Though, maybe? "It's Taryn. She invited me to dinner with Emily and Gwen."

When I look up at him, he looks mildly amused.

"What?" I demand.

"You're trying to come up with a logical excuse why you can't, aren't you?"

My glare is still in place as I say, "No, actually, I'm not." I 100 percent was.

"Then why aren't you going?"

"I never said I wasn't."

He tilts his head at me. "Are you?"

"No," I say, and his expression is far too pleased. "But only because I don't think she really means it. She's . . . she's really nice. She's probably just being nice."

The amusement in Parker's face vanishes. "Elle," he says, "why is it so hard for you to believe people might actually like you?"

Because I *don't even like me,* is what I don't say.

He can read something similar in my face, because he searches my eyes, his own narrowed. "You really don't know, do you?"

"Know what?"

"That you're fun, Elle. You're fun to be around."

I almost snort out the hot chocolate I'm sipping. The word "fun" and me have never been in the same sentence before.

"Why do you think I'm spending the summer with you?" he asks.

"For your image," I say. "For the acquisition. To cover up all this press."

He looks annoyed, but he drops it, and I'm grateful. I start typing out an excuse on the group chat just as excited messages start pouring in with a startling amount of emojis. *They* seem fun.

I stop my typing.

Penelope would tell me to go. Parker clearly thinks I should too. I can feel him staring at me, though he doesn't say another word.

This summer is supposed to be about growing beyond the confines of my hermetic life, right?

I delete my message and send a new response before I can backtrack.

"I'm going," I say, before opening my laptop and starting on the scene again. I can't see his expression, but I can guess he's pleased.

This time, I'm gentler on the keys.

WE MEET FOR DIM SUM AT A PLACE CALLED GOLDEN UNICORN IN Chinatown. It was Emily's turn to pick. Apparently, they do this dinner thing a lot.

"The guys are never invited," Taryn tells me, as we walk down the busy blocks. "Charles tried to show up once, and we called him an Uber home."

Before I laugh, I glance at Emily. She looks right back at me and waves a hand. "I broke up with Charles a few days ago," she says casually.

"It's the reason we're celebrating," Taryn says.

Emily doesn't look too torn up about the breakup. She doesn't seem too *anything,* really. She is the definition of easygoing, not letting any single emotion rule over the rest.

I strive to be Emily-level cool. Nothing seems to faze her.

The restaurant is busy, but it isn't long before we're sitting down. The carts come by, and we fill every square inch of the table with a variety of dumplings, reaching over each other to grab the ones we want. We keep saying we're stuffed, and can't possibly eat any more, yet also keep packing our plates. I try melon rice balls. Egg custard tarts. Swan-shaped dumplings. Vegetable dumplings. Coffee jelly that I have a love-at-first-bite situation with. Conversation quiets as we chew. We're all so absorbed with our meals that it isn't until we leave, and walk a few blocks to a bar, that we start to talk again.

Gwen, apparently, oversees drinks. "We play a game," she says, "where I order, and everyone tries to guess what, exactly, is in their cocktail. You don't have to drink, of course. It's only if you want to."

I don't normally drink. But I also don't normally go out. Penelope and I usually order takeout and eat it on pillows in front of the TV because our apartment doesn't fit a dining table.

We've lived in the same place since we moved to LA, even as our circumstances changed. We could get something bigger, better, but I hate moving. It's the ultimate state of change.

We moved constantly when I was a kid, before my mom went back to school and got a better job. Nothing ever seemed permanent, until it was. It took a year living in our house for me to fully unpack, but once I did, I was rooted there. I held on to that house with claws, until the bank took it away.

Gwen's waiting for my answer. She's smiling. I don't think I've ever seen her not smiling. "I'll drink," I say, and she retreats into the menu, fingers drumming against the side of the table. She orders in hushed tones, and we're supposed to do our best not to listen.

The drinks arrive, and Taryn goes first. Hers is slightly gold. Muddled. "Lychee?"

Gwen nods excitedly.

Emily takes a sip. Another. "I have no fucking clue, but it's good," she says, then downs the rest.

My turn. I take a small sip and wince. All I taste is alcohol. I try to let it sit on the tip of my tongue. There's something floral, fragrant. "Rose?"

"Close. Lavender."

"How is that close?" Taryn says. Gwen ignores her.

Gwen takes a sip of her own non-mystery drink. It looks like coffee. "Espresso martini," she says. "Always."

A few sips of my own drink make me bold. I glance over at Emily, who's sitting back, watching as Gwen and Taryn debate which couple is going home on some summer reality show.

"Can I ask why you and Charles broke up?" I say, then find myself immediately regretting it. We don't know each other well. It's too invasive.

But Emily just hits me with the full radiance of her gaze and says, "You can ask anything you want, Elle." She takes a sip of the tea she ordered after her drink. She doesn't even lower her voice when she says, "I found out that he's been selling stories about Parker to the press."

Taryn and Gwen go silent. They look at me.

I wonder if I should act surprised, but being with these women makes me not want to fake anything.

Taryn's eyes narrow at me and my lack of shock. "You suspected?"

I nod. "And Parker."

Emily scoffs. "Well, Parker might be fine hanging out with Charles knowing that, but I'm not." She takes a sip of her tea. "If he'll do that to one of his friends, what would he do to me, you know?"

We all nod. We all know.

I frown. "But . . . if he's been selling stories about Parker, why hasn't he told the press about us?" The Billionaire Bachelor having a girlfriend should have been on the homepage of Page Six by now.

Emily sits back in her chair. "Because I told him if he sells them any story involving you, I'll forward his boss the emails he sent to the press." She purses her lips. "I'm guessing having a mole on the exec team of an internet security company would be highly frowned upon."

I stare at Emily in awe. "Thank you," I say, even though getting media about Parker's and my relationship was the goal since the beginning. She doesn't know the relationship is fake, though. She doesn't know about Parker's and my deal.

We barely said a few words together at the basketball game, yet she wanted to protect me.

It makes me feel guilty about lying to them. But how could I explain to them why I would pretend to be Parker's girlfriend without revealing my own secret?

Emily just shrugs. "If we women don't watch out for each other, no one else will."

Taryn toasts to it.

And we all drink way too many cocktails.

WE'RE ON A PLATFORM THAT MIGHT AS WELL BE A GLORIFIED TABLE, belting out a song from the early 2000s like it's our job. The crowd probably can't hear a thing through our laughs and Gwen loudly messing up the lyrics, but our arms are intertwined as we save one another from falling off the definitely-doesn't-earn-the-name stage.

Drinks turned into more drinks at a karaoke bar in K-Town. We were all piled into a taxi to take me home, and Taryn insisted we stop here because it was *on the way*. It was in the exact opposite direction, but we all screeched in excitement, and what I thought would be a night of watching other people belt out songs that don't play on the radio anymore turned into *us* standing on the stage, squinting at the too-small words on the teleprompter, wondering if we all needed glasses, linked like the chain of a charm bracelet.

If Penelope were here, she would be in the crowd, cheering us on, doing the whistle that requires putting a large percentage of your hand into your mouth.

When our song is over, we all stumble off the platform and weave into a hug that's all elbows, hair, dry shampoo, and giggling. Just like their restaurant tradition, we all take turns choosing each other's songs, which are revealed only once the singer in question is onstage.

"I don't know this one!" Gwen insists.

"Good luck!" Taryn says.

Emily steps onto the platform to help, and they somehow turn a dance pop song into a duet.

This is fun. This is something the characters in one of my screenplays would do. For the first time in a while, I'm living life instead of just writing about it.

It feels good. I can't believe I almost made an excuse and missed this. There are moments in life, I think, that make you grateful you didn't just stay in your room.

By the time I'm walking out of the elevator and toward the apartment door, I'm humming to myself, smiling, and slightly stumbling. And my phone is dead.

Wait. My phone is dead.

I rapidly click the buttons on the side like they're a defibrillator that will magically bring my phone back to life. No matter how hard I press, or how many times, my phone only flashes a sign telling me, in very clear terms, *Yes, I am dead.*

I knew this stupid technologically savvy lock would be the ruin of me. There's a backup key, but of course, that is in the apartment.

The lobby doesn't have a copy since Cali gave the extra one to Luke.

He'll be here first thing in the morning. I check my phone for the time and curse when I see that it is, yes, very much still dead.

It must be past midnight. We stayed in the karaoke bar until closing. Two a.m. I briefly consider knocking on Parker's door and asking for a charger, but then I remember he has the latest model, with the new hardware.

I've never been so happy to see the previously impractical decorative couch. I collapse onto it, tuck my legs beneath me, and wait for Luke.

THERE'S A TALL MAN IN FRONT OF ME. HE'S SAYING MY NAME, I think. He's blurry, until I blink a few times and make out gray sweatpants and a T-shirt stuck against muscle.

My first thought is Luke, but no, I know this body—a little more intimately than I should.

It must be a dream. Or some alcohol mirage.

I can't be dreaming about Parker looking like this: sweaty, and muscled, and leaning toward me. It's just not healthy.

"Go away," I croak, hoping my dream or hallucination or whatever this is will disappear.

The mirage frowns. "Are you sure? This doesn't look comfortable."

It's not. My neck is twisted in a position that has alerted the nearest exorcist.

I move, and a bolt of pain drags me into reality. This isn't a dream. No, in a dream my back wouldn't hurt so badly. And my feet wouldn't sting. And my head wouldn't have its own heartbeat.

I sit up on the couch, only to find that I'm barefoot. My heels are tipped over on the carpet.

Right. I decided to dress up nicely. I'm wearing a skirt and button-down shirt that's a little more sheer than I expected. The material is scratchy against my skin. Definitely not meant to be slept in. I'll have to give Penelope that feedback the next time she decides to sneak items into my luggage.

"You got locked out, didn't you?"

I yawn. "No, I actually prefer sleeping like a contortionist. You should try it."

His hair is ruffled. He looks tired. I've never seen him so disheveled, or casual, even when we've gone running.

"Did you just . . . work out?"

He nods. "At the gym downstairs."

I frown. "This building has a gym?" Not that I have much use for it. "Wait—is it morning?" I turn to the window in the hall and see it's still dark out.

"No. I just . . . I couldn't sleep," he says. "I work out to release stress." He looks confused. "You weren't out here an hour ago . . ."

Strange. Even the idea of working out causes me stress. "What time is it?"

"Around three."

I groan. Six more hours on this chaise. Lovely.

"You don't have this charger, do you?" I ask, holding up my phone.

He shakes his head.

I sigh, then start folding myself back up.

A few moments of silence tick by. He just stands there and watches me turn into a human pretzel. Finally, he says, "You can sleep in my apartment."

I give him a look.

"I have four bedrooms."

Right. It's a nice offer . . . but being his fake girlfriend is one thing. Sleeping within feet of each other is another.

"No thanks," I say. "It's actually not that uncomfortable." I wait to see if I'll burst into flames for my egregious lie.

"Right," he says.

"Luke will be here in a few hours anyway."

His body tenses. "The contractor?"

I nod. "He'll let me in."

He shakes his head. "I'm not leaving you out here. I'll get a hotel if it makes you uncomfortable to sleep in the same place. You can have my apartment."

I give him a bewildered look. "I'm not going to kick you out of your own apartment."

"I don't mind," he says. "It wouldn't be any trouble."

That's ridiculous. I wave his suggestion away. "Don't worry about me. I'm fine."

We have a stare-off, until he finally sighs. He walks to his door. Unlocks it. Then he turns back to me. "Come inside, Elle," he says.

His voice is uncharacteristically sincere. Something twists within me.

He's trying to help. Putting my barbs away for one night won't kill me.

"Fine." I nearly lose my balance in the few steps to his door, even though my heels are in my hands, not on my feet.

He steadies me and plucks Penelope's stilettos from my palm, like he's afraid I might accidentally stab myself with them. He carefully places them just inside the doorway, in front of what, in my sister's unit, is a coat closet.

"Did you . . . drink?" he asks, which is about the politest way of asking, *Are you drunk?*

I nod. "I did. I'm okay. Don't worry." I had two and a half drinks throughout the night, which normally would have me vomiting all over Parker's apartment, but luckily, I ate enough to settle my stomach.

I walk past him and stop. His place. It's surprisingly . . . warm. Not as sterile as I thought it would be.

I hear him step next to me. He must sense my shock, because he says, "What? Were you expecting a bunch of monitors everywhere?"

That was exactly what I was expecting.

He makes an amused sound at the expression on my face. "I'm the CEO of a tech company, Elle. Not a hacker."

I glance at him. "So, you couldn't hack into the government's satellites if you wanted to?"

"I didn't say that," he says, before casually strolling through the living room and into what must be his bedroom. It's just a few seconds before he returns, holding a nicely folded T-shirt and cotton pants. He hands them over.

I let the pants uncurl in front of me. "Thanks," I say. "If I decide to spontaneously grow fourteen inches, these will be great."

Instead of smiling at my joke, he looks genuinely disappointed in himself, like he should have anticipated his fake girlfriend might accidentally get locked out of her apartment in a miniskirt and need something to wear to sleep. "Sorry I don't have anything in your size," he says. "I just thought—if you wanted to change . . . but you don't need to if you don't want—"

"Thank you," I say, genuinely this time, because it was thoughtful. He seems surprised at the softness of my tone, and I realize I've never genuinely thanked him before, even though he's objectively done nice things for me these last few weeks.

He motions for me to follow him, and I do, my blisters-in-the-making stinging against the cold hardwood floor. He opens a door in the hallway and turns on the lights. The room is bigger than both Penelope's and mine back home and looks like it's never been used. The sheets are pristine.

"There are towels in the bathroom, if you want to shower," he says, before hesitating. He's looking at the way I'm leaning against the wall, like I don't trust myself standing upright without swaying (because I don't). "Though . . . I wouldn't advise it." His forehead creases with concern. "Do you need something, Elle? Can I help you?"

"I'm fine," I say, and I mean it, though I will most definitely need

Advil and a breakfast burrito tomorrow morning, when the hangover and regret hits.

He doesn't look convinced, but he doesn't press. "I'm going to shower," he says. "I'm just over there if you need me."

I nod, then do my best impression of someone who doesn't feel like the world is spinning and shoo him out of my room, even though this is his apartment.

As soon as he's in the hall, I sink to the floor. Yes, the world looks a lot less in-the-middle-of-a-sea-storm on the floor. I sit there for a while, looking around the room, wondering if he bought it this way or hired a decorator, and why I'm even thinking of the decor when I'm minutes away from potentially throwing up all over it, before peeling off my top. The fabric is scratchy, and I sigh in relief when it's gone. I sigh even more in relief when it is replaced with Parker's shirt. The fabric is as soft as bedsheets. It smells like detergent. Like *him*.

When I stand, it reaches a little longer than my skirt did. No matter how many times I roll the pants, they slip down my hips, so I kick them into the corner.

I groan, back of my hand against my forehead the way my mom would put hers when I was sick at home. This was very much a self-induced nausea, however. Tomorrow is going to be terrible. I need to drink water. I need to have it injected into my veins like those reality stars after a night out on the town.

The door only slightly creaks as I inch it open. "Parker?" I say tentatively. There's no answer. He must still be in the shower. I creep down the hallway and into the kitchen, which looks far too lived-in for someone who likely has a private chef.

Though, now that I think about it, I haven't seen or heard anyone else enter his apartment in the weeks I've lived here.

The kitchen has a waterfall marble island (thank you, HGTV shows that always pair well with coffee and morning anxiety), sleek appliances, and dark blue cabinets. The mental house I build every time I watch any of these shows, as if I too will someday soon be undergoing a major renovation project, has *white* cabinets. But this is . . . nice. Masculine. Sexy?

I frown. Everything except for a hideous vase filled to the brim with five different shapes of dry pasta. It's sitting awkwardly at the edge of the island, like it kind of knows it doesn't belong.

Why am I here again?

Water. Right. Normally, I would use the tap, but there's a sleek, slightly humming machine nearby that looks too fancy not to try. All I need is a cup. I start opening cabinet after cabinet and quickly find an impressive stash of snacks. Everything is annoyingly semi-healthy ("kale chip" should be an oxymoron), but there's a big bag of popcorn, some pretzels, and chocolate-covered almonds. I shamelessly fill my arms with the stash like it's Black Friday and I've forgone a cart, grinning like a thief whose main goal is indigestion, so pleased with myself that I turn around too quickly and knock over the hideous vase.

It shatters on the floor, throwing up pasta everywhere.

A door somewhere slams open, and Parker races into the kitchen, wet hair still dripping down his forehead, in nothing but sweatpants.

I try to look anywhere but the upper body that is somehow more muscular than I could have even imagined. His shoulders are wide, he has every muscle like he's collecting them, and are those *abs*—

"Sorry!" I say. "I was looking for a cup of water."

His gaze falls to the bags of snacks still clutched against my chest. "In the snack drawer?"

I nod like that makes sense.

Then I remember the pile of shattered glass in front of me. I make to take a step, to find a broom or something, but I'm barefoot and slightly off-balance—

Before I step into the pile of glass or do something stupid like try to clean it up with my bare hands, Parker grips my hips. I tense, but all he does is seamlessly lift me out of the middle of the broken glass and onto the edge of the kitchen counter.

My every nerve seems to flicker on. The marble is cold against the backs of my thighs, and I remember, very suddenly, that I'm wearing only a shirt.

His shirt.

And I'm not wearing anything but underwear beneath it.

Parker seems to have the same realization as he looks at me. My hair is over my shoulders, and I watch as his gaze drops to my chest, prickled from the cold, clearly visible in this white shirt. He seems to go unnaturally still. I wonder if I should be embarrassed or cover myself, but I don't want to. He quickly looks away.

Then he's on his knees in front of me.

Suddenly, this perfectly air-conditioned apartment now feels like a furnace. There's a heat dropping directly between my legs. But all he's doing is cleaning up the shattered vase. I watch, transfixed, as he carefully picks up the large pieces of glass, not cutting himself the way I have exactly 100 percent of the times I've ever dropped anything fragile. Then he finds a vacuum and gets rid of the rest, including all the pasta. The entire time, his shoulders and arms are flexing, and I have no business studying him so closely, but I also feel like I might not be able to stop. He has muscles I didn't even know existed.

By the time he's standing in front of me again, I think I've forgotten how to breathe. The alcohol has made me bold.

He swallows as I slowly reach a hand toward him, but he doesn't make a move to find a shirt or somewhere else to be entirely.

"I didn't think real people actually had abs," I say, my nails lightly dragging down them.

His voice is tight. "Only the computer-generated ones?"

"Only the Hollywood-generated ones."

"Ah," he says, and my hand drops against the marble again.

"I'm sorry about your . . . pasta holder?"

He looks faintly amused. "It was a vase."

My transparent walkway face must be even worse when I've had something to drink, because he says, "What is it?"

I shrug a shoulder. "I don't know. It didn't really match everything else. It looked a little out of place."

"Out of place?"

The truth stumbles out of me. "It was . . . so ugly."

He's still amused. "My mom gave it to me."

I make to hop off the kitchen counter. "Right. Should I throw myself down the elevator shaft? Or do you want to push me?"

He laughs and puts a gentle hand on my hip, keeping me in place. The heat within me turns into a wildfire. His fingers are so long, curled so close to exactly where I want them.

"You're barefoot," he says. "There might be pieces I didn't get."

I shake my head. Swallow. "No, you were thorough. I was watching."

His eyes meet mine.

"I—I wanted to make sure you didn't get cut or anything. You didn't, obviously, which was kind of impressive. Your fingers are . . . they're very . . ."

"Impressive?" he supplies, a slow smile forming on his face. His eyes are pinning me on the kitchen counter. His hand is hot against my hip. I straighten and his thumb dips, just slightly, smoothing down the fabric.

"Dexterous," I say, though it comes out more like a whisper.

He's closer than he was before. He towers over me, even perched on the island.

My blood is thrumming; my skin feels like it's about to catch fire. My knees slightly widen, an invitation, and Parker steps forward, settling between them. He's still too far away. I haven't felt like this since that night in the stairwell. Electric. Needy.

"Can I lift you again?" he says softly, breath hot against my forehead, and I nod, wishing he would ask for far more.

A moment later, his dexterous—*Really, that was the best word you could come up with?*—fingers are curling around my waist, and he's lifting me with an ease that I now know is thanks to an extensive gym routine. He turns, circumventing where the glass fell, and then slowly brings me back down to my feet.

He makes to drop his hands, but my fingers curl over his before I can think too long about what I'm doing. Logic has left the premises. All that is left is this deep, thrumming need. He swallows. Eyes locked, I rise on my toes. Our lips are just inches apart.

"Parker," I say, not recognizing my voice. It's just a husky rasp. He leans forward, like he can't help himself. Our foreheads press together. We're just barely touching, and it's not enough. I want to be far closer.

He must see the want all over my face, because he says, "Elle. You hate me, remember?"

"I do," I say, nodding. "I hate you so much."

We stand there, sharing breath, our chests touching with every inhale. Every scrape of the thin fabric against my heated skin is torture. His hands are still on my waist, and I want them higher, lower, everywhere. I want to tell him just how much I hate him while he bends me over the counter.

I'm shocked by my thoughts, my wants. I slowly bring a hand to his face. I run my thumb across the slash in his eyebrow and down his cheek, gently, so gently, and I swear he shivers. My other hand is on his bare chest. His heart is beating wildly beneath it.

"I missed you, when you were gone," I say, because apparently I am at this moment someone who acts on her desires and voices the truth.

"I missed you too," he says, one hand now cupping the side of my face. He does the same thing I did, explores for just a moment. His callused fingers lightly scrape against my cheek. Down my temple. Across my lips. I swallow, and his fingers trace down my neck. His thumb runs across my collarbone. I'm ready, aching.

But he steps back. I carefully fall back onto my heels and watch as he walks over to a cabinet I hadn't investigated, gets a fancy glass, fills it with water from the fancy machine, and carefully puts it in my hand.

"Drink, Elle," he says. I do.

The cold water almost immediately puts out the fire burning beneath my skin. I'm suddenly too aware of my peaked chest and his lack of shirt entirely, and the fact that I just broke his mother's vase.

"I—"

"You should get some rest," he says, turning away from me, and I nod.

"Absolutely." I raise the glass. "Thanks again."

And then I rush back to the room.

"WE'RE NEVER DRINKING AGAIN," I TELL MY REFLECTION. MY MASCARA and eyeliner have headed south for the winter. My hair looks like I've spent the morning on a roller coaster.

I woke up against a silk pillowcase way nicer than the one I currently sleep on, tensed, and groaned as the memories came flooding back.

Me on that decorative couch in the hallway.

Me and Parker, entering his apartment.

Me again, becoming the world's worst snack thief and breaking a vase.

Parker, cleaning up the glass on his knees, after lifting me onto the kitchen counter.

Us, staring at each other. Me, still in his shirt.

Part of me hoped he would take pity on me and be gone before I got up.

But, as I inch out of the room, dressed again in that scratchy top and skirt, his shirt folded on top of the made bed, I hear the gentle chime of glass bowls clinking against each other. A light sizzle. And . . .

Bacon?

I walk into the kitchen, slowly, only to find Parker turned toward the stove, hand expertly around a pan's handle.

He's wearing a shirt now, thank goodness—yeah, right, who am I kidding?—and the same sweatpants from yesterday. As much as I'd like to admire his back muscles flexing as he flips something in the pan, my eyes go to something far less attractive.

A pasta-filled vase on the counter.

I freeze.

The same exact vase is sitting in the same exact place, and it's even uglier in the summer light.

Panic races through me.

Has it returned from the dead to haunt me?

Did I have some weird dream about breaking it last night?

Can I see the future?

Parker turns around, and any fear of awkwardness I had anticipated between us after last night is put to rest. His face lights up, like he's genuinely happy to see me. Maybe he's relieved I didn't choke on my vomit in my sleep. He looks slightly disheveled, even more so than after the gym. This is Parker Warren before he puts on his suit and smooths down his edges to face the rest of the world.

I stop by the edge of the counter and motion toward the pasta vessel that has decided to haunt me. "I was going to apologize again for breaking your mom's vase, but . . . it's been resurrected?" I press two fingers against my forehead, wincing at the pain pulsing behind it. "Did I—did I imagine last night?"

Last night.

His eyes slightly glaze over, like he's remembering too. Me perched on the edge of the marble. Him between my knees. His hands on my waist—

"No," he says, his voice just slightly deeper than usual. "It was part of a set." I must look horrified at the idea that there were at least *two* of these in circulation, because he says, "You know, I'm starting to think you pushed the other one on purpose. If something happens to this one, I'll really be suspicious."

I almost smile. "Don't worry, I'm not a pasta-vase serial killer. Just single homicide for me." He flips something in the pan again, effortlessly. I realize now that he's making an omelet with what looks like spinach and mushrooms and pieces of bacon. "What . . . what are you doing?"

"I'm making you breakfast." He tilts the pan, and the omelet slides onto a plate. He looks up at me. "Please tell me you're not one of those people that doesn't eat breakfast."

"Oh no, I eat breakfast," I say. He looks relieved. "Just not vegetables."

He looks horrified.

"Don't you have a chef?"

He nods. "Normally, I do. But not for the summer."

Right. This is his summer of normalcy. His summer of cosplaying as someone whose net worth isn't equivalent to the GDP of a small country.

"So, you . . . learned to cook?"

"I learned when I was a teenager. My mom taught me. I was rusty, though, so you're lucky you caught me with some practice. At the beginning of the summer, this would have been a sad scramble."

The idea of Parker learning to cook when he was a teenager is at odds with whatever story I've already written for him in my head.

Maybe I don't really know him.

He pushes the plate toward me. "I can make you something else if you don't want it. Though I do think you should look into the concept of eating vegetables."

I take the plate. He hands me a fork. "Yes, I have heard they're good for you," I say in mock seriousness.

"Essential to human life, some might say."

Penelope says it's a miracle I haven't keeled over in front of my laptop by now. I've told her that it's a miracle I haven't gotten a new roommate after she's killed three consecutive blenders by trying to make green juices at home.

I lean my hip against the kitchen island and stab a bite of omelet. Parker stands there, hands braced on his side of the counter, watching me.

"Aren't you going to eat?"

He shakes his head. "Already did."

I frown at the clock. It's only just past nine. "How long have you been up?"

"Since six." He motions toward the plate. I take a bite. He looks on expectantly, like he really does care what I think of what he made me.

"It's good," I say, taking another bite. "You know. For vegetables."

He smiles, genuinely pleased with himself. He gets me a glass of water. I sit on one of the high stools at the counter and watch as he begins to do all the dishes.

"So?" he asks, when I'm done, and he's taken my plate. "Does it look like your unit?" He motions around.

I shake my head. "No. And it's not mine, it's my sister's." I look around. "I like yours better, I think," I say. "You have a sexy kitchen." I really don't know why I said that. I blame any lingering alcohol in my system.

He stills. Looks over at me. "A sexy kitchen?"

I nod. "Like, sex could happen. In this kitchen." Oh my god, I need to just sell my voice like the Little Mermaid, so I never say anything like that again.

Parker only smiles. He's bracing himself against the counter again. His arms are flexing in a way that makes my chest tighten. His eyes darken. "Is that a proposition?"

I think I forget to breathe. "No," I say quickly, shaking my head. I can feel the heat spreading across my face. He looks amused. At his grin, I say, simply, "I take contracts very seriously. Even oral ones." Why do I even bother talking?!

"Right. No sex. Almost forgot."

I slide off the barstool. "Yep!" I chirp, hoping I look and sound more casual than I feel. I need to get out of here before I keep saying things that will inevitably be replaying in my head tonight in a sad anxiety reel.

"Well, thanks again. For . . . taking me in. And for . . . feeding me!" I sound like a stray dog.

"Any time, Elle," he says. I collect my heels from the doorway.

"Oh," I say, the rest of the night collecting in pieces. "Emily broke up with Charles because he was selling stories about you."

Parker doesn't look too surprised that his suspicions turned out to be true.

"She told him if he went to the press about us, she would get him fired."

He looks impressed. "I've always liked Emily." His lips press together pensively. "So, we'll need another way for our relationship to go public, then."

"Fake relationship."

He moves on as if I haven't said anything. "We'll need a highly publicized event. One with journalists and photographers."

I frown. That sounds like my worst nightmare. Also, not common. "What kind of event like that happens in the summer?"

His eyes meet mine. They're glittering with something. "How do you feel about art auctions?"

"My sister loves them."

He seems surprised that I've offered him another little kernel of information. "Okay. What do *you* think of them?"

I don't answer immediately, not the way I normally would. Instead, I pose myself the same question, as though I haven't lived with this mind and body my entire life. *What* do *I think of art auctions?*

Art history has always fascinated me, though not as much as my sister. I took a class on it at Columbia as an elective, with Penelope. All I really know about auctions is what I've seen in movies: the ping-pong-looking paddles, the hushed phone calls from bidders around the world. It might be interesting to see.

This summer is about doing things outside of my comfort zone.

"Sounds fun," I say, trying to make my tone convincing.

Parker looks a little surprised. "Have you ever heard of Christie's?"

15

WE MIGHT AS WELL BE AT A MOVIE PREMIERE. MY NERVES BEGIN TO STIR AS WE pull up to the building. There's a photo op station and dozens of paparazzi already lined up, down the block. There are even a few journalists holding oversized microphones.

"Is there always this much press at auctions?" I ask, wondering if it's too late to turn the car around.

It is. Parker's already out. He's reaching for me. "No. We got lucky. There's a rare pink diamond for sale, but the main attraction is a necklace that has the biggest diamond ever discovered. All the heads of jewelry companies are going to fight over it." He nods toward the growing cluster of cameras, all still pointed in the opposite direction. "They're here to see which one wins."

"Ah," I say. My knowledge of pink diamonds comes exclusively from the *Pink Panther* movie with Beyoncé.

I hadn't known what to wear, but, mercifully, there was a dress waiting on the hallway couch again. A simple, strapless dark blue dress with matching heels.

We head to a side door, circumventing all the press. "There will be photos afterward," Parker says in my ear, tracking my view. *Great,* I think, dread already sinking through my bones.

This is what I signed up for, though. I knew the conditions from the beginning. And, as much as I hate admitting it, our agreement has made me far more productive. I'm already well into the second act of my screenplay.

A few pictures are a small price to pay.

An associate from Christie's greets us. "Mr. Warren," the man says, shaking his hand. Parker then turns to me.

"My girlfriend, Ms. Leon."

The man shakes my hand next. He smiles. "Elle. Pleasure to meet you. Would you both like a final preview of the pieces?"

Parker nods and takes my hand in his. I look around for cameras, but there aren't any inside. The message is clear, however. Out in public, I am Parker Warren's girlfriend, whether we can see the press or not.

All the jewels are set up behind a sheet of glass, laid out like a feast. Diamonds, it turns out, can come in a variety of shades and shapes. They remind me of ripe fruits. I see blue, yellow, green, even orange.

There are also pieces made of other precious stones. Some are more beautiful than others. Behind a strangely mushroom-resembling bracelet is a pair of teardrop ruby earrings. I had some just like them, from a play set, made of plastic. My mom used to clip them onto my ears, and we would walk on our tiptoes around the house, pretending we were fancy, while she was pregnant with Cali.

Normally, she was serious. Firm. She locked herself like a prison, like it could keep the hurt from spilling out. Like being strong meant being unfeeling. Like being smart meant being alone.

It was one of the only times I remember her throwing her head back and laughing. As if she had forgotten, for just a moment, that life didn't always have to be so heavy.

I smile, remembering. My fingers catch against my necklace. It's not worth anything, especially compared with any of the stones behind this glass, but it means everything to me.

What would she think of me, here, with a tech billionaire? About to parade myself in front of cameras?

I wonder if she would understand, given the circumstances. If she wouldn't mind, as long as it was all pretend.

"And, of course, the pièce de résistance," the man says, pointing toward the only necklace that is encased in another layer of glass. "Winston, De Beers, and Tiffany all want it."

I can see why. The diamond is shockingly large, even from far away. It's like a piece of art.

We get ushered into a room full of chairs and led to one of the front rows. Parker is handed a paddle.

The auction begins.

Parker doesn't seem too interested in anything. Most of the time we just sit there, bored, and I try not to flush when he starts to absent-mindedly trace shapes on the top of my hand. Then the shapes start to turn into letters. He's writing me notes.

Help, one reads.

I shoot him a look. He's still looking straight ahead, expressionless.

Boring, another says.

I start to trace my own message across his ridiculously large hand. *Your fault,* it says.

Luckily, there's supposed to be a break after this piece. I look at the clock, only to see that strange mushroom bracelet fill the screen.

The bid starts at a hundred thousand, a startling amount for something so ugly. I almost laugh.

Parker raises his paddle.

I glance at him, perplexed, but he doesn't look my way.

Someone else bids one fifty.

He bids one seventy-five.

Someone bids two hundred.

Parker looks annoyed. "Three hundred thousand," he says, and some people behind him gasp. There's no way that bracelet is worth that much. I wonder what in the world he's going to do with it. Maybe it's a gift for his mom? It seems like something she might like . . .

The gavel comes down, and the item has been sold. Parker puts his arm around my shoulders, and I try not to tense. I know what we're doing. We're pretending. I can feel the curious glances at our backs. Still, the stutter in my chest feels very real.

When we walk out of the room, I'm grateful. It felt too full in there, like all the air was slowly being sucked out. I don't know how I'm going to sit in there for the remainder of the auction.

People try to talk to him, to congratulate him, but when we finally end up in a quiet corner, I frown at him. "Why did you want that bracelet so badly?"

Parker's answer is immediate. "It made you smile."

I blink, not sure if I'm more shocked at the fact that he just spent *three hundred thousand dollars on something that made me smile . . .* or the fact that I don't remember smiling at it at all.

Then it hits me. "Parker," I say very carefully, "I was smiling at the earrings behind it."

"Fuck," he says, and turns around.

Just like that, I'm alone. And more than a little confused. I'm about to pull my phone out of my purse when someone comes up to me. Her blond hair is braided into a crown against her head.

Carissa, from the dinner. Great. This time, at least, she's wearing a dress that obeys the laws of physics. "I have to admit," she says, "I didn't expect this to be anything serious."

I frown. "The auction?"

She gives me a scathing look. "No. You and Parker."

Oh. *Well, it's not,* I want to tell her. But I'm not supposed to. And, come to think about it, I don't really like what she's implying. "And why wouldn't it be serious?"

Carissa smirks as she looks down at me. She's wearing heels far taller than mine. "Everyone wants him. He has his pick of the city. I'm just surprised he picked you."

Anger is building behind my ribs. I might be a hermit and not the best at having friends and might intake an alarming amount of caffeine daily but I know my own worth as a person. I keep my mouth shut, knowing this is what she likely wants, to get a rise out of me.

In response to my silence, she says, "Well. Perhaps it isn't serious after all. Summer flings happen all the time, of course."

I smile. "Better luck next summer, I guess."

She gives me a grating look as she walks away.

Parker has returned. Carissa tries to talk to him, but he strides past her as if he doesn't even notice her. No. His eyes are on me.

"The earrings are in the next lot," he says.

"Parker," I say very clearly, "I don't want the earrings. Please, don't buy me anything. Give your mom the bracelet. I'm sure she'll love it." I hope he doesn't think I mean it's because she has awful taste. "Moms—they love bracelets, I mean," I say, clarifying. "My mom loved them, at least, and—"

His hand is steady on my back. He looks amused. "Don't worry," he says. "You're right. My mom will love it."

I nod. Good.

We're not actually dating. A real gift, *because I smiled at it,* is well beyond the scope of our agreement.

Is it all for show? Is Parker going to tell the reporters he bought the bracelet for me? It's the first time we're in a large crowd, acting like we're together. I'm not used to this—my pulse is racing every time he gets close to me, my body doesn't understand that this is all fake.

Suddenly, I need some distance. Just for a little bit, to recalibrate.

There's a sign for the preview of another auction, coming up next month, in the next room. It's featuring impressionist paintings. That was my favorite part of art history. "Do you mind if I sit this one out? I want to see the preview."

I wonder if he'll tell me this isn't part of the plan.

He doesn't. "Of course," he says, no hint of annoyance in his expression.

Conversations are happening around us, small groups forming, speaking about the pieces that were snatched up and those yet to be auctioned off. Still, they seem fixated on us. On Parker's hand along the bottom of my spine. He reaches down and lightly presses his lips against my cheek. It's just a whisper of a kiss, but then he's gone, and his heat has somehow been left behind, and it's falling through me.

Breathless, I walk into the preview.

Calm down, I tell myself. *It's all for show.*

I try to distract myself by carefully studying the paintings. Some of the artists are familiar. The rest, I google.

The last one, carefully positioned behind glass and a warning sign in several different languages, is a Monet. A woman in an elaborate hat is sitting among long grass and flowers, reading a book. A parasol is upturned behind her. She's lost in the words, in another world. Part of me wants to be there, like her, buried in daffodils.

I remember sitting in front of the television, so close my nose almost brushed the screen. *It's like you want to crawl inside the movie,* my mom would say, amused.

She got me a library card, but books never had the same escape. It wasn't until I found out you could borrow movies there that I enjoyed it. Every week, something new to watch. Another life to get lost in, if only for a couple of hours.

When I've seen all the pieces, I wait on a bench and scroll through my phone, then put it away. I have a sudden, strange, and concerning urge to talk to Parker. To have his messages traced on my hand. To look at him and have an understanding pass between us. I realize, in that moment, that we don't even have each other's numbers. Texting isn't necessary when we live next door to each other.

I need to get it together.

It's another hour before the doors burst open again, and I immediately hear the excitement. The auction is over. People are loudly discussing it, the pieces, the ridiculous prices. *Fifty million dollars.* One of the diamond companies bought that necklace for *fifty million dollars.*

I stand, and Parker finds me immediately. With a simple hand against my back, he leads us toward the double doors, where I can see flashes of cameras and commotion. We linger at the side.

It's time. This is what we came for.

My chest feels like it's been overtaken by the bundle of balloons from *Up*. My throat is tight.

No one has ever paid much attention to me. That's on purpose. I don't *like* the attention. I've lived my life exclusively in the shadows, in anonymity.

Now, that's about to end. At least for Elle Leon, the person. Not me, the screenwriter. I frown, wondering when I started to give my profession most of the attention.

Who is Elle Leon? I find I barely know. I'm better at writing everyone else's story than I am my own.

"Elle." I look up to see Parker's face, clear of any nerves or uncertainty. "We don't have to do this. We can leave out the back."

"But our deal," I say, my voice thin. This is why I'm at this auction. Because—if it's not part of our agreement—then what am I doing here with him?

He doesn't even hesitate. "Fuck the deal. I don't want you doing anything you don't want to."

I almost take him up on it. I almost escape out the side door from which we came.

But even though I believe Parker would continue our deal, that wouldn't be fair. We made a promise. And I don't intend on being the only person getting something out of this agreement.

Besides, he needs this press to outweigh the headlines about the trouble with the acquisition. If this helps him . . .

"I want to do it."

Parker studies me for a few moments. Then he nods.

Security guards are walking toward the doors, in the direction of the paparazzi. They have a box between them. I can only guess what's inside: the star of the show.

I frown, watching the chatter intensify. I start to doubt Parker's plan.

"Wait. No one's even going to be looking at us. They're all going to be looking at the fifty-million-dollar necklace."

"Then it's a good thing you'll be wearing it," Parker says, as the security team stops right beside us. Before I can react, the box is clicked open. He doesn't waste a moment before clasping it against my neck.

"I—I can't wear this," I tell Parker, eyes wide.

"Why not?"

I motion wildly. "This belongs in a museum! Or on a statue! Or behind a glass box!"

He shakes his head. "No," he says. "It belongs to me."

His finger runs down the chain, dragging against my bare skin, all the way to the stone, and I shiver.

"It belongs *on* someone who can outshine it." He lightly tugs the diamond. "It belongs on you."

Parker turns us toward the doors.

Before I can even process the situation, we're led through them, and I'm nearly blinded by the cameras.

Lights, everywhere, staining my vision, stars bursting then fading, only to be replaced, an endless galaxy. The roar of excitement sounds like a storm. The press is loving this. We're led in front of the photographers. They start *yelling* at us.

"Look this way!"

"Right here!"

"No, over here!"

"Let's see a kiss!"

"Move your hair!"

"Who are you?"

I blink and can barely see, my vision is all flash, all I hear is a dozen increasingly urgent orders from every direction. My heart is beating way too fast, my shoulders are hitching up, this dress is suddenly too tight and—

Parker's hand flexes on my waist. He's like an anchor in the chaos. I look up and, through flashes, can see him staring down at me. *Green.* A peaceful color, I think. The shade of the forests I used to hike through with my mother, to find the redwoods, during our brief stint living in Northern California. She loved nature as much as I do. More, even.

I remember his fear at the Summit. I remember telling him, *Don't look down. Look at me.*

I can almost hear him saying the same thing to me in response to my panic.

Don't look at them. Look at me.

I do. The world dims. It's just us, staring at each other. Helping each other through a tough moment. Communicating in this wordless way, a language we've developed through a mosaic of a hundred small moments. One I wasn't even aware I was learning.

I take a shaking breath that has nothing to do with the photographers, but Parker seems to sense my stress and says, "That's enough," before leading us away, ignoring all the yells for interviews and *one more pose!*

"Elle, are you okay?"

We're in a hallway. I'm blinking too many times, hoping it will do something to melt the stars from my vision. I nod. "Yeah. I'm just trying to see clearly again."

His thumb rubs gentle circles against the bottom of my spine, as he leads me down the corridor.

He's good at this, I think, as he looks over at me . . . as he looks at me like I'm more important than the two-hundred-carat diamond resting on my chest.

Suddenly, the strapless dress makes sense.

"You were planning this," I tell him, voice quiet, as we walk through a room of press, filled with publicists, Christie's associates, and security. Carissa is there, with another group of socialites, glaring at me. We stride right past all of them, despite rising protests.

A corner of his lip raises. "Of course I did," he says. "I don't make fifty-million-dollar spur-of-the-moment decisions."

I almost choke, remembering the price. The circles along my spine get bigger. "Why? Just for this? Just to make a statement?"

He lifts a shoulder. "My financial advisers have been telling me to diversify my portfolio. I just did."

I frown. "Aren't diamonds, like, terrible investments?"

"Not when they hold records."

I shake my head.

He closes the door behind us, and I look around, relieved to find us alone. There's just a single couch inside.

Once I sit, the full weight of what just happened sinks in. *My mom's necklace.* This one is on top of it. As if it's nothing, as if it's meaningless, as if it can just be *replaced,* because it isn't worth tens of millions of dollars.

What would she say, if she were alive, and saw me pictured next to Parker Warren? Wearing a necklace like this, like some sort of trophy?

"Take it off," I say, sharper than I meant to.

"If that's what you want." Parker casually unclasps it, then opens the door. Hands the necklace back to the guards. Closes it again.

I shake my head, breathless. I'm relieved to have it off me. My hand reaches up to my mom's necklace. I roll the charm between my fingers, like it can remind me of who I am, who my mom raised. "This is why I could never be with someone like you."

He was reaching toward me, as if to tuck a loose strand behind my ear, but he stops dead. "Someone like me?"

"Someone with so much money."

His arm is now firmly at his side. "Why is that, exactly?"

I sit back against the couch cushions, suddenly exhausted. Drained. "My screenwriting fee is exorbitant. It took years for me to get there. But I would have to write, like, a hundred movies to buy that necklace, before taxes, with my every last dollar." I shake my head. "It just . . . my work wouldn't matter anymore. Why would it? It would be like a drop in the bucket."

Parker looks more wounded than I expected. Any softness in his expression has sharpened again. "You write movies just for the money?"

I'm oddly defensive. "No. Of course not."

"Then why would it matter?"

He wouldn't understand. I'm not going to explain it to him. "It just would."

Parker smiles at me, but it doesn't reach his eyes. Not even close. "Then it's a good thing that this is all pretend." He reaches into his pocket and drops a pouch into my lap. "For the pictures," he says, before going into the other room. I guess he changed his mind about talking to the press.

I open the pouch. Turn it over.

And the ruby earrings drop into my lap.

THE CAR RIDE BACK IS LONG AND AWKWARD. WE'RE STUCK IN TRAFfic. The Escalade doesn't move for several minutes. Fifth Avenue might as well have become a drive-in movie theater, like the one my mom took us to once, on the first birthday my dad didn't bother showing up for.

It closed down soon afterward, but there were free movies at the park every day of the summer, and we would go to every single one. We'd bring blankets, and popcorn my mom made on the stove, and chewy candy, and I would stare up at the screen, fascinated.

After one night, my mom noticed I was quiet on the ride home. "What's wrong?" she asked.

"I didn't like the way the movie ended. It was stupid."

She just laughed. "You think you could write it better?"

I narrowed my eyes at her. "Yeah. I think I could."

She shrugged. "Okay. Then do it."

Then do it. That was her phrase. Whenever I complained about something, whenever I wanted something, it was always *Then do it.* It used to annoy me as a child, but I came to appreciate it. It meant action—not just thinking, not just wishing, not just dreaming, but *doing.*

That night, I wrote a new ending for the movie on a piece of printer paper. I showed it to my mom. She read it, folded it into a square, put it in her pocket, and said, "Good. Why don't you do it again?"

"Again?"

She shrugged. "Maybe it will be even better."

That, again, was *very annoying.* Scowling, I tried to write the same thing by memory, but I couldn't. I got most of it right, but, after she handed the other one back, I realized, begrudgingly, that the second one was better. So, I wrote a third one. Then a fourth. The ending kept getting better and better. It would be a while after that until I even thought about writing movies again, but that lesson never left me.

A honk brings me back to the car. We've moved exactly half a block in the last ten minutes.

Pedicabs wrapped in lights and blasting radio songs zip by. I'm almost tempted to throw myself into one and pay basically a month's rent to get back to the apartment, just so I don't have to be next to Parker Warren for another second. I haven't thought about my mom this much in a while, and guilt is starting to gnaw at me, knowing she wouldn't approve, knowing she would be disappointed.

With a look to make sure there aren't any bicyclists, I wrench the car door open.

I can hear Parker turn immediately. "Elle, what—"

I slam the door before I can hear any more.

Yes, I'm in heels that have already imprinted themselves on me in some horrible blister anklet. Yes, there are ruby earrings in my purse probably worth more than a sports car. Yes, I can see the dark gray clouds swirling above, as if my mood has decided to synchronize with the weather.

None of it matters.

I'm not even a step onto the sidewalk when I hear another door slam closed. Then I feel a presence at my side.

"Get back in the car, Parker," I say, my voice withering.

"Not unless you do."

My feet are killing me, but the strides I'm making in these heels are impressive. "A decent chunk of your net worth is in the trunk. Wouldn't want to lose it."

There is a security vehicle behind it, provided by the auction house. They're probably wondering what the buyer of a fifty-million-dollar necklace is doing, abandoning it so casually.

"Not even one percent, Elle," he says.

I roll my eyes. "Wow. So impressive. Are you sure there's even room for me in the car, with you and your ego inside?"

Parker lets out a startled laugh. I don't even look up at him.

"Look," I say, jogging to cross the next intersection in time. The clouds above have gotten increasingly darker. "Our appearance ended a few blocks ago. I'm walking. You're free to take a phone call or do whatever important business stuff you need to—back in the car."

A minute later, he's still by my side. Whatever. If he wants to get soaked on his way home, that's his own business.

We walk the next five blocks in silence. My eyes keep darting up past the skyscrapers, wondering if luck might actually take pity on me and let me get home dry. It's like we're traveling against a current, a sea full of people wearing backpacks on their fronts and carrying an array of colorful, logo-covered shopping bags. Who knew there were so many Lego stores in the city?

A rumble of thunder makes me jump as we wait for the next light to turn.

"Scared of the rain, Belle?"

I shoot him a glare. "You really think I would shorten my name by a single letter?"

He shrugs a shoulder.

The light changes, and I sprint to the other side. I'm walking as fast as I can in these heels, and Parker looks like he's moving in slow motion next to me, one of his steps is like three of mine.

Even with the impending rain, Fifth Avenue is full of tourists going in and out of stores that act more as giant billboards.

"You know, this wouldn't be a problem if we stayed in the car," he says.

I roll my eyes. "I hate traffic," I say, nearly tripping when my heel gets stuck in a grate. I wrench it out. "I hate this *city,*" I say, cursing under my breath.

"Really? Why?"

I don't know why he's still talking to me. I don't know why he's still here. The auction is over. He got the press he wanted. The words rush out of me, and my eyes are prickling, remembering the worst years of my life, going back and forth between California and New York, making decisions I would soon regret, even though I thought I was doing the right thing for my mom. "Because it's heavy with memories—bad ones. The city is practically painted with them."

I don't know why I'm telling him this, something *true,* when he said it himself—this was just pretend. Especially when one of my last bad memories in this city involved *him.*

Parker just looks at me. "Then paint over them," he says. "Make it new."

If only it were that easy.

There's another rumbling of thunder. I start basically half running, my feet screaming in protest. I'm going to have to soak them in hot water when I get home. I keep going, picturing the nice steam shower that Cali had installed.

Just ten blocks away. Less than ten minutes, at this pace.

I almost convince myself I'll make it.

Then, the sky breaks open. It's not a subtle, ombré type of rain. No, it comes down in thick sheets, like the clouds have been building up their arsenal for the most effective attack.

I'm drenched in a moment, gasping, and then Parker is at my side, curling his arm around my waist, pulling me from the curb. A moment later, water splashes the place I just vacated.

Still, I shove myself away from him.

He's dripping wet. Rain is clinging to his eyelashes. His white shirt is stuck against his torso, as if his abs have suddenly gone on exhibition.

"Your suit is ruined," I say over the roar of the rain.

"Do you really think I care about my suit?" he yells back. We race across the street, beneath some scaffolding. Parker makes to stand there, like we're going to wait out the rain, but I just want to get home. We're so close.

"Yes," I hiss, wondering if he can even hear me. "All you care about is your money and your company."

He looks over at me. "Is that really what you think?"

Of course that's what I think, I say to myself, remembering that night in the stairwell, the one he so clearly doesn't. Anger fills me, flamed by the thunder above. I dart back into the rain to cross the next street. Then another.

"You think I'm some sort of villain, don't you?" he says, eyes flashing with intensity, mirroring the lightning that cuts the sky in half behind him. "That's my trope, right? The heartless CEO who could never actually care about anything other than my business?"

Yes. I thought that two years ago, and I've read almost every article and interview since, all cementing the same thing I thought in that stairwell. He'll do anything to make sure the acquisition goes through, even pretending to be in a relationship. And I can't even complain, because I'm the one who agreed to it.

When we verge off onto our side street and into the building, relief is dripping through me more than the puddle I'm making across the lobby. I race into the elevator, Parker at my back. We ran the last few blocks. Our chests are both heaving. I stare at him through my wet curtain of hair, only to find his eyes burning into mine.

We get to our floor, and I dart away, only stopping when he says, "You're wrong."

"What?"

He steps toward me until my back hits the wall. He's so close, droplets from his hair are falling against my forehead. "You said the only thing I care about is money and my company. You're wrong."

Something within me heats at his proximity. At the way his wet suit is pressed against his body. At the fact that he's staring at the raindrops dripping down my neck, my chest, and disappearing into my dress.

No. He doesn't get to stand there and pretend he cares about anything else, when his priorities were clear as day when we first met. Shame had kept me silent before, but now all my anger and bitterness come rising to the surface.

I lift my chin and look right into his eyes as I say what I've been wanting to since the day we both pressed the same button in the elevator: "We've met before. And you were an asshole."

He just blinks.

"You thought . . . you thought I was the complete opposite of who I am, you *judged me* . . ." For some reason, I'm flustered, I'm breathing too hard, my face feels flushed.

He's standing there, so close, watching me, his expression revealing nothing.

I throw my hands up. "And the worst part is you don't even *remember*—"

"I remember you, Elle," he says.

My thoughts stop in their tracks. The world seems to still. "What?"

His head tilts to the side, wet hair curling around his ears. "Did you really think I wouldn't remember you?" He leans closer, until he's practically pressed into me. "Did you really think I would forget a night like that?"

Night like that. Please. "It was five minutes."

"I was trying to gather the courage to talk to you for far longer."

He had been . . . watching me? He'd wanted to talk to me?

No. He's lying.

"Prove it," I say. "Where did we meet?"

"The Next Big Exits party, two years ago, at a nightclub. You practically dragged me into a stairwell with you."

"*I did not,*" I scoff, and a whisper of humor dances in his eyes.

"You're right. I went *very* willingly," he says. He lifts his hand, and his knuckles brush away the raindrops on my face, then slide down my neck. I let him. "I would have gone on my knees to get you to come home with me that night."

"Instead, you just offered payment," I say bitterly.

He frowns. "I didn't—"

"You thought I was a *gold digger.*" I shake my head. "I can't get past that."

"Sweetheart," he says bitterly, "you judged me just as much as I judged you."

"I did not," I say with all the conviction in the world.

He raises an eyebrow at me. "You thought I was a bouncer. You judged me because of my looks, the same way I judged you." I say nothing. "Would you have believed I was the founder of a big tech company?"

No. The answer, if I dig down deep, is no. Of course not. I thought he was a model, not a former computer science major from Stanford.

He's right. I did the same thing to him that he did to me. Almost. I'm not the one who offered a helicopter ride in exchange for sex.

"I'm sorry," he says, any humor dropping from his expression. "I'm sorry for judging you. I'm sorry for not knowing just how special you were. I'm sorry for implying you were after anything but a good night."

"I thought about you for so long . . ." I say. *I hated you for so long.*

"Me too," he says, his voice a dark rasp. "I looked for you after that night. I tried to find you online, but there was nothing. You were a ghost. Now, I know why."

I don't want to believe him. I don't want to feel this incessant pull in my chest toward him, like we have our own form of gravity. I break our gaze.

It doesn't matter, I tell myself. *None of this is serious.* I can be attracted to him and still kind of hate him.

His hand curls around the back of my neck, gently positioning me so our eyes meet again. For a fluttering moment, I think he might kiss me, but he doesn't. His hand slowly drops, callused fingers slipping down my wet skin, making me swallow. His thumb traces the low neckline of my dress, causing a chill to lick down my spine. My skin is all prickled. *From the cold rain,* I tell myself, even though it's a lie.

I gasp as his warm fingers dip below my dress. His thumb curves, tracing the edge of my chest, and I'm breathing too quickly, I'm wanting this a little too much. He pauses, as if giving me a chance to ask him to stop, but I don't. No, instead, I arch my back in an attempt to get even closer, hoping he'll touch more of me.

Parker makes a pleased sound, and his other hand curls around my hip bone, pulling me toward him. His thumb makes wide sweeps across the sensitive skin there, just inches away from where I'm aching. Then his hand slips down to grip my ass, the same way he did that night in the stairwell, as if reminding me, as if he's showing me *he remembers.*

His other thumb is circling my chest beneath my bodice, getting closer and closer to my sensitive peak. He finally brushes against it, and my shoulders hike. I press my lips together to keep back any type of moan.

He leans his forehead against mine. We're both soaking wet. His warm lips slip against my cheek as he brings them to my ear and says, "I remember everything."

Then, suddenly, he's gone, and I'm left cold and wet and panting alone in the hallway.

16

PARKER WAS RIGHT. THE NEWS IS EVERYWHERE.

"Billionaire Bachelor No Longer a Bachelor! Mystery Woman Wearing His $50 Million Purchase!"

Penelope is the first to call. Of course, her first words are "So, when can I borrow it?"

I snort. "The necklace? It's not mine. It was just for the photos."

"No," she says, not missing a beat. "The hot billionaire boyfriend."

I roll my eyes, even though she can't see it. "You mean the *fake* boyfriend?"

"Even better," she says. "Real relationships can be such a drag." She isn't wrong. "Besides . . ." she continues. "I saw those pictures. There doesn't seem to be anything fake about it."

I hadn't pressed any of the links. I do now and see the photos Penelope's talking about. I swallow. She's right. Parker and I might be better at this fake-relationship thing than we thought.

We're looking at each other like there isn't fifty million dollars between us. We're looking at each other like we're not surrounded by dozens of cameras and rude questions.

This specific article has decided to comment on how *different* I am from the women he's been photographed with before. It includes a list, and I click out of it without looking. The idea of seeing Parker with those other women sends a tearing through my chest that I don't want to examine too closely.

"Little is known about Parker Warren's mystery woman," a caption of us says. Good. It better stay that way.

"There's something else," I tell Penelope. "He—he says he remembers."

"What?"

"The night in the stairwell."

"No."

"Yes," I squeak.

"Oh my god. Maybe he has a photographic memory?"

"Maybe," I say, not telling Penelope about the other stuff he'd said, about watching me for a while or trying to look me up afterward. Those were probably embellishments. I'm sure he says that to all the women he hooks up with.

I *definitely* don't tell her what happened afterward.

It was nothing, I tell myself. We didn't even kiss.

"This just made everything more fun," Penelope says, sounding delighted.

"I'm glad my misery is amusing to you."

"Whatever keeps you writing," she says. "It sounds like you're making good progress, Elle, but CAA will probably kidnap me and demand your screenplay for ransom if you don't turn it in the day after Labor Day."

Sarah has left me two voicemails in the last week, checking on its status. Penelope's not wrong.

"You're right," I say, even though part of me never wants to see him again. Something has shifted between us, a wall crumbling, bit by bit. I need to fortify it.

I manage to avoid Parker Warren for three days. The press might think we're living together and "on our way to the altar" (yeah, okay), but the time apart is only proof that all of this is very much fake.

He doesn't knock on my door. I don't knock on his. We don't go on our daily runs. Instead, I walk, listening to music. Luke and his crew are finishing up with the second powder room, and I head down to the coffee shop, mourning the memory of that perfect scone.

I write. A lot. Writing has always been the best distraction, and it works like a charm. I write well into the night, then sleep in. Walk. Write. Rinse, repeat.

By the fourth day, there's no denying it. I've written everything I need to and have gone over the rest twice. I need to go to my next location.

I tell myself he isn't mad at me when I knock on the door. Being mad would mean he cares, which he doesn't. As he very clearly pointed out, this is *pretend.*

That's how I find myself in the back of a taxi with him, both of us *pretending* like he didn't have his hands all over me a few days ago. It's a long drive. Thirty minutes, at least. Still, we sit in silence, as if neither of us really knows what to say. That's fine, because the radio and a talk show host on the tiny screen in the back seat are happy to fill the quiet. I see the same segment so many times, I memorize it.

When we arrive, Parker helps me out onto the worn cobblestone.

There's a castle looming above. Fine, not a real castle. But it looks like one.

"Have you ever been to the Cloisters?" he asks, as we make the trek up to the entrance. He's serious. Guarded. All business.

I shake my head. "No. Never."

We arrive right at opening. It's mostly empty, just the way I like it. Our tickets get scanned, then we walk right into the first room. The ceiling is high and vaulted, and a tapestry eats up almost the entire left wall.

Parker stays by my side as I go piece by piece, reading each of the little plaques, taking notes in my notebook, trying to get inspiration. Would the characters stop to admire this piece? Would it spark a conversation?

One depicts a fourth-century hermit. I look up "hermit" on my phone to get more historical information and find a group that lived on an island in the middle of Lake Como.

I kind of want to be a hermit in the middle of Lake Como.

"They're like you," he says.

"Hermits?"

I look up and he's not staring at the hermit statue. He's looking around the room. He frowns. "No. I mean, a little bit. But, I meant . . . they're storytellers."

I take in the statues. The tapestry, the source of what must have been endless cataracts and carpal tunnel. All of it must have taken years. Decades, maybe. All just to tell stories.

"I never really thought of it that way," I say, though it seems obvious. I feel a surge of gratitude that I live in the time of Final Draft, and my laptop, and hand yoga (yes, it's a thing, and I should probably do it more).

Especially when I see a giant illuminated manuscript open to a page with a floral border. It must be thousands of pages long, and each letter is painstakingly drawn.

There are stories everywhere: on the borders of the walls, on the stained glass, on the enormous dressers. Every few minutes, a high-pitched alarm screams when someone gets too close to one of the works of art. Everyone in every painting seems to be wearing a crown. Entire doorways have been carved out and put here. I wonder where they used to lead. There are little faces on everything, even on the sides of laughably small chairs.

"Oh my god, there's a unicorn room," I say, because that is really the only acceptable response to a medieval *unicorn room*.

That is, until I realize the room is dedicated to depicting the *hunt* of a unicorn.

A set of massive tapestries adorn each wall. They each tell a piece of a story, a different chapter. One shows the hunters gathered around, wearing a perplexing mix of blue vests over red long sleeves and caps with feathers in them. A guide tells a tour that's just started that historians know almost exactly when the tapestries were created, because fashion trends moved nearly as quickly as they do now. I wonder if the men in the tapestries looked at them years later and cringed at their past fashion choices, the way Penelope and I do when we look at our college photos. Two large initials are woven into the corners of each piece, leading some to believe they were made as a wedding gift.

"Imagine putting a four-piece hand-woven tapestry on your registry," I mumble to Parker.

"I've seen worse."

I look up at him, intrigued.

"I've seen private islands."

"No."

"I swear."

I burst out laughing, and the guide gives me a scathing look.

We back toward the corner, where a high pitch screams into my ear, because I've nearly bumped into a massive unicorn horn.

No, apparently it's a narwhal tusk.

A narwhal tusk?!

The guide's look is withering.

I can't get over the narwhal tusk and the fact that they thought it was proof unicorns existed. "How are whales with majestic horns more realistic than horses with horns?" I whisper to Parker.

He lifts a shoulder. "I thought *Elf* made up narwhals until five seconds ago."

I put a hand on his arm. With mock seriousness, I say, "Am I going to have to tell you unicorns aren't real too?"

He puts a hand over his heart, feigning crushing shock and disappointment.

We both start laughing, then leave the room, right behind a guy telling the person next to him, “No wonder there’s no unicorns left. They killed them all!”

We make our way out to a courtyard lined with what are labeled, very clearly, “Poisonous Plants.” Then into a room filled with large frescoes.

“Is that . . . a dragon?” I say.

It looks more like a cobra with a spiral tail, wings, chicken feet, and horns. Right across from it is a depiction of a camel. As if they were both just as likely to exist.

Across from that is a concerning depiction of a lion from someone who had clearly never seen a lion before.

I feel a stutter in my chest, thinking of my mom. She used to call Cali and me her *little lions*. She used to tell us we were strong enough to face anything.

“Why did the studio clear all these places?” Parker asks. “It doesn’t really seem like there’s a theme.”

“They wanted a *New York* movie. Something that showcased some of its biggest draws. I don’t know.”

“So, all of the locations are in the city?”

“All but one.”

He looks intrigued.

“The last one is in Paris.”

At that, he looks even more interested. “We should go,” he says.

I laugh. He must be joking. “That’s about the *last* thing we should do,” I say, as we wait at the curb for our car. It’s taking a while.

“We could walk home,” he says, and he only half sounds like he’s kidding.

I snort. “I wouldn’t even make it to Central Park.”

“No, you would. You’ve gotten better. Haven’t you noticed?”

Yes, begrudgingly, I have. We were running every weekday up until a few days ago. And, even on my own walks, I found that I could go for over an hour without much strain at all.

"That should be our goal," Parker says. "Before the end of the summer, we're going to walk the length of Manhattan."

I look at him like he just suggested we streak through the museum. "What?"

"People do it. They walk down Broadway. We could end at Battery Park, watch the sunset, and tend to our blisters."

Speaking of blisters—the ones from the heels and my brilliant idea of running home in the rain have only barely started recovering. I'm wearing a mosaic of different Band-Aid shapes and designs beneath these weather-inappropriate booties.

I shake my head just as our car pulls up. "You've said a lot of unbelievable things in our time together," I say. "But that has to be the worst."

"Believe in yourself, Elle," he says, in a way I can feel in my bones. "I do."

I STOP IN MY TRACKS, THE SMELL OF FRESHLY BAKED BUTTERY sugar filling the space. I blink a few times, wondering if I'm imagining it, but no. Right there, in the bakery case, are three scones, like ghosts from my best memories.

"That's—is that—" I say to the barista behind the iPad, like I've encountered a mythical being behind the counter.

"Yeah, it's back on the menu," he says, like he couldn't really care less. "And we carry them every day now. Want one?"

"One?" I say, nearly choking on the word. "I'll take all of them." Then I think. "No, that's too selfish. I'll take two."

"All right then," he says, using the tongs to place them on my plate. "Hot latte, whole milk?"

I nod. "Thanks, Jeremy."

"No problem, Elle," he says, and the fact that he remembers my name, my preferred (first) coffee, and my unnatural love of these blueberry scones makes me feel warm inside. Like maybe it can be nice to talk to strangers and become friendly with them.

I hold the plate of scones with a reverence usually reserved only for my laptop. I walk toward my favorite table, only to find it occupied.

Then, miraculously, just as I'm about to consider another option, the cups on the table are swept away, like they were never there at all. My table is right there, waiting.

Strange. Mornings aren't usually this nice to me.

I take the seat, lean back, and think that if I could write here every day of my life, I would be happy. As much as I enjoy being a goblin in my apartment, hunched over the keys, alone, and mumbling to myself in between shoving dry snacks into my mouth, being among people . . . is better.

Parker walks in and finds me immediately. He grins as I wave dramatically in the air. "You'll never guess what happened," I say, surprised by how much I want to tell him something that has made me happy.

"They recontinued the scone," Parker says, very clearly seeing them on my plate.

I nod enthusiastically. "This might be the best day of my life."

Parker laughs. "Challenge accepted to somehow dethrone *return of the blueberry scone*."

I shake my head. "Impossible." I take a bite and groan. It's even better than I remembered. I look down at my plate and make the ultimate sacrifice.

"Here," I say, motioning toward the second scone.

Parker's lips twitch. "How generous of you."

I take another bite. He watches me, transfixed, like he somehow is getting happiness by watching me be happy.

"This day has just been perfect," I say. "You know this is my favorite table, right?"

"It's the only table you ever sit at," he says.

I nod. "I get here at opening most days, just so I can have it."

"And?"

"When I got here, it was taken. But right when I was walking by it, it was suddenly free. It was so . . ."

Lucky.

Now that I think about it . . . was it an employee who moved the cups, freeing up the table? Was it strange for there to still be three scones left, when it's late enough in the morning that they should all be gone?

"Parker," I say very slowly, trying to remain calm, "did you buy the coffee shop?"

He's leaning back casually in his chair, not a care in the world. "No," he says.

I melt in relief. "Oh, good, I thought—"

"I bought the chain." He looks at me earnestly. "They have a location in Brooklyn and one in the Hamptons. Did you know?"

I don't move. For a few seconds, I'm stunned. I don't know why. It's not like he doesn't have the money. It's not like he hasn't done outrageous stuff like this before.

"Why?" I ask. He leans forward, a tad less casual, when he hears my tone. "And don't tell me it's because your financial adviser told you to *diversify your portfolio.*"

He rests his arms on the table, looks me right in the eyes. "I bought the coffee shop because you love it. I bought it so that you can have your favorite scone, with your favorite latte, at your favorite table, every morning." He leans forward. "I bought it because it makes you happy, and that, to me, Elle, is priceless."

I don't know what to say. I don't even really know how I feel.

"Is there . . . going to be an article about this?"

His eyes flash with something. Anger, maybe. Or hurt. "No, Elle," he says.

That doesn't make sense then. Not when this is pretend.

Unless . . .

"Parker, this could never be anything. You know that, right? We—*we* can never be anything. I told you that I—"

"I know," he says, serious as ever. "I understand. I just want to make you happy, Elle. That's all."

I rear back, feeling a sudden bite of hurt. "You think buying things for me is the way to make me happy?" I remember the night in the stairwell, the one he *remembers*. The *type of person* he assumed I was. Clearly, that hasn't changed much.

He thought he could buy my affection then, and he thinks he can buy it now.

I stand. "You can't buy me, Parker," I say. "You can't buy my happiness. And if you think you can, then you don't know me at all."

I leave him and the pastries behind as I leave the coffee shop.

17

THERE'S A KNOCK ON MY DOOR. FOR ONCE IN MY LIFE, I ACTUALLY USE THE peephole, hoping to get myself back in the serial killer podcasters' good graces.

There's a familiar hulking figure there, leaning against the wall, with something I can't make out in his hands. "What do you want?" I say through the door.

"To apologize," he says. He looks up directly at the peephole now, meeting my gaze, and I fall back onto my heels.

I take a breath, open the door, and start my tirade. "If you think you can—" I stop short, frowning at what he's brought. "What are those?"

There is a stack of scripts beneath one arm, a bag of popcorn in the other.

I frown. "Are those . . . mine?"

"No." He straightens. "I'm sorry. You're right. I'm not used to having much time, so I use money to make up for it. Buying things for people instead of spending time with them. It works, mostly. I've gotten used to it." He swallows. "That's not meant to be an excuse. It's an explanation. And I . . . I don't want to be that person.

"I want to spend time with you, Elle," he says. "I want to know you."

He looks down at what he's brought. "I thought we could do something simple. A movie night. I found scripts for the newest releases."

I told him that weeks ago. I'm surprised he cared enough to remember.

"I don't have a TV," I say, looking behind me. "It's still in the box. It hasn't been set up yet."

He could easily suggest his place, but instead he says, all too eagerly, "I'll set it up. It'll only take a few minutes."

"I . . . don't have any furniture."

That doesn't seem to faze him. "I'm fine on the floor. That is, if you are."

The idea of Parker Warren sitting on the floor, watching a movie on a television also on the floor, almost makes me laugh. "Really?"

He nods. "I told you. I just want to spend time with you. The rest doesn't matter."

You won't be saying that when your lower back starts hurting, I think, considering how many hours I've spent sitting on this same hardwood, plotting my screenplay. We'll see how long he lasts.

"Fine," I say, opening the door, waiting to see any hint of disappointment that I didn't suggest his place.

But I don't see any. If anything, all I see is relief.

THE FLOOR SEEMS TO BE DETERMINED TO BE EXTRA UNCOMFORTable tonight, but Parker doesn't say a word as he watches the movie, not seeming annoyed at the sound of flipping pages as I write notes in the margins of the script.

"Good line," I say to myself, before pressing my lips together, not used to having an audience when I'm watching movies.

Parker only grunts in agreement, and my self-consciousness loses some of its gravity.

"This is the midpoint . . . right?" Parker says, glancing over at me. I'm used to him looking reassured, confident. There's a bit of hesitance there.

I frown.

"It isn't?"

"No, it is. But how do you know that?"

He turns back to the television. "I looked up some stuff about screenwriting. I wanted to learn a little bit about what you do." He motions toward my sticky note plot monster a few feet away. "You use a three-act structure, right?"

I'm about to keel over. I nod, a little unnerved. "I don't know the first thing about what you do," I say, feeling like I'm coming up short.

He smiles. "I could explain it to you. But it might put you to sleep."

Even though I have never had any interest whatsoever in tech, I'm surprised by my desire to know him. To know what it is he created. To know what he'll be working on, after this summer. I shouldn't.

Maybe I can want to know him and spend time with him, just for the summer. Maybe it really doesn't have to mean anything. Like a one-night stand. Only without the sex.

"That's perfect," I say, shoving a fistful of popcorn into my mouth. "You can be my podcast."

He raises a brow.

"I have to listen to one before I go to bed every night. It replaces the voice in my head, the anxiety. It's the only way I can sleep."

He nods, understanding.

I face him. "So, if you could just record yourself talking about your job in nice forty-five-minute segments, that would be great."

He smiles again. I look toward the screen and am happy to see he paused it a long time ago. "I'll get right on that."

He unpauses it, and I keep scribbling. The movie's plot is good, but it's long. And I'm tired.

So tired, that I don't make it to the end of it.

ONE OF THE RULES I LIVE BY HAS BEEN BROKEN. THERE WAS NO PODcast, yet here I am, in the middle of the night.

With my head in Parker's lap.

He's slumped against the wall. His hand is in my hair. The script is folded in front of me, and my pen has rolled across the room. The apartment is quiet.

I slowly rise, but Parker must be a light sleeper. His eyes open immediately.

"That's good," I say, still partially asleep. "For the serial killers."

He suddenly looks concerned. "What?"

"Being a light sleeper. It's good. Maybe you would stand a chance." I yawn. "I sleep like a rock. I always think, *If someone murdered me in the middle of the night, I'd sleep through the whole thing.*"

"Elle," he says, very carefully, "what the fuck are you talking about?"

"My podcast. The one I usually listen to. It's true crime."

"Ah."

I frown. "I don't know why, but saying that out loud . . ." I'm scared. Why am I scared? "I don't want to sleep alone tonight."

"Then don't sleep alone," he says, gently pushing me back down. I let him. And then I drift back into sleep.

THE DOOR CLOSES, AND I SHOOT UP. I'M IN MY BED, ON TOP OF THE covers.

I frown. Before I can wonder too long how I got here, Parker is leaning against the frame of my bedroom door.

"You really are a heavy sleeper," he says. He's holding a latte from his coffee shop. There's a pastry bag in his hand.

"Weren't we on the floor?"

He nods. "The whole night," he says, wincing as he stretches his neck. "I carried you here a few minutes ago, when I went to get us coffee. It felt weird leaving you alone on the floor."

"Oh."

"It's Saturday," he says.

Usually, that wouldn't be immediately obvious to me. When I write, especially on deadlines like this, I often forget what day it is, since I don't take weekends. It's like summer break in elementary school, all the days blurring together.

Now, though, I know. A schedule has taken shape. I feel every day of the week again.

"Do you already have plans?"

I shake my head no. Then I think about it. "Well, I was going to do something probably stupid."

He looks unconvinced. "I don't get the sense that you do anything stupid."

I raise a brow at him. "*Most* of the things I do are stupid." I stretch my back. "Like insisting we sit on the floor." And deciding I can potentially *just have fun* with Parker this summer.

"It was great," he says, though I can tell his back is also killing him. "So, does the probably stupid thing have to do with your screenplay?"

I nod. "It's going to sound weird."

He waits, undeterred.

"There's a part in my screenplay where the main character says, 'X has the best pizza in New York City.' And it's kind of a running joke between the two of them, because he has another favorite." I lift a shoulder. "I like to do research for my screenplays. It makes it feel more authentic—truer, in my opinion. It's just one line . . . but to me, it matters."

"So, you want to try all the pizzas in New York," Parker says.

"Not all of them. There's a list on some website." I look at him. I think about the snack cabinet filled with healthy choices. I wonder if pizza is part of his diet at all. "Are you in?"

He shrugs. "Why not?"

WE TAKE THE SUBWAY. PARKER SITS THERE, STUDYING THE MAP WE made, complete with little pizza stickers across the city, indicating our stops, and I just look at him.

He's wearing casual clothes. Or more casual than usual, at least. Slacks, a T-shirt, and shoes that look comfortable but are from one of those designers that don't have labels.

He glances over at me. "What?"

"I'm wondering if you've ever taken the subway."

Parker gives me a look. "Before a few years ago, I was paying myself barely enough to eat ramen. I was sleeping on my friends' couches. I lived here for a summer during an incubator and literally—and I mean literally—rented out someone's closet."

That doesn't make any sense. "Your company has been worth a lot for a long time."

Parker nods. "True. But without a liquidity event, it was basically just a number. When the media started calling me a billionaire, I had less than a thousand dollars in my bank account and was living in my friend's living room. It wasn't until a little over three years ago that I was able to sell some of my shares in secondaries."

"It must have been weird, then, going from not having a lot to having . . . everything. Overnight." I think about Cali.

"It was."

"So, what did you do with it?"

The subway car is nearly empty. He stretches his long legs out in front of him. "The first thing I did was pay off my mom's mortgage. The second was get black-out drunk at a nightclub." Sounds about right for any twenty-something with sudden access to that much money. He looks pensive. "Then I bought the nightclub."

"You did not." I don't know why I'm surprised at all. "Let me guess. Your financial adviser was thrilled that your portfolio was *so diverse*."

That makes him laugh. He shakes his head. "It was, apparently, a massive liability, and not good for my image either. The board made me sell it, but only after I had an amazing party with everyone I had ever met." He sighs wistfully. "How about you?"

"Oh, are we trading first-time-we-bought-a-nightclub stories?"

The corner of his mouth twitches. "What did you do when you got your first big screenwriting check?"

"I cried."

He looks confused. "From happiness?"

I shake my head. "No. I—I felt this immense sense of guilt. Like, if only it had landed a year sooner . . . things could have been different."

He waits for me to continue. I'm not entirely sure why, but I do.

"My mom got really sick when I was in college," I say. "By the third month of treatments, her life savings were drained. The new experimental trials, the medicines, they were all way too expensive. She didn't have good insurance." I swallow past the knot in my throat. "When I got that first check, I thought, *If only this had come a little bit sooner, I could have paid for everything.*"

Parker's hand curls around my knee. "I'm sorry," he says.

I try to smile. "After I cried, I transferred a big chunk of it to a charity Penelope and I volunteered at in college, then used the rest to pay off my student loans."

Parker considers this. "You never dreamed of buying anything? You never wanted anything?"

There is one thing.

He waits. He must see it on my face. "Let's hear it."

I can't believe I'm telling him this. "In college, I tutored a kid in English. His family lived in a navy-blue town house right on Gramercy Park. It had a skylight on the top floor and a marble kitchen, and sometimes, I would stand in front of it for a while and think, *I'm going to write as many movies as I need to so that one day I can buy it.*"

I don't tell him how, when I had writer's block or during stressful times, I would take the subway and walk around the park, staring at the house, as some sort of inspiration. Motivation. That just seems too sad to admit.

I don't tell him that I've done it recently. That I've looked it up online, to see if maybe it might be on the market. It isn't. Hasn't been in years.

"I'm guessing they had a key to the park."

"Yeah." I always secretly hoped they would invite me, but they never did. And why would they? I was hired only to help with homework.

The train comes to a stop. "Ready?" I say.

He sighs before getting up. "Is this the time to tell you I don't really like pizza?"

Our first stop is Patsy's Pizzeria in East Harlem. The exterior is painted dark green. Articles hang in the windows. Families walk by speaking Spanish. We arrive right at opening, at 11:00 a.m.

There's an option to sit or take out. I shrug. We choose the restaurant. It's cash only. The tables are draped in white tablecloths, framed photos cover the walls.

"So," Parker says, as we study the menu. "Are we going to order the same type at each place? Does that make it fair?"

"Yeah. We'll just get whatever seems closest to *cheese*."

We order the Old School Round pizza, which has a thin crust, tomato sauce, and grated mozzarella.

It arrives quicker than I thought it would. We grab a slice—me wincing as my fingertips get singed—then do an awkward cheer above the elevated plate.

Our gazes don't break as we each take a bite. There's a pause, a consideration, then we both nod at each other, chewing. *Good,* our expressions seem to say to each other. *This is good.*

There's a char on the bottom, rough against my tongue. Just the right amount of cheese, hot in my mouth, melting across my taste buds. It pulls in perfect strands, trailing down my wrist. It's delicious. I have to stop myself from going next door and getting a slice on our way to our next location, reminding myself that I will be approximately 60 percent margherita pizza by the end of the day. We head back to the subway.

Our next stop is L'Industrie Pizza in Brooklyn. A small cardboard sign says "This is the menu" above one of those blackboards with the stick-on letters. The first letter of every menu item is dramatically oversized. "Margherita" is missing the "g," and that's what we get.

Cookies are sold by the register. Pizzas are made right in front of us. Everyone I see behind the counter has short sleeves and tattoos. The ovens are stacked and have glass doors, pizzas crisping inside. This time, we order two slices instead of a whole pie. A guy with a mic calls our names when they're ready. They're handed to us on the thinnest of white paper plates. A few basil leaves are sprinkled on top, along with some curls of freshly grated cheese.

"Ready?" Parker says, and I have an excuse to stare into his green eyes again. Who knew trying out pizzas would turn into a test in maintaining eye contact? There's an audible crunch when we bite, and that makes us both nod. *Yes, this is what it should be, right?* our nods say. *This is the makings of a good pizza.* Our gazes stay locked as we chew, as we compliment the slice, as we consider getting another flavor.

We do the same thing all day, but it never feels the same. It never gets old. Every time we're trying a new variety—at Philomena's in Queens, at Joe's in Greenwich Village, at Scarr's in the Lower East Side, at Emily in the West Village, at Rubirosa in Nolita—our eyes widen like it's the first bite of the day. We spend a lot of time walking or on the subway. Sometimes we go back and forth through the city, inefficiently, because of opening times and new recommendations we get from anyone who sees our map. Everyone seems to have an opinion on the best places to try. Some, like Una Pizza Napoletana, open late and are nearly impossible to get into. There is one, though, that everyone insists we must make it to, even though the wait times are in the hours. That's how, in the late afternoon, we make our way back to Brooklyn.

Lucali has a redbrick exterior and a striped green awning, looking like it belongs in a small town. Only a velvet rope in front of the door marks it as one of the city's iconic restaurants.

Oh, and all the people.

It hasn't even opened yet, but there's already a line curling around the block, past a row of brownstones. I look over at Parker, wondering when he last waited in a line, wondering if this will be the moment he wants to head home. But he doesn't look annoyed, not at all. We join the back of the queue and face each other.

"So," I say. "Do you have a favorite already?"

He considers. "I do. But I don't think it's fair to judge until we've had this one."

I nod. "Same." I bite my lip. There's something I've wanted to ask him all day. "Be honest. When was the last time you had pizza?"

"About twenty minutes ago."

I give him a look.

"Five years, give or take."

My eyes widen. "Really?"

"I never was a big pizza person. My mom is one of those people who doesn't buy anything with preservatives in it. We never did delivery pizza or anything. Almost everything was made from scratch." He looks at the brownstones. "She would come home after working all day and then be in the kitchen for hours. I always told her we could get something faster, that it would be fine. But she always insisted. She didn't want us eating prepackaged stuff, and it's not like we could afford restaurant food."

"That's why you learned to cook," I guess. "To help her."

He nods.

"And your dad?" I ask. I remember reading that both of his parents are still alive. There isn't much about his parents online.

Parker laughs bitterly. "My dad was barely home, and when he was, he was in front of the TV. He never did a single thing to help her."

"His job took him away from home?"

Parker looks at me. He almost looks . . . sad. "He was laid off when I was a kid and never got a job again. I don't know where he went, but it wasn't to work. He left when I was a teenager. Started a new life on his own."

I swallow, realizing we might not be as different as I thought.

"Do you have a relationship now?" I wonder if I'm asking too many questions—and how many of these I would answer if he asked me.

But he doesn't hesitate before saying, "Only the type where he calls me when he needs a bill paid." His jaw tenses. "I bought him a house and a car a while back, and sort of thought I would never hear from him again. I was so happy when he called one day. I thought maybe he just wanted to talk to me, but no. Someone wrecked his car. Somehow, he lost the house. It's always something."

"So," I say, frowning, "that's the thing we have in common, isn't it?"

"What?"

"Our dads weren't around much."

He looks surprised but doesn't press. I don't know why I'm even saying anything. I haven't talked about either of my parents this much in a while. Him opening up makes me want to be more open too.

The couple in front of us are standing several feet away, deep in their own conversation. I take a steadying breath.

"My parents are both from Colombia," I say. "They moved to California, and they didn't have much. My dad was a student, and my mom got pregnant quickly. Then, just before my mom had my sister, they separated. At first, it was okay. My dad came around a decent amount. Then, I guess, he found something better. We saw him less and less, until finally . . . he was just gone.

"My mom's English wasn't great. It was hard for her to find a job. I remember helping proofread her applications when I was still in elementary school. Things were rough for a while, we moved a lot, but eventually she went back to school and became an accountant. She always found a way to give us anything we needed."

It wasn't meals from scratch, like Parker's mom—we ate fast food probably way too much—but she always made sure we had enough and that we were grateful for it. For fun, she would find free activities, like the summer movie screenings in the park.

"Then, when I was in college, she got sick." I hate talking about it.

I always inevitably end up crying, and I hate crying in front of people. I look around in an effort to keep the emotions from surging up. Parker's hand weaves through mine. His other hand is steady against my back. *He's got me,* I think. "She died when I was a junior." That's all I can get out.

"That's her necklace, isn't it?"

I don't even realize I'm touching it. I nod. "It is."

A little before five, the line starts to move rapidly. Reaching the door feels like its own type of victory. It happens quicker than we thought it would, but only because we have solely reached the right to put our names down for a table. There are only ten of them. The estimated wait time is at least two hours.

The people in front of us do this every month. They've perfected the Lucali line, they tell us, as we mill around the entrance. "You should walk around and check out Carroll Gardens and Cobble Hill while you wait. There are lots of bars and shops."

We take the advice. We walk and talk about nothing and everything.

We pass a bookstore with a line that wraps around the block, just like the pizza shop. I recognize the books in people's hands. Some readers even brought carts full of them.

"Do you ever think of writing books?" Parker asks.

"No," I say. "You have to be on social media nowadays to get anywhere, and I would rather die." I nod at the woman inside the bookstore, the one they're all waiting for. She's recording some sort of promotion on her phone. The moment she puts it down, her smile wilts. "Look at her. She looks miserable."

We keep walking.

"So, if not books, why screenwriting?"

It's a fair question. There are several types of writing.

"The first thing I ever wrote creatively was an alternate ending to a movie. Then, after that, I got really into reading and started to write chapters that I thought might turn into books."

I pause. I haven't told anyone this before. I'm anonymous; it's not like I've done any interviews. Parker is waiting, interested.

"I can't see images clearly in my head when I read. It's called aphantasia. Or I've heard it referred to as 'mind blind.' I didn't even know other people see full-on movies in their head when they read, until my sister told me. When I learned that, I knew the only way I would ever be able to *see* my writing was to have it be made into movies. So, I started writing screenplays."

Parker looks far too fascinated. "And the first time you actually saw your story?"

"It was one of the best moments of my life."

By the time we get the call that our table is ready, we both agree, *It doesn't seem like it's been two hours, does it?* though a quick look at the time confirms that, yes, it has been.

"I'm expecting the best pizza on the planet," Parker says.

"I don't even think I can eat another slice of pizza for the rest of my life," I say, as we're seated at a rustic table. The space is small. There are pizzas everywhere, more pizzas than there are people. I wonder if there's a pizza max capacity.

"This is the final stop," Parker says. "I think we should try two varieties."

I repeat, "I don't even think I can eat another slice of pizza for the rest of my life," then proceed to eat three different slices as they come out.

It's good. Wait-outside-in-the-summer-heat-for-two-plus-hours good.

When we're done, and the check is taken care of, I sit back against my chair, satiated and, also, a little nauseated.

Parker is staring at me. "Can I take you somewhere?"

"More pizza?" I say automatically, my voice horrified.

He cracks a smile, shakes his head no. "Somewhere nearby. I have a surprise for you."

I give him a look.

"It didn't cost anything. Just a favor."

We walk a few blocks to the subway and take the F from Carroll Street to York. Soon, the Manhattan Bridge is right there, above us. The buildings are brown and industrial. We pass Main Street Park and Pebble Beach. I've been here once, in college. Penelope and I took photos on the rocks, trying to get both bridges and Manhattan behind us. "Where are we going?" I ask, as we keep walking past everything.

"You'll see."

Will I? "My eyesight is pretty terrible," I admit. "I blame all the reading in the dark and writing."

"You'll see it," he promises.

And then, very soon, I do.

A carousel in a box, like a jewel. It's lit up and empty, as if it's waiting for us. I turn to him. I've seen this place before but never paid much attention. Right now, in this moment, it feels like the most beautiful thing in the city.

I break out into a smile. Parker can't stop staring at me.

"What?"

He shakes his head. "I don't think I've ever seen you smile like that. Like . . . you're happy."

I am happy, I want to tell him.

But it seems like giving him too much. So instead I say, "Should we get on it?"

There are tiny bulbs everywhere. The horses look handmade and hand-painted. There are dozens of them.

I choose a majestic brown horse with a golden saddle. Parker sits in the closest place next to it, what looks like a carriage. Before I can ask how it turns on, the ride starts moving. The exact music you would imagine starts playing. It's whimsical. It feels like a fantasy.

The Manhattan Bridge is right there, filling our view. The water is dark. We might not be able to see many stars here, but the city lights make up for it. The other bridge is next. This, I think, must be the best way to see the skyline. I sit in pure wonder as we pass it all by.

"I don't think I've ever seen anything so beautiful," I say.

Parker says, "I have," and I get the distinct feeling he's looking at me. I don't check. I don't want to know. I don't want to explore this feeling that's been spilling through me since that night in the kitchen.

I might have made the wrong choice with my seat. The horses move up and down, and my stomach is currently at max capacity. "I—I think I want to get off the horse," I say.

Parker gets off his chariot. He starts walking toward me.

"That seems like it's against the rules," I say. "A capital carousel offense." I'm gripping the pole in front of me for dear life.

"Here," Parker says, reaching toward me. "Let go."

I shake my head. "No, I don't think I can."

"You can. Swing your leg to the side."

I do as he says and then immediately slip off the horse's smooth exterior. I gasp—but land safely in his grip. He slowly lowers me to my feet. We're standing there, still spinning on the platform, in between horses rising and falling around us.

I'm looking up at him.

He's looking down at me.

Maybe it's the ride. Maybe it's the view. Maybe it's the day we spent together. But he starts to lean down toward me, slow enough to give me more than enough chance to stop it. But I don't want to stop it.

Our lips are just inches apart.

Just before they meet, the ride slams to a halt, and all that pizza comes racing back up.

18

"PENELOPE. HE TRIED TO KISS ME, AND I THREW UP ALL OVER HIM."

"Right," she says on the other line. I hear her moving some stuff around. "So, when can I expect you? Tonight? Tomorrow?"

"Penelope, I threw up on him, and he *still* wants to date me."

"What?"

"I mean, fake-date me."

"Sure."

To my surprise, Parker didn't seem to care about his shirt or the fact that I literally threw up all over both of us. He only cared about me.

While I was dealing with an antibiotic-resistant level of mortification, he was taking me home. Running to CVS to get me Pedialyte. Asking, every fifteen minutes, if I was okay.

"Yes," I said. "Just dying of embarrassment."

Imagine my surprise when, the next morning, instead of ghosting me for eternity (which I would have understood), he showed up at my door, with a latte and my favorite pastry, asking if I was doing okay.

"Last night, I told you I would never be able to eat anything again for as long as I live, right before you left," I reminded him.

"I know," he said.

He put the pastry on a plate, pushed it toward me. I ate every last crumb.

"Feeling better?" he asked.

I nodded.

"I have a day planned," he said. "But if you already have plans, or if you want to rest—"

"Wait," Penelope says, butting in my story. "He planned a *day*?"

"Will you let me finish?"

"What did you have in mind?" I asked Parker.

"Yesterday, when we were racing across the city, it made me think. I've lived here for years, on and off, and there's so much I haven't experienced. I have a few things on my own New York City bucket list. I've planned everything. None of it is expensive," he said. "Let me surprise you."

"So, here I am," I tell Penelope, "talking to my best friend, standing in front of my closet, wondering what to wear."

"Well, did he give you any hints?"

"He said to dress casually and comfortably. And that we would be outside."

Penelope takes a second to think. Then she says, "Have you gotten a package lately?"

"It might be with the doorman. Why?"

"I thought I might come to visit you soon, so I mailed a bunch of my clothes over in a box."

"What?"

"You know I hate checking bags at LAX."

It's true. We travel exclusively with carry-ons, unless we can snag a flight out of Burbank.

I would die to have Penelope visit. I haven't gone this long without seeing her since we met. I go downstairs and collect the box, then open it.

Inside, there are summer clothes galore. I thank Penelope again.

Then I think that I might have to start buying clothes that aren't exclusively meant to be worn inside, now that I have a reason to.

NOTHING ABOUT PARKER WARREN REALLY SCREAMS NEW YORK Botanical Garden. I stare at the sign in wonder. "This is where you wanted to go?" I say, glancing at him.

He looks back at me. "You love plants," he says, like it's obvious.

Oh.

I do love plants.

"Wow, everyone's doing merch these days," I joke, as we walk through the garden's version of a gift shop—an area full of plants available to buy. "Should we get a plant in case there's paparazzi in the hedges? Nothing says committed relationship more than sharing a gardenia."

"No, we should get one of these miniature Christmas trees," he says in mock seriousness. "It'll show we see this going past the holidays."

I'm pretty sure the thing he's standing next to has a technical name that is not, actually, *miniature Christmas tree,* but it looks enough like one for me to laugh. "The ornaments would have to be so tiny," I say.

"Or just, like, three regular ones."

It's sunny outside, and I'm happy with my choice—okay, basically Penelope's choice—in clothing: shorts, a tank top, and an unbuttoned cotton button-down shirt. I can stick it in my bag if I get too hot, according to Penelope's texts. She added fire emojis, so I actually, in retrospect, don't think she meant the sun.

"They have those in the Amazon," I say, grinning, pointing at a set of massive water lilies clustered in the center of a pond. "I would love to take a nap on one, wouldn't you?"

Parker looks amused. "I move around when I sleep. I'd end up in the water."

"Remind me to get my own water lily, then. I wouldn't want you dragging me down."

"Noted."

We walk down endless paths, framed in trees and flowers. Little signs next to them tell us a little bit about themselves. I keep saying, "Did you know flowers could look like that?" and Parker doesn't seem annoyed.

No, he seems just as interested. I become momentarily obsessed with a patch of aggressively tall flowers with thin stems leading to a halo of tiny purple flowers. "How do these not fall over?" I marvel.

"Strong core."

Some flowers have their bulbs closed, like miniature turnips. We see daylilies.

We walk into a massive conservatory. The ceiling and walls are glass. We're greeted by palm trees, and it feels like a little slice of home. There are ponds. Plants with leaves larger than our heads. Vines that curl down from the ceiling. Bright purple tropical flowers.

The gardens stretch on outside. There's so much nature, so much variety, colors that I haven't seen around me in a long time. "I can't believe this is still the city," I say.

"I was thinking the same thing."

We stop in front of a rose garden. It's sunken below—the wind carries its bright scent.

Moments later, we're in the center of it. "I didn't even know roses grew in this color," I say, staring at a magenta bulb. Roses, it turns out, can be almost any color, almost like diamonds. Butter colored, cherry colored, ballerina pink; some are striped like candy.

He's wearing a crooked smile as he studies me. "So, I should get you roses."

I shake my head. "No. I . . . hate getting flowers," I say, meaning it. "I hate watching them die."

A memory makes my throat go tight.

No, I much prefer seeing them like this. Alive. Thriving.

I turn around, only to see Parker lowering his phone. I frown at him. "Did you just take a picture of me?"

He nods.

"Why?"

"Why does anyone take pictures? I want to remember this."

I don't know what to say, except for "Well, then, at least be in the photo with me."

A passing older woman stops and asks if we would like her to take one for us.

"Yes, please," I say, and Parker looks like he would rather die. Still, he stands there while I smile next to him.

The woman frowns and lowers the phone. "You should look happier for someone with such a pretty girlfriend," she says.

I look up at Parker, who scowls. "Yeah, Parker," I say. "Try to look like you like me for a second. Who knows where this photo will get picked up?"

He's glaring as he glances down at me. Slowly, his arm curves around my waist. He's staring at my lips. I'm staring at his. I'm wishing I didn't throw up on him the last time he tried to kiss me.

"Perfect!" the woman says, and Parker breaks our stare to get his phone back.

My skin still feels like it's on too tight as he says, "Next stop?"

I can't believe he's planned this day. For someone who admittedly hasn't had time in years to spend with anyone but his company, he's doing a good job. "How many are there?"

"Just two more."

Before we leave, I stop to marvel at the forest behind us. It looks so undisturbed. So unlike the glass, steel, and concrete we'll eventually go home to.

"It's the original forest that used to be New York City," Parker says. "It's an old-growth forest."

That sounds almost like a fantasy. I look at the last remnant of the original, untouched forest and feel sad, then relieved that at least a tiny piece of it is still here.

Then . . . I feel a surprising surge of peace. Forests are dead plants feeding new ones. Forests are proof that nothing dies forever.

The Bronx Zoo is nearby. But that's not where we're going. "Should I even try to guess?" I say, sitting up in an attempt to see the Uber's screen. Parker shakes his head.

We drive and drive. We're still in the Bronx when I see it: Yankee Stadium. I turn to him.

He looks amused. "Has any piece of you ever wanted to go to a baseball game?"

"None. Absolutely zero piece."

I hate crowds. The idea of sitting outside, on a sticky seat, surrounded by people, watching a game with rules I'm not sure I understand, sounds like my personal hell.

But not right now. Right now, next to Parker, after the day we've already had . . . it sounds like something I want to do with him.

"We don't have to go to the game. We can go to the next stop."

I shake my head. "No, I want to go."

We follow the crowds through security, through ticketing, then make our way up different sets of ramps. Our seats are right in the middle, behind home plate. I can tell they're good seats, but it's nothing wild, nothing extravagant.

"Is this good?"

"It's perfect," I say, and I mean it. Because he listened. I told him how I felt, and it's clear he heard me. Something in my chest seems to give way as he smiles down at me.

"Wait here, I'll be right back." And then he's gone.

I wait in the seat, furiously googling the rules of baseball while people find their places around me, holding my phone to my ear to hear a video about the different parts of the game, and nearly jump up when something overtakes my vision.

A baseball cap. Parker's just pulled it down over my head. He's wearing the same one, his dark hair curling around his ears beneath it, and . . . it's a far cry from the suits I'm used to seeing him in. I swallow, stuck in my surprise, as he hands me a bucket of popcorn, a hot dog, and a water bottle. He has his own. Finally, I recover enough to say, "You really don't half-ass anything, do you?"

"Never," he says, still standing there, watching me.

The sun is blazing down on us. The seat is, yes, as sticky as I imagined it to be. I'm holding a flowerpot-sized popcorn box with a hot dog resting inside it. I've just put a fresh coat of foul-smelling and far too pasty sunblock on my cheeks and nose. And, somehow, I'm smiling.

Penelope would never in a million years believe this. Good thing there's proof.

Parker takes out his phone and takes a picture of me.

Then he sits down.

After the first pitch is thrown, a section of the crowd starts a chant at the players. The players chant back.

"Do you think it's real grass?" I say, watching the players run across it.

He shakes his head. "I'm not sure. All my plant knowledge was left back in the botanical garden."

Parker surprisingly knows a lot about baseball. He leans over and explains the rules to me. Every time, he gets a little closer. So close that I'm nodding without really listening to what he's saying. I'm just focused on the way his shoulder is brushing against mine. I get closer too. So close that he eventually just puts his arm around my waist, pulling me to his side.

I look up at him, but he's watching the game. His hand starts to make small shapes beneath the button-down shirt, against the side of my tank top, and I'm suddenly too aware of my skin. There's no sunblock for this, no way to temper the heat of his touch, and I try to breathe through the want that curls in my stomach with every scrape of his fingers.

"Hey, aren't you that guy?" someone says. We look up to see a guy who looks around college age, stopped in the stairs, right next to our seats. "It is you!" he says. "Whoa. Congratulations on everything. Can I get a picture?"

Parker politely declines. The guy seems to take it in stride, though, and asks Parker a few questions.

Parker might not be generous with his likeness, but he is with his time. When their conversation gets a little too long, he stands to talk to the guy a little ways off, so they're not interrupting anyone's game. Then he comes back down to me.

To my delight, his arm immediately reaches around my waist again. His fingers resume their roaming.

I look up at him. "Why'd you say no to the photo?"

"I fucking hate taking pictures."

I nod. I remember the photo of him on the cover of the magazine now, how he was practically scowling at the camera. "Right. So that one of us in the rose garden is already in the trash, right? Already 'are you sure you want to permanently delete this' deleted?"

"No" is all he says.

People around us eat buckets of chicken and fries and drink the largest beer cans I've ever seen. A man is selling them in a giant cooler, up and down the stairs. Parker gets one, and we split it, passing it back and forth between us. I've never had beer before, but it's good, especially when shared.

"How do you know so much about baseball anyway?" I ask him.

I watch his eyes almost wince, like the question is a scalpel poking at something sensitive.

"It's okay, you don't—"

"My dad taught me." Our eyes lock. "It was one of the only things he liked, so I pretended to like it too. He would take me to games occasionally. Most times, we'd watch them on the couch together. I guess . . . the pretending turned real. I started actually liking the game."

He seems conflicted about sharing this with me, as if it might erase what he said before, as if it might make his dad sound like a good guy, when he clearly isn't.

But I know what that's like. Before my own dad left, I remember going to rent movies with him. My mom might have taken me to the daily summer showings, but my dad introduced me to my favorite film. And it's complicated, knowing someone I resent planted a seed in me that grew into something that became almost everything.

Relationships are complicated. People are complicated. There's a gamut from good to bad, I know that.

I don't think too hard about the fact that Parker took us here, of all places, like he wanted to paint over the bad memories with good ones. The same thing he told me to do with the city.

The game is hours long, but the time passes quickly.

When there's a home run, we both stand. We grin at each other.

It's easy, sitting here with him. Putting our popcorn in one bucket so we can rest it between us. Leaning against his shoulder. Looking up at him and discovering that small crinkles appear next to his eyes when he smiles and they make him look boyish, so far removed from the man on the cover above a ridiculous number.

It would be so easy, I think, *to fall in love with him. To pretend life is as simple and straightforward as a baseball game in the middle of the summer.*

It isn't, though. This is just pretend. It has an expiration date. And, unlike Parker's love of baseball, pretend rarely becomes real.

When the game's over, I find myself grieving something. Maybe those carefree moments, where I didn't think of my screenplay at all.

Come to think of it . . . today is the only day this summer we've done something technically outside of our agreement. This wasn't for his image. It wasn't for my movie. It was for us. I'm not sure how I feel about that.

It's late afternoon by the time we leave Yankee Stadium.

"There's one more place," he says, "if you're up for it."

With you, I'm up for anything, I want to say, but I don't. Instead, I just nod.

It's called Arthur Avenue, in the Bronx's own Little Italy. Some shop owners tell us, very emphatically, that it is the *real* Little Italy. Freshly made bread is stacked in the windows, lines across their crusts; fold-out signs advertise different types of cheese. We go into a bakery and leave with *pane di casa,* or "house bread," a round variety that we eat from the bag, tearing off pieces. We both look at each other, giving the same expressions from yesterday, no words needing to be spoken.

There are butcher shops, markets with fruits and vegetables, and restaurants with their menus outside, encased in glass. We haven't eaten anything but the snacks at the game all day, so we head into a place called Enzo's. There are brick walls, white tablecloths, and homemade pasta that we quickly devour.

For dessert, we walk to Gino's, another shop that is clearly family owned; you see the family on the walls, in shiny gold frames, with flowers pressed to their portraits. The walls themselves are faded white, there are colorful cookies behind the glass, and a dollar is pressed just behind the register, covered in tape.

We're told we need to try the cannoli, so we do. We get two, and they're massive, or maybe I've just never had a real one. They're filled with cream and rolled in chocolate chips on one side, bright green pistachios on the other, then topped with powdered sugar.

It gets everywhere as we eat, all over our fingertips and faces, but we smile at each other, never breaking eye contact, like we've quickly developed this rule when trying new things. It's oddly intimate, seeing his eyes widen, watching his smile grow, as we have these new experiences together.

I mourn the last bite of cannoli, only to find Parker grinning down at me.

"You have some sugar on your nose," he says, and wipes it off with his thumb. "It's all over your mouth too."

Powdered sugar has to dissolve, it doesn't get wiped away, I want to tell him, but I don't want to imply anything. Instead, I quickly lick my lips, and that was a bad idea, because now, he's staring at my mouth.

I'm remembering yesterday, when he was about to kiss me. Look how that ended.

"We should get coffee," I say quickly, spotting the machine in the corner.

They serve massive cappuccinos in mugs you might find in someone's home, topped with freshly whipped cream. It's too late for coffee, probably, but I finish half of it before passing it to Parker to try.

"Sharing your coffee with me," Parker says, giving the mug back. "Now I'll never truly believe you hate me."

My skin prickles, remembering that night in his kitchen, only his T-shirt between our bare chests. *You hate me, remember?*

I do. I hate you so much.

We walk around some more. We visit a deli that sells a dozen different types of olives, in a variety of colors, and fresh mozzarella.

"You're right," Parker says, "everyone has merch these days," when we pass a shirt that says "No Pasta, No Party™."

By the time we're done for the day, and are in the car going home, I feel . . . full. And not just because we went back and got another cannoli before we left. No, some part of me, some part I didn't quite realize was so empty, has been poured into.

I fall asleep on Parker's shoulder on the way back, to the rhythm of the shapes he's tracing down my arm.

"YOU'RE ALWAYS FALLING ASLEEP ON ME," PARKER SAYS AS HE wakes me up. "I don't know if I should be offended."

I laugh, then yawn. "Actually, apparently it's a good sign if you're always falling asleep on someone. It means you trust them. It means you feel safe."

I'm just repeating something I saw online one time, but the way he looks at me, like he's suddenly honored I was probably drooling on his shoulder for the past forty-five minutes, makes something inside me flip.

"I lied," he says. "There's one last thing, if you're up for it."

I look around. We're back in Manhattan. The clock in the car says it's just past eight. For all we did today, I expected it to be far later.

"Okay. Let's do it."

We're dropped off on a corner, not too far away from our building. There are crowds outside, like people are waiting for something. I turn to Parker, frowning.

He points at the street. There's nothing there except for some cars waiting at the intersection. "Just wait," he says.

I do. And, a few minutes later, rays of gold begin to fill the place between the buildings, like the sun is trying to squeeze through them.

Of course. Manhattanhenge. Penelope and I caught one of them in college. The sunset is completely aligned with the street grid. It happens only four days a year.

I don't remember it being so beautiful, but for a few moments, it's like the city that never sleeps has gone still. Everyone stops, facing the same direction.

The city, I think, can be wondrous.

I don't realize I'm smiling until I look over at Parker and find he's watching me. I roll my eyes at him and turn his head toward the sunset. My hand brushes down his arm, and he takes it. I let him.

These minutes feel enclosed, like a moment trapped in a snow globe. It seems like the gold could keep spilling down the block forever.

But, just like summers always end, so do sunsets. The city goes dark. We walk home in silence.

Upstairs, we linger outside our doors.

"Next weekend," he says. "There's a party. I wasn't going to go, but I thought it could be fun. With you."

With you. Those two words make me feel warm, like some of that sunlight has been trapped in my pockets. "What kind of party?"

"The magazine is throwing it to celebrate the cover." His expression slightly darkens. "It's at—it's at the club."

The same one where we met.

The words sink through me, and suddenly, the empty place, the place he filled, feels hollow again. The warmth withers.

I remember the stairwell. The words he said.

He looks at me, something like hope in his eyes. Part of me wants to crush it. Part of me wants to slam the door in his face, and I wonder if I'll haunt him the same way he and that night have haunted me for years.

But the other part wants to go, wants to look for proof that he's not the guy in the stairwell. He's the guy who took me to the botanical gardens and a Yankee game, and ate cannoli with me, and let me fall asleep on him on more than one occasion.

"I'll be there," I say, if only because it will be a reminder that no matter how good today went, this was never meant to last past the summer.

19

THE WEEK GOES BY IN A BLUR. I'M IN THE COFFEE SHOP EVERY MORNING, WITH a latte and my favorite pastry and my favorite table. Parker's ownership has some perks, and not just for me. New flavors are added to the menu. More baked goods. Outdoor seating becomes available.

I've broken into my story, and it's like I can't write the words fast enough. This is my favorite part of the screenplay, where it feels like I've fallen into it. I'm at its mercy. I stay up late at night and wake up early in the morning, just to fold myself back into the story. I crave it like a drug; I live it like a second life.

My normal anxieties fade away. It's like meditation, being so singularly focused on one thing. This is the point when I usually go long stretches of time without leaving my apartment. When Penelope usually has to feed me vegetables and point out that I haven't had any water that day. It's the part when my laptop dies because I've been so buried in my pages that I have missed all the alerts telling me about low power. My screenplays swallow my life, for months at a time.

This time, it's different. I take breaks from my story when Parker comes to say hi. I don't get annoyed when he interrupts me to leave a mug of hot chocolate in front of my laptop. When Taryn asks if I want to get lunch, I go. We laugh for two hours straight, and I ask about her job working in marketing at a clothing company, because I care. On Thursday, we meet Emily and Gwen for chardonnay and pottery painting in Tribeca. We eat doughnut holes Gwen brought in her purse. We walk along cobblestone roads, going in and out of shops just to browse. Three times during the week, Parker and I go for runs in the morning, and out of nowhere, my body and mind seem to crave them. We visit Little Island and marvel at its construction—whimsical, with winding roads like a walkable board game. We run down the West Side Highway.

"You're getting good," Parker says, as I'm folded over, breathing warm summer air into my lungs, sweaty palms slipping against my knees. I look up at him, incredulous. I'm just short of needing to call an ambulance.

He laughs at the look I give him. "I'm serious. You couldn't run for a block a few weeks ago, and we just ran a mile."

A mile? He nods at my surprise.

"A mile. We'll be walking the length of Manhattan in no time."

I roll my eyes, remembering his goalpost he set at the Cloisters.

I've built a life outside of my writing, outside my apartment. It happened suddenly, without warning. One day, I woke up, and there was a little city built around me.

I'm no longer a deserted island.

By Friday night, I'm halfway through my screenplay. I sit back, marveling at the pages. Half a movie. I've written half a movie. It never gets old. I tell Sarah, and more champagne is delivered. This time, instead of letting it bubble in the corner of my fridge, I make plans for it. Maybe I'll invite Taryn, Gwen, and Emily to share both bottles with me. Maybe I'll take it over to Parker's apartment.

Before I know it, it's Saturday night.

And it's time to wear the dress. The one that has hung in this closet all summer.

"You win," I tell Penelope over FaceTime, as I grab the hanger.

"Great, what's my prize?"

"Helping me get ready."

We've been on the phone for an hour and a half, as she gave me careful instructions for how to blow-dry my hair, and I tried not to burn my scalp. Then she watched me put my makeup on while telling me about her latest date with the hot doctor, cutting herself off to say, "No, smokier. *Smokier.*"

By the time I'm done, I have more makeup on than I've ever worn in my life.

Now, as I look at myself in the mirror, I don't feel like a different person, the way I might have before.

I still feel like me. Just . . . a different version of me.

"Wait," Penelope says, as I put the phone on the bed, facing the ceiling, while I change. "Did you pack the nice underwear?"

She means the black lacy set that I bought a year ago, in case my dates ever went anywhere. They never did.

"Yes," I admit. I don't even really know why.

Penelope doesn't say anything else. I want to tell her I won't need them. That *nothing* is happening tonight. But I slip them on anyway without a word.

I'm going to a nightclub. I want to feel sexy. This is for *me*.

Then I put the dress on.

"You're too quiet. What is it?" Penelope says from the bed. "I can't see anything!"

I pick up the phone. Turn the camera so she can see the mirror.

She gasps. A dramatic stretch of silence. Then, "Does Parker suffer from any preexisting heart conditions?"

I frown. "I don't think so. Why?"

"Because he's going to go into fucking cardiac arrest when he sees you."

Penelope is being dramatic. But I do look . . . different. The dress is almost too scandalous to wear outside, at least to me. It's short and black. There are two thin straps, then tight fabric that clings to my waist and hips, riding up my thighs.

As if that wasn't revealing enough, there's a slit.

In heels, the dress feels even shorter. I swallow.

I flip the camera around. "I'm scared," I admit. "I don't—I don't know what to do at a club. I don't dance, I don't know how to make small talk, I don't know how to wear something like this and not feel ridiculous."

"Breathe," Penelope says. "The music will be too loud to talk to too many people anyway. It'll be so crowded that dancing will be more like swaying, holding a drink. Keep your chin up, shoulders down, posture straight. Take all the confidence you have and wrap it around you like a damn cashmere sweater, because you look amazing and you are amazing, and yes, I'm biased because you're my best friend, but I would say it even if I wasn't."

My eyes prickle. "I wish you were here," I say.

"Me too," she says. "If only to see the look on Parker's face when he sees you."

PARKER'S WAITING IN THE LOBBY. HE SAID HE DIDN'T WANT TO rush me.

I stand in the elevator and wonder if maybe I should just go back upstairs. If maybe I should just tell him I'm sick.

Then the doors open, and I see him.

Parker's on the phone. It sounds important. When he looks up at me, it slips out of his hand and cracks against the marble, shattering into pieces.

He doesn't even look at it. He's looking at me.

"I think—I think your phone just broke," I say, stepping toward him. I feel the rush of the air-conditioning on way too much skin.

"I'll get a new one," he says, his lips barely moving at all as he studies me. His eyes inch up my bare legs to my waist, to my chest, to my face, like he's taking in every detail. He does it again. "Elle, are you trying to kill me on the night of my cover party?"

I smile. "Maybe that's been my plan all along. A long game."

He steps forward until he's right in front of me. "Maybe I wouldn't even mind."

THE NIGHTCLUB LOOKS THE SAME AS IT DID TWO YEARS AGO.

My heart is in my throat when we enter. This could be bad. All the feelings I pushed down about him could come rearing back up. The hatred . . . or the desire. I'm not sure which is worse.

I glance over at Parker as we make it past the bouncer, and he's already looking at me. It's like stepping back in time. Security walks us downstairs, past a blown-up version of Parker's cover. "I'll help you carry this back to our building after," I assure him, and he flips me off.

His hand finds my lower back. The fabric of my dress is thin enough that I feel his fingers almost like they're on my skin. The main room is packed, just like it was that night we met.

Unlike that night, the moment we step into it, everyone turns in our direction. A few cameras go off, photographers for the event.

Parker's hand curls around my waist, pulling me toward him, almost protectively, as we're swarmed.

Everyone wants to talk to him. There are a few people from the magazine, then some colleagues in the industry, and a few women brazen enough to try to flirt with him while his hand is making lazy circles down my side. He brushes all of them off, indifferent, and converses with the people who want to talk business. He expertly handles questions about the acquisition, and it's interesting to see him in this mode. Work mode. His eyes are intense, his expression cold, just like he looks on the magazine cover.

For some reason, I put a hand on his back. He glances down at me, midconversation, and I wonder if I shouldn't have, but then his body relaxes, just a little. He always introduces me to every new person who comes up to him, but I don't say much, beyond answering a few of their questions.

Finally, someone else from the magazine comes over and leads us to our table.

It's just a slice of couch, barely enough room for both of us. The tables are overflowing with people who have clearly been here a lot longer, empty bottles sitting in ice in front of their knees. Designer purses stacked behind them, they squeeze in tight or sit on each other's laps to fit.

A woman comes to take our order. Parker asks me what I like, and I tell him the type confidently, silently thanking Gwen for explaining the different kinds of alcohol and the best brands to order at our dinner. When the bottle is delivered, he pours me a glass first. We're sitting so close together, his thigh is completely against mine. "Sorry," he says, trying to give me more room, but I shake my head.

"It's fine." I lift my drink to him. "Congratulations," I say, because I'm happy for him. Whatever he wants, whatever he does . . . I'm happy for him.

I can barely hear the glasses clink together over the music, and we don't break eye contact as we drink.

"Warren!"

Parker's eyes narrow before he turns away, toward a short man who looks to be in his thirties, walking over to us. Two women walk with him.

"Benson," Parker says flatly, reaching out to shake his hand. "This is Elle, my girlfriend." He turns to me. "This is Benson. We were in the same incubator a few years ago."

"I recently had an exit," Benson says, shaking my hand for a little too long. "Not as big as Warren's, of course, but not too bad."

I force a smile, trying to remember when I asked. I stand and extend a hand to the women, and Benson startles, like it never occurred to him to introduce them. I'm not even sure he knows their names. I sidestep Benson and introduce myself. They're both tall and beautiful. Mira has red hair and freckled skin, and Adriana is from Brazil. She has brown skin, dark hair, and hazel eyes. They're both getting their master's at NYU and happened upon Benson while trying to get into the club.

"He got us in," Mira says, shrugging.

Adriana laughs. "He clearly wanted to look cool walking in with two women, but who cares? We're here, and we're going to dance. Without him. Want to join us?"

I look over my shoulder at Parker. He's still sitting down, arm extended where I was, talking to Benson. He seems to sense my gaze, and our eyes lock. He smiles just the slightest bit.

"Sure," I say, because why not? I've already had half a drink and can feel it humming through me. I pour two more drinks for Mira and Adriana, and we carry our glasses with us to the dance floor.

It's chaos, just like I remember it from two years ago. But this time, I don't really mind. My hair dips into someone's drink, but it doesn't matter. Bodies press against me, but it doesn't make me shudder like it did that night.

Songs are played that I haven't heard since college, and I dance with Mira and Adriana, laughing, and belting out the words, and moving without a care in the world. We're in the middle, framed by bodies. No one is watching. No one cares. We're all just trying to have fun. We dance for what seems like hours, until I feel sweat in the roots of my hair. I haven't even had much to drink, but I'm drunk on the excitement, on the freedom, on the music. I'm swaying my hips, dancing to the rhythm, when I turn and see that part of the crowd has cleared. Parker is sitting there, watching me, the intensity in his green eyes nearly bringing me to my knees.

Adriana taps me on the shoulder. "We're headed to another party. Want to come?"

I shake my head. "I'm going to stay." We hug goodbye, and then I turn back around. Parker is still watching me.

I don't shrink under his gaze. No, tonight, I savor it as I walk toward him, through the crowd. He's watching my body like he's committing it to memory.

There's even less space on the couch than before, thanks to the next table having too many people, and he moves to stand to let me sit, but I gently push him back down by the shoulders and sit on his lap instead.

He goes still beneath me.

"Elle," he says, a whisper like a warning against my shoulder.

I turn to him. "We're dating, remember?" I scoot closer up his thigh, and I don't think he's breathing. "I'll get up, if you want." I make a move to stand, but his arm curls around my waist.

"Don't," he says, his voice just a tortured rasp.

For some reason, Benson takes this moment to walk up to the table again. "Where are the girls?" he asks, and it makes me want to forcibly remove him from the premises.

"The *women* left," I say.

He gives me an appraising look. "If you ever get bored with him, let me know. I just bought a two-hundred-foot yacht. It's parked in the harbor."

I just look at him, not wanting to waste my breath shouting over this blaring music.

"Sorry, Benson," Parker says lightly, though his gaze is cold. "Elle isn't impressed by money."

Benson must finally take the hint, because he mumbles something about getting gin at the bar and leaves us alone.

I turn to Parker. "That's not true," I say. "I'm sometimes impressed by money."

"Really?"

I nod. "When a big donation comes in when Penelope and I are volunteering. Then I'm really impressed."

Parker doesn't waste a moment before pulling out a brand-new phone. I blink. Somehow, in the time I was dancing, someone clearly delivered one to him.

He hands his phone to me.

"Pick your favorite cause," Parker says. "And then pick a number."

He can't be serious. I type in the URL for an endangered animal fund. It's the first one I think of, and I know it takes donations by credit card, since it's one of my monthly charges. I go to the donation page and type in an absurd number. A ridiculous one. One that could buy a house. I tilt the phone toward Parker for approval.

He frowns.

I grab the phone back. "Sorry, I know that's a lot, I'll—"

His fingers slowly curl around mine. "We can do better than that," he says, voice right at my ear.

And then he adds another zero.

I blink. The charge goes through. I didn't even know it was possible to put a number that large on a credit card.

I should have picked another charity, I think. *Another cause. There are so many—*

He seems to sense my concern, because he says, "Make a list for me. I'll give the same to all of them."

The sincerity in his tone melts something in my chest..

It's not just the money, because he *should* be giving that much, given how much he has.

But he cares about what I care about. He's making an effort.

Parker pockets his phone. We sit in silence for a while, the music blaring, the dancing getting more and more chaotic. People are making out at the table to our left. The group to our right has left, and there's more room again, but I don't get off his lap.

He's warm. His hand is resting on my hip loosely. My hands are firmly laced together in front of me.

I reach forward to grab a bottle of water from the table and feel him tense beneath me. The motion has dragged my ass down his thigh—

And he's hard.

My mouth is suddenly far drier than it was before. My skin is on fire. I forget the water and sit back, slowly sliding against his length. He grips my hips, keeping me in place, and says, "Careful."

I look over my shoulder at him. His eyes have darkened; his skin is slightly flushed. I don't think he's had more than a sip to drink, and I've only had a couple more sips than that. "Not tonight," I say. "Tonight, I don't want to be careful."

For a moment, he's just still. He's staring, like he couldn't possibly have heard me correctly. When my words finally sink in, his hold on my hip tightens.

Slowly, so slowly, his fingers begin a trail down my thigh, to the hem of my dress. He starts to trace it, very carefully, middle finger slipping up the slit, then retreating down, leaving me burning. I start to gently rock against him, desperate for any friction.

"Fuck," he breathes against my neck, as I press closer, hips grinding back. The club is packed. No one is looking at us anymore. Everyone's too caught up in their own night to care.

I turn to face him and say, "I need you."

That's how we end up back in the stairway. I'm pressed against the wall. He's towering above me. His eyes are hungry, desperate, even more so than they were that night.

That night.

I hesitate. Parker can feel it.

"I'm sorry," he says, apologizing for the second time. "I'm sorry I didn't act like a decent human being that night, because if I did, maybe I could have had more summers with you." His fingers slide down my temple, then tuck my hair behind my ear. "You're looking at me like you might be about to bolt or call this whole thing off, but I hope you'll stay, because this is the best summer of my life, and I don't want it to end. I don't want to spend the rest of it without you."

"What *do* you want?" I say, chest moving a little too quickly, repeating his words from that night.

"You," he says immediately. "I want you."

I look down. I can see how much he wants me. It makes my throat go dry, how much he wants me.

"I want you too," I say in a voice I barely recognize. But not here. Not in a stairwell. "Can you leave?"

He looks like he might be losing his mind. "I can do whatever I want," he says, and then he's taking me by the hand and leading me to his car.

WE DON'T SPEAK ON THE RIDE BACK TO THE BUILDING. WE JUST LOOK at each other in a way that can only be described as hungrily. We walk through the lobby as fast as we can and race into the elevator.

He's against one wall. I'm against the other. There's an energy surging between us, an electricity I can practically taste, a gravity I want to give in to. I'm staring at him, shaking my head, brimming with emotions I wasn't sure I would ever feel again.

"What is it?" he asks.

Sixty floors have never passed slower. I watch the numbers grow and will them to go faster. I'm so impatient, so full of feeling, I can't be anything but honest. "For years, all I felt was hurt, but at least hurting means feeling something. Then, I went through a period of not feeling anything at all." My chest rises and falls too quickly. "It's why I couldn't write."

It was like all the emotion had been drained out of me. It was like I had forgotten how to feel.

"What got you out of it?" Parker asks, hands pressed against the elevator steel, fingers flexing, like it is torture not to be touching me right now.

My voice is a whisper. "Hating you."

His eyes are burning through mine. It's like he can't take it anymore.

"Come here," he says, and we collide in the middle.

Our lips crash together, and it's a frenzy, just like the first time. We can't taste enough of each other, touch enough of each other. My arms wrap around his neck, his fingers curl around the back of my head, pulling me closer, closer.

His tongue slides against mine, flicks against the top of my mouth, and I'm gasping. Digging my nails into his shoulders. His hands slide down to my ass. He lifts me, my heels lock behind him, and we both groan as he drags himself against me. Slowly. The friction is almost too much, and I want more, grinding against him greedily. He finds my mouth again.

The elevator opens, and he carries me to his door, seamlessly unlocks it, and nudges it open.

We don't make it far.

Inside, he presses me against the door, like he can't wait another moment. We're both breathing too heavily, watching each other as I slowly lower to my feet. In my heels, I don't have to tilt my head fully back to meet his eyes, but he's still towering over me, breath hot against my temple as he leans down to whisper in my ear, in a voice that skitters down my bones, "I want to buy you this dress in every color, just so I can tear it off you."

That's it. I want him. I want him right here, against his door.

My chest is heaving. My nipples are straining against the silk. His hand trails up my thigh, his gaze never leaving mine. It finds the slit of my dress. Moves past it.

"Is this okay?" he asks.

"Yes," I say. "*Please.*"

He quickly finds the lace at my hip, then follows it down, slowly, torturously, until he reaches just above where I want him. He lingers there, for a moment, two, then, just as I start to say something, his knuckles drag straight down my aching core, and I gasp.

"Fuck," he says, feeling the soaked lace. He pulls it to the side.

At the first press of his callused fingers against me, my back arches off the door. He makes a pleased sound, watching me writhe as he slowly circles my center. His fingers are long and capable—*dexterous*—and, maybe, a little teasing. I look up at him, glaring really, lips parted as I breathe too quickly, as he takes his sweet time. "Please," I say, taking his wrist. Slowly dragging him lower.

"Just because you asked so nicely," he says, and then his finger slips inside me. I gasp, my head falling back, hand still gripping his wrist as he pumps into me. Slowly, then harder. Faster. Sparks race up my spine. My skin is electric, needy. I make a sound I've never made in my entire life. "Is this what you wanted, Elle?" he asks, mouth at my ear, his voice sounding both domineering and strained.

I nod furiously, and his lips dip to trace my jaw, back and forth. His teeth drag down my neck, ever so lightly. He pauses. Hums approvingly. Then, I go wholly liquid as he slowly licks across my pulse like he wants to feel it racing below his tongue. Like he wants to taste my pleasure.

Reason and thought and what happened two years ago have vanished. All that is left is this blazing want. I'm breathless, gasping, clinging to his shoulders as he pumps into me at an unforgiving pace.

"You can take another one," he says, then waits for me to confirm. I do, then cry out as he slips in a second finger. I tense around the building pressure, clenching, but then he starts to move again, and I'm panting. His palm starts to hit my center, and I see stars.

I start to shamelessly ride his fingers, hips grinding, and Parker braces his other hand against the doorframe. His eyes are wide as he watches me. His erection is straining against his pants.

"That's it," he says. "Fuck my fingers, Elle."

I do. I'm moving with abandon, and for once my mind is emptied out, blissfully bare, save for the cresting pleasure traveling up my spine. Nothing has ever felt this good, this all-encompassing, this right.

His thumb brushes against my center, and I cry out, pulsing around his fingers as he keeps going, cursing as he watches me break and mend again in front of him, shivering, gasping, before slumping against the door.

Slowly, he pulls his fingers back, and I'm immediately empty, needy.

"What do you want?" I say for the second time that night, my hand going to the front of his pants. A shock goes through him as I stroke him, and his hand covers mine, stilling it.

"What do I want?" he says, shaking his head.

I nod, pressing harder against the door.

His voice is a tortured growl. "I want to go on my knees and make you come again, this time on my tongue. I want to peel this dress off you. I want to bend you over every single piece of furniture I own. I want to hate you, because you're all I can think about, even in important meetings, and sometimes, it's fucking annoying."

I'm ready for all of it. He has no idea how ready I am.

He takes a step back. "But not tonight."

"Why not?" I say, breathless.

"Because it's only July, Elle," he says. "And you promised me all summer." His eyes drag down my body. He's looking at me like he wants to devour me. "I intend to take my sweet time enjoying you."

20

HE DOES TAKE HIS TIME. THAT MORNING, WHEN I WAKE UP IN HIS BED, WEARING one of his shirts, he's making lazy strokes down my back. That turns into him gripping my ass. Which turns into me straddling him, grinding my hips against his, and him nearly giving me everything I want. Instead, he gives me his fingers again, and I ride them until release finds me, and I collapse against his chest.

It's a distraction. We kiss, far too much. When he leaves me at my door after our next run, we end up making out against it. His hands end up under my shirt.

The week goes by quickly. I invite Taryn to get dinner with me. We talk about her roommate moving out and her plans to see her family this fall, across the country.

I tell her about Penelope and my sister, then a little about what Parker and I have done this summer.

"You look happy," she tells me. "Happier than before."

And I am. That happiness seems to be radiating out of me. I'm like an alchemist, gilding everything I touch. The words come easier. My moods are mellower. The things that would once bother me just . . . don't.

Parker goes to San Francisco for yet another acquisition meeting, and I work on finishing my second act. July turns into August.

When I walk home that night, taking in the buildings, laptop beneath my arm, I think New York City might not have been deserving of my hatred.

There's a charity gala tonight. Parker was invited. He says he wasn't going to go, but the benefiting cause was on the list I gave him a few days ago.

Press will be there. It'll be good for him, given the latest of several snags in the acquisition.

Our relationship, as a PR distraction, is working. Photos of us are everywhere, all over the tabloids.

"Billionaire Bachelor and Mystery Woman Spotted at Yankees Game"—insert the least flattering photo of me possible, about to unhinge my jaw to take a bite of a hot dog. "Billionaire Bachelor and Mystery Woman Stun at Nightclub"—insert a far more flattering photo of me, but also insert a comment section talking about my body in ways that both horrify and confuse me.

A charity gala appearance would be good to round it all out. I don't have a gown in my closet—Penelope is good, but she's not prophetic—but right as I begin to panic, a woman shows up at my door with a rack of clothing. She wheels it into the unit, along with a stack of shoe boxes.

Naskia is a personal shopper from Bergdorf Goodman, and she's about the most stylish person I've ever met—the type of effortless chic I have only seen pulled off by celebrities.

"We have a car waiting to take you to the store, but Mr. Warren said you might prefer trying them on in the comfort of your home," she tells me.

"Did he?" I say flatly, wondering if I should be mad at him for this.

I try the dresses on in my room, trying to find the price tags. There are none. I don't even recognize the brands.

"This one," Naskia says simply, when I walk out wearing the third option, as though I don't have any choice in the matter.

I nod, trusting her implicitly. "Okay. This one." I fumble for my tote. "Do you take credit cards?"

She laughs as though I've suddenly become a Comedy Cellar comedian, leaves a box of heels on my counter, then rolls the rack back out. "Have fun," she says.

And then I'm left standing in the middle of the apartment in a gown.

It's red. It has a tight bodice and thin straps and goes all the way to the floor, in a sheet of silk. It's simple, but stunning. The heels she's left are black stilettos. With the toe showing.

I curse and run to CVS (sans gown) to get tools to give myself a pedicure. It comes out okay "if you squint," Penelope says when I show her. "But no one's going to be staring at your feet. I hope."

"Very reassuring," I tell her.

I straighten my hair. I decide to use red lipstick, to match my dress, even though I've never worn it before. I wonder if it's a bad idea.

Parker meets me at my door this time. I open it and forget how to breathe.

Nothing could have prepared me to see Parker Warren in a tux.

My lips part. I temporarily lose the ability to control my facial expression at all. I stare greedily, shamelessly.

I'm not even embarrassed. Because he's doing the same thing to me.

When his gaze finds my face again, he stills. He reaches over to brush my hair behind my ear. "You're wearing them," he says, so gently.

The ruby earrings. "It seemed like a waste not to."

He traces the shell of my ear, and I shiver.

"If I don't make it out of this apartment now, I never will," he says.

Part of me wants to drag him down to the floor and take off every layer of his tux.

But I take his hand and lead him to the elevator.

THE GALA IS AT A MEMBERS-ONLY CLUB IN NOHO, AN INDUSTRIAL building turned into a place where phones are forbidden and paparazzi are parked outside.

Flashes go off as we enter the massive double doors, helped through by security. "Over here! Parker, over here!"

I wonder if he wants us to linger. Get a good shot for the paper, to guarantee another headline. But Parker doesn't even look at them. His arm is protectively wrapped around me.

He's a member of the club. We're led into an elevator and out into a gorgeous space with big arched windows, high ceilings, modern art, and faded brick walls. The lighting is dimmed. There is an array of seating options.

"This looks pretty casual for a gala," I tell him.

"It is. Usually they're in a museum or something. I think they're trying to draw in a younger crowd."

The room is already filled with guests, all in gowns and tuxes. They stare at us while we walk by. Whisper. I spot Carissa in the corner, sitting in one of the chairs, next to another woman. I smile at her like we're old friends, and she glares at me.

The charity benefit is for art programs for children. I've volunteered for their LA branch and am excited to meet the organizers here. They tell me about their plans to expand their volunteer teaching program, and I wish, for one of the first times, that I wasn't anonymous, so I could be part of it. Instead, I sign up on the spot for a yearly donation. All the while, Parker watches me, like every word I have to say is important, like everything is interesting.

When we finally walk away, he says, "You care."

"Of course I do. Art... saved me. Giving kids access to art programs is important. It's something I believe in." I lift a shoulder. "Everyone needs something to care about."

Just like any charity gala, everyone's already donated big to be here. There's a performance by a pop star, followed by a seated dinner by a

Michelin-starred chef. Mostly, though, it seems as though the attendees would like to see and be seen. Dozens of people come up to Parker. They ask him about his acquisition. More than a few of the much older men leer at me and any other passing woman, even with their wives standing right next to them.

A few minutes after Parker leaves me in the center of the room to get us drinks, one of the older men suddenly grabs my arm. I rear back and turn to face him, then freeze when I see who it is.

He's the CEO of one of the biggest pharmaceutical companies in the world. He's one of the most revered minds in business.

I must look horrified, because before I can make a single move, I hear Parker say behind me, "Get your fucking hand off her."

The crowd around us seems to tense. Voices hush.

Parker doesn't look like he gives a shit.

The man looks up and sneers at him. "Who do you think you are?" he says. His hand remains firmly around my arm.

Parker takes a step forward. I genuinely think he might commit assault in the middle of this room. The people around us have completely stopped talking.

"I'm her boyfriend," he says, his voice lethally calm. "Who do you think *you* are?"

The world seems to fall off its axis as he says, "I'm her father."

21

PARKER LOOKS STUNNED, BUT HIS ANGER DOESN'T FALTER. HE SAYS, "I DON'T care who you are. You're hurting her. Let go."

It's true. His hand is like a vise around my arm. He doesn't move, and I finally find my voice. "Get off me," I say, ripping my arm away.

My father stands there, smirking at me. "I saw the photos. Didn't think it was true. *My* daughter, dating this tech protégé? What could she possibly offer him?"

My nails dig into my palms. It takes every ounce of self-control to keep my head held high as he continues.

"Your sister said you write movie reviews online, and not even for a big outlet." He laughs. "I knew you had to have had someone supporting you in LA, if it wasn't me." He looks at Parker. "Now I know who."

I can almost feel the anger coming off Parker in waves, but I'm grateful he doesn't say a word. Contradicting him would mean telling him my secret.

There are a million things I want to say to my father, but he doesn't deserve any of them. "Bye, Dad," I say. "I'd like to say it's nice to see you, but it never has been."

I turn. To my back, he says, "After everything I've done for you, this is the thanks I get?"

Everything he's done for me.

I'm so tempted to let the dam break, to let it all come spilling out, but I would be the only one who drowns. He doesn't care enough to hurt. So, I keep walking.

I can feel Parker looking at me as we walk out of the members-only club. I don't look back. I manage to keep the tears in until I'm in the car, and then I face the window and let them fall.

"YOUR FATHER IS DAVID SALAZAR," HE SAYS. WE'RE IN HIS APARTMENT. I'm sitting on the couch, staring at the floor.

I nod.

"I don't understand," Parker says, sounding truly confused. "You said we can't be together because of my money. But your father . . ."

I look up at him. "Is the CEO of one of the biggest companies in the world?" I finish.

He nods.

"It's because of him that I can't," I say, my voice breaking.

He sits beside me on the couch. I tuck my knees into my chest and face him.

"You assumed, because he was absent, he wasn't doing well, right?"

He nods. It's the story of his own father, after all.

Assumptions. We all make so many.

"It was the opposite. My parents didn't have much, but they were both smart. Really smart. My dad got into the MBA program at Stanford, and my mom moved with him, even though she hadn't finished her own degree. He said she didn't need one, that he would take care of them. She didn't speak English and planned to learn, enroll in classes, but then she got pregnant. With me.

"At first, it was great. They were happy. My mom said she fell in love with his mind. He was the smartest person she had ever met; he could always figure out any problem. And he was caring. He liked to take care of her, maybe a little too much. When they first met, he found out driving stressed her out, so he would take her everywhere himself. She let her license expire. He knew she hated getting her shoes dirty on the dirt patch outside her house, so he would literally carry her to the car. It was so romantic, she said. Then, when they moved here, caring slowly turned to control. First it was *Oh, you don't have to learn English, I can speak it for the both of us.* Then it was *I'll be in charge of the money, I'm the one with the MBA.* He got a great job in Silicon Valley, and the more he made, the more my mom relied on him. One day, she realized she relied on him for *everything.* To speak for her. To make decisions for her . . . and for me.

"And he liked it. He liked her being dependent on him, because he thought that meant she could never leave. Success was like poison, she said, it amplified the worst of him. Made him truly believe his way was best, and she should simply follow. When she was pregnant with my sister, he got an even better job, he became even more controlling, and that was when she knew it would only get worse. She didn't want him to control us too. She started taking English classes. She started saving her money. And then, one day, she left him.

"He was upset, of course, but he still tried to control her. He would withhold child support if she didn't do what he wanted. He would use his connections to interfere with her job search, so that she wouldn't have her own money.

"Money was always at the center of it. So, finally, she started refusing the child support. She moved south where she could finally find work. She worked two jobs, and went to school, and gave us everything we needed, on her own. Once it was clear he didn't have power over us, we never saw him again. He had no interest in having children he couldn't control."

I shrug. "She told us what happened to her as a cautionary tale, as a lesson, and it made me hate my dad. I never looked him up over the years, because we didn't need him. And he didn't want us anyway.

"I remembered some of his treatment of my mom. I remembered his visits, with gifts that always came with strings attached. My sister didn't. She googled him when we were teenagers, and, lo and behold, he's this big shot in New York City. My sister wanted to go see him, she wanted that life, but my mother refused. Then . . . she got sick."

I feel the tears falling down my face, clinging to my jaw.

"I was in college. I was going back and forth all the time, taking her to treatment. At first, we tried to make it work. I got another job. We used up all our savings." I give a sad smile. "But it was all too expensive. It was impossible. The trials . . . they were the only chance she had." I take a shaking breath. "So, I went behind my mom's back and did the one thing she always told me not to. I went to my dad for help.

"It was sophomore year. I still remember going into that office building. Telling the receptionist who I was. Her not believing me. Me insisting, until she made a few phone calls. Those phone calls led to me being escorted into an office that took up half the floor, floor-to-ceiling windows, New York sprawled out behind his seat like a blanket. Then watching as he looked up at me and smiled.

"*Of course he would help.* The money was a drop in the bucket to him. I left, feeling like I made the right decision. The next day, her first trials were paid for. I told my mom it was the result of a charitable grant. She started to improve. Then the phone call came. The string. *I'm doing so much to help you. The least you can do is have dinner with me.* I still hated him for what he had done to my mom, but he was helping her. Dinner seemed harmless enough. Then it turned into meeting his new family. Fine. Then it turned into him wanting to control my internships and major, which I refused. Then it turned into wanting to meet my sister."

The guilt ratchets up in me.

"She was going on college visits. I was meant to host her here, in the city, while she visited NYU. I took her to meet him." I wince. "It's one of my biggest regrets. What he couldn't get from me—a genuine connection, forgiveness—he got from her. The same control my mother had told us about started again. He would pay for my sister's college, as long as he chose where she went. He would pay for her spring break trips, as long as he chose what she studied. He would pay for a single in the dorm, as long as she broke up with the boyfriend he didn't approve of. My sister didn't care. It all seemed fine to her. He was *helping* us. But I could see the pattern. I could see where it would lead. For him, money means control. Complete power over the people who rely on him for it.

"My mom eventually found out, and I'll never forget the look on her face as she said, *What have you done?* By then, it was too late. All the treatments were paid for, and, because I begged her, she continued. She lived her last year in comfort. I was so busy going back and forth between school and her treatments, so lost in grief when she died, that I didn't realize how much the money had changed my sister. Instead of studying, she partied every weekend, flew off to different cities whenever she wanted. *Who cares?* she said, when I told her that grades were important, to get a good job. *Dad says I don't need a job, if I don't want to work.*"

I shake my head. "Every lesson my mother had drilled into her, every ounce of ambition, every sacrifice she made, was gone, because of me. Because of him." I shrug. "After she died, I hated him more. Hated that he had hurt her, that he had made her so untrusting of men, so closed off to love. I stopped speaking to him. He still tried to control me, though. I worked all through college and sold my first screenplay my senior year. I was so proud that I was going to be able to pay off my student loans with my own money. But when I called, guess what? They had already been paid for. By my father."

I remember the rage, the betrayal, like he had ripped something important away from me.

"I demanded they give the money back, given that he wasn't even listed as my family or authorized on my account, and they did. I paid for my college myself. But, after that, I was careful. I knew he would try to insert himself into my life, try to control it in any way he could, so that I would feel indebted to him."

"That's why you are anonymous," Parker says softly. He's been so quiet this whole time.

I nod. "I wanted to be certain that any screenplay I sold was because of me, nothing else. That's why I've kept my whole career a secret. He doesn't even know what I do, so he can't interfere with it."

I don't think too hard about the fact that my mother would *hate* that I was anonymous, that I refused to put my name proudly on my work, because of a man. Because of my father. She always told me not to let the men in my life diminish me, and I had allowed him to *extinguish* me.

It's a choice I made, though. Even if it was made from fear.

"I'm sorry," he says. "I'm sorry any of that happened to you."

I hope he understands now why this would never work between us. "I've worked too hard, Parker, to be the woman my mother raised, just to throw it all away. To be . . . erased, inadvertently or not, by the person I'm with. I—I won't allow it."

He lets me talk. He listens. Then he says, so softly I could cry, "I'm not your father, Elle. I would never try to control you."

I know that. God, I know that. But still, I shake my head. "I just . . . I can't."

He doesn't try to change my mind. He just nods. Then he says something I would never expect. "I admire you."

"What?"

"The way he was talking to you . . ." he says, his jaw tensed. "You handled it really well."

I laugh without humor. "I stormed out. I wouldn't say I handled it greatly."

He shakes his head. "No. The first time I saw my dad, after the company was valued at a ridiculous number, and all he cared about was how much I was going to give him . . . I went off on him. I couldn't hold it back. I told him exactly how I felt." His hand is on mine. "You did much better than I would have, under the same circumstances."

I take a deep breath. I guess he's right, in a way. Old Elle might have screamed at him in front of everyone. Might have cried right in front of him, let him see how much he hurt me.

I was strong today.

What I don't tell him is that his mere presence was like a support beam, holding me up. My personal scaffolding, making me feel steadier.

"Your last name," Parker says.

"It isn't Salazar. Leon was my mother's maiden name. I changed it when my dad left."

He nods, understanding. "Sometimes I wish I had changed mine."

I know how that feels. Names are so important.

Seeing my dad, having him assume Parker is supporting me, it reminds me why we could never work. But, right now, while it's still summer . . . I want to let him in just a little bit.

"It's Elle," I say softly.

He looks up at me, confused.

"My first name. It's just Elle. It's not . . . short for anything."

Parker smiles, as if another level of his favorite game has been unlocked. "Really?"

I nod. "My mom liked it. It was the name she wished she had, when she was younger. So, she gave it to me." I take a shaky breath. "She gave me so much."

That's why I won't let myself forget her and what she taught me. It would be like losing her again, disappointing her.

I don't know why I'm telling him this, but I say, "My mom had dreams. It's weird, thinking about that, right? That our parents once wanted something they never got? Well, one day, I asked her what she wanted. To my surprise, she told me she also dreamed of being a writer. I asked her why she didn't do it, why she never tried. She told me some generations are for working, so the next can dream." I feel tears slip down my face.

"When I was seventeen, I got into a state school with a full scholarship and Columbia with incomplete financial aid. She knew it was my dream to study creative writing there, but it didn't seem possible. I was going to choose the state school. Then she showed me that she had been saving money from her second job since the day I told her it was my dream to be a writer. It wasn't much, but it was enough for me to consider Columbia. She said, *None of the women before me ever got to do anything but work. But you're going to do more than that. You're going to dream. You're going to do it.*

"All that money ended up going to medical bills, but it was the best thing anyone has ever done for me. She gave me a chance. I never would have gone to Columbia, or thought I could do any of this, without her. She used to call me her *little lion*. She said I was stronger than I thought I was."

"You are," Parker says, with all the conviction in the world. With the same certainty my mother had. "You're strong, and you're smart, and you're creative, and I'm glad you write, because it's a way to be let into your perfect mind."

"I'm not perfect," I tell Parker. He's said the word so many times when it comes to me, and it's a lie.

He just smiles. "You are, though. To me, you are. It's like your mind and soul and body and everything was made for me. It's like you're perfectly mine."

"But I'm not," I say. *I'm not yours. I can't be.*

"I know," he says. "But sometimes, I pretend."

22

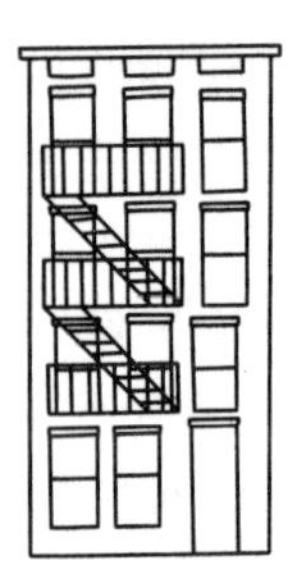

I EXPECTED MY EMOTIONS TO BE EVERYWHERE AFTER SEEING MY FATHER. IN the past, any phone call, any attempt from him to claw his way back into my life, would have me reeling for weeks. Doubting myself. Unable to write.

This time, though, I feel nothing. No—if anything, telling Parker about him makes me feel better.

My sister calls. If my father told her about our meeting, she doesn't say anything. She tells me about her hotel room in Palermo, how it's *literally on a cliff!* And I try my best not to hyperventilate. Finally, I coax Paola into emailing me a detailed itinerary as long as I promise not to call every day.

I've gotten past the midpoint in my screenplay, the dramatic revelation that changes things and puts the fun and games into perspective.

There's drilling in the apartment, as Luke and his team begin installing new flooring, putting in custom cabinets, making mosaics out of marble in the bathrooms. The apartment is starting to transform before my eyes, change, become something different. Every day, there's a new decision to make—this tile or that, these drapes or those—and I try my best to channel my inner Cali.

The nursery is almost done. I find myself leaning in the doorway long after they've left, a pinch in my chest. I might not agree with my sister's choices, I might not absolutely love her husband, but I will love her child more than I think I can contain in my body.

I feared Parker might be mad at me, after I wasn't exactly forthcoming from the beginning about my father, but he isn't. He's just busy. He leaves for days at a time, back to San Francisco, because of the acquisition.

The first week of August comes to an end, and I can't help but feel like I did when I was still in school—like the summer has slipped by me.

There's still almost an entire month left, I tell myself, but it doesn't seem like enough. Before, I feared I wouldn't be able to finish my screenplay in time for my deadline. Now, I'm afraid for entirely different reasons.

Thinking Parker was going to be away this weekend, I went ahead and signed up to volunteer to do Street Tree Care through NYC Parks, an organization I learned about through Taryn. We were supposed to go together, but she got sick. I Postmated her chicken soup, then got dressed in some of Penelope's overalls, with a cropped white T-shirt underneath.

I'm slipping my sneakers on when there's a knock on my door.

Parker. I throw my arms around him before I can help myself. "I thought you were coming back Monday," I say into his chest.

He tenses beneath my grip, then holds me close, his fingers running down my sides.

"I decided to come back early." He looks down at my outfit and smiles. "But I can see you already have plans. Don't let me keep you."

I tell him about volunteering.

"Do you think they need an extra set of hands?"

I laugh. "The description was 'mulch, tools, and supplies will be provided.'" He's wearing a suit. I frown. "Did you wear that on the plane?"

He ignores my question and shrugs. “I’m a fast learner.”

That’s how we end up in the East Village, sitting on the pavement, wearing gloves, with black trash bags beside us. For each square of tree, we clean the waste from the area, weed, and cultivate the soil, to give these trees the best chance of survival. Mulching will be taking place later. We hear about other opportunities to make curbside gardens. They tell us you don’t need a permit to garden in a local tree bed.

“There’s one of these in front of the building,” I tell Parker. “What do you think Richard would think if we filled it with flowers?”

Our doorman has been giving us strange looks ever since the news of our relationship came out.

“I think he would personally rip them out one by one,” Parker says.

I always vaguely knew that trees were good for you, but then we’re told how important they are to the city. When we’re done, Parker’s cheeks and nose are slightly pink from a sunburn, and sweat is sliding through the roots of my hair, but I feel like I’ve done . . . something. Something meaningful.

“I didn’t really think I would enjoy that,” Parker tells me, as we return our gear and say goodbye to the other volunteers. “But it was . . . nice.” He frowns. “I’m used to just writing a check, not actually getting . . .”

“In the weeds?” I supply.

He smiles. “Yes. Yes, literally in the weeds.”

On our walk home, we pass Gramercy Park. My eyes immediately go where they always do—to the town house right on its edge. I frown. There’s a construction crew going in and out. It’s clearly going through a renovation.

There’s a deflation in my chest, a dream being punctured. I move to cross the street, but Parker doesn’t join me. He’s standing by the gate. He pulls a key out of his pocket.

That’s when I remember what he told me during that first dinner. He has a key to Gramercy Park.

I rush to his side, excitement humming through my bones. How many times have I walked this park's perimeter, looking longingly inside? How many years have I waited for this moment?

The door opens, and Parker smiles as he motions for me to go first.

I don't need to be told twice. I rush inside and turn in all directions, taking it all in. There's a statue in the middle and endless empty benches, and I look around as I take each path, marveling at the flowers. We're alone. There's no one else inside but us. It's like, for just a moment, this slice of New York City is ours.

I whirl to face him. "How did you get a key?"

He shrugs. "I rent an apartment on the park for it."

Of course he does. It's excessive and ridiculous, but right now, I'm grateful. We sit on a bench and talk, until the top of my hair gets too hot and Parker looks in fear of getting a worse sunburn. Only then do we leave, me looking wistfully back at the park.

We both promptly need showers. We take them, then I meet Parker in his apartment. My damp hair is tied up, I'm wearing sweatpants, and I've never felt more comfortable. We watch TV, and, during a commercial break, he pulls me into his lap, and I kiss him like I'm starving, like I've been waiting days to feel him.

His fingers weave through my damp hair, and it feels so good, every time he touches me.

"Sometimes I pretend too," I tell him, brushing against his lips. "I pretend you're mine."

"You don't have to pretend, Elle," he says. "You have me. I'm here."

Maybe this isn't wrong, I tell myself. Maybe we can find a way to make this work. Maybe people can change, just like I have, this summer. Maybe money isn't a good reason not to be with someone.

He kisses me until my head empties of all the reasons we can't do this, he touches me until I'm breathless, and I smile until my happiness feels like something I can drown in.

23

MY PHONE WAKES ME UP. IT'S PENELOPE. I FROWN. IT'S SIX O'CLOCK IN THE morning in LA. She's never up this early on a weekend.

"Hello?" I say, my heart in my throat.

I'm relieved when I hear her voice. "Elle," she says. But then my chest clenches when I hear her tone.

"What's wrong?"

She doesn't say anything for a few seconds, and I don't think I'm breathing. Then: "You haven't seen, have you?"

"Seen what?"

"I'm getting on the next plane. I just bought my ticket. I'll be there by late afternoon."

I rise out of bed. My body feels like it's bracing itself. My heart is thundering. "Penelope. *What's wrong?*"

She sighs. There's a ding against my ear as a message comes through.

"I'm sorry, Elle."

That's when I see it. My face, in the preview, and the headline beneath it:

"Billionaire Bachelor's Mystery Girlfriend Revealed to Be Previously Anonymous Screenwriter."

No.

My world turns over. I can't breathe. I sink to the floor.

I click the link. They know everything. Every screenplay I've ever written. Who my father is.

There's a quote from him in the article: "I'm proud to have supported my daughter from the beginning of her career and helped her become one of the world's leading screenwriters."

I'm going to throw up. Anger chokes me.

"How dare he?" I say, the words scraping against my throat. My phone is on the floor now.

It's everything I was ever afraid of. Every reason I became anonymous. The moment the world knew my dad is some big-time CEO, they would assume he's responsible for my career.

And here he is, not even having *known* what I did for a living a few days ago, now taking *credit* for it.

The comments below the article might as well be my own worst fears, typed out plainly. "Her boyfriend probably funded the last movie she wrote." "I always hated the last movie in the franchise, now I know why." "Wow, it must be nice to be handed over your entire career, some of us actually have to work for it."

These people don't know me. They have no idea what my life has been like. The wider population—the people who go see my movies, the people who matter—likely won't even hear about this, or care.

But I do. Because my mom would be *furious*. She would see all my accomplishments being reduced to the men in my life, and she would have hated it.

Someone is banging on my door.

I pick up the phone with shaking fingers. "Thank you for telling me," I say to Penelope.

"It's going to be okay. I'll be there soon," she says. I hang up.

I don't entirely feel my body as I walk toward the door. I hear his voice through it. "Elle," he's saying. "Elle, please open up."

I do, and he goes still.

He sees my face. I must look like a wreck. My eyes are burning. I can feel the tears, frozen on my cheeks.

Parker shakes his head. "Elle, I'm so sorry. It was Richard," he says. "He gave the mail to the journalist. He's already been let go. It was illegal what they did, my lawyers can—"

I put my hand up. I don't care who did it or what can be done, it is *over.* That kind of information can't just be unsaid. There will never be a yesterday again, when I was blissfully unknown. "It's my fault," I say. "I never should have done this, I never should have trusted it would be okay."

It was stupid, putting myself out there, when my anonymity meant so much to me. Thinking that my identity could remain a secret when linked to someone the media is so obsessed with.

He shakes his head. He runs a hand through his hair, making it stick up wildly. "I'll buy the newspaper. I'll have them retract it."

I just blink at him. Of course that's his solution. Of course Parker thinks this is something he can buy his way out of. That's how he thinks about everything. I remember his words in the stairwell: *I can buy anything I want.*

"I'll buy every goddamn newspaper, I'll—"

"It's done," I say. "This . . . development . . . should tide over the press for the rest of the summer, until your acquisition goes through."

Parker's entire body tenses. He straightens. "Elle," he says very slowly. "What are you saying?"

The words are out of me before I can regret them. "It's over. This whole thing, it's over. You got the PR you needed. My screenplay is almost done. We both got what we wanted."

Parker doesn't look like he got what he wanted at all. His eyes look glassy, but no—why would he be upset? It's not *his* entire life and career that's been turned upside down.

"Elle—"

"I think it's best we don't see each other again." A clean break. No need to make things harder than they need to be. Parker isn't to blame, but none of this would have happened if we hadn't made this stupid agreement.

Regret sinks its teeth into me. I never should have put myself out there. I never should have taken this risk. I should have known this would only end badly.

"Bye, Parker," I say, before he can say another word.

Then I close the door, sink to the floor, and cry.

TRUE TO HER WORD, PENELOPE IS AT MY APARTMENT LATE THAT afternoon. She has a carry-on behind her and a CVS bag full of ice cream.

I burst into tears again when I see her, and she's ready, wrapping her arms around me, ice cream cold against my spine.

"I know it doesn't seem like it, but it's not the end of the world," she says.

"It is," I say, because it completely feels like it. "It really is."

"It's not."

She shuffles inside, still hugging me, and says, "Did Sarah call?"

I nod. CAA's been calling me all morning, mostly to calm me down.

"How are the studios taking it?"

I sigh. "They don't really care. Their movies did well, and they've underpaid me for years."

"And your current screenplay?"

"They still want it the week after Labor Day."

Penelope nods. "Well, then that's settled. Your career is fine. See? The world isn't ending."

I shake my head. "You know it was never about my career, P. Not really."

"I know," she says. And then she hugs me again.

Taryn calls half an hour later. "I've been offline all day, but I just saw the article. I have a take-out order placed, and Gwen and Emily on standby. Can we come over?"

That's how I end up with an apartment full of takeout, more ice cream, and women in loungewear.

Penelope loves them immediately. They immediately love Penelope. Without furniture in the living room—*You've been on the floor all summer?*—we open the plastic-wrapped linens and make a "Princess and the Pea" situation, with blankets instead of mattresses, on the floor. We line the wall with pillows. Then we watch a rom-com. When the all-is-lost moment makes me burst into tears, Taryn pauses the movie and says, "Is it something you want to talk about?" And that's how I tell them all about the fake dating, about the entire summer.

"You can't stay here," Taryn says. She lowers her voice to a whisper and points behind her. "Not when he's a wall away."

"What am I going to do? Get a hotel?"

"Of course not," Taryn says. "You can stay with me. My roommate just moved out, I have an extra bedroom."

It's a nice offer. So nice, I can hardly think what I did to deserve such a great group of friends.

"She has a terrace, it's super cozy," Gwen says.

Emily pops a chocolate-covered almond in her mouth. "Yeah, Taryn's place is objectively amazing."

It sounds incredible. "I'd love to, but the renovations last another week. I promised my sister I would oversee them."

"I'll stay here, then," Penelope says, like it's an easy solution.

I look at her, like, *Do you suddenly not have a job?*

"I'm doing work from home for a week." She looks around. "Or, I guess, work from *your* home."

I consider it. It is, at least, nice to have the option.

Half an hour later, everyone is asleep around me, the movie is still playing its credits, and I'm staring up at the ceiling.

I am not an island. I am not deserted. I have friends. I'm not the same person I was at the beginning of the summer. Screenwriting is not my entire life.

Still, I don't know how I'm going to get through this.

24

THE NEXT MORNING, WE GO TO BRUNCH. THERE'S A NEW DOORMAN AT THE front desk. There's a lone paparazzo at the entrance, who snaps furiously when we leave. Penelope gives him her middle finger.

"So," Taryn says. "Yesterday was a shock. How do you feel now, the morning after?"

Part of me doesn't want to even think about how I feel. Another knows that anything I bury down will surface sooner or later.

"Still raw," I say. "Still unbelieving. Hurt. I'm thinking about how people will receive my future work, knowing it's me behind it. I'm thinking of all the meetings I'll have to go to now, the executives I'll have to face, the insults online, the pressure to start social media accounts." I sigh. "Part of me is, I guess, a little relieved. This big secret I've kept for years now . . . I guess I never realized how much it was weighing on me."

This morning, for a blissful second, I had forgotten. Then it had all hit me with the force of a battering ram. *This is real. Your life has changed.* My email, typically empty save for a few pings from Sarah, was flooded with media requests. My phone log was filled with calls from people I haven't talked to in years. A guy I'd gone on a single date with fifteen months ago texted, asking if I could look at his TV pilot.

I had, promptly, locked my phone in another room. It couldn't hurt me, I told myself. It wasn't real.

Then why did I feel like someone had scooped my chest out?

Most of the interest is because they think I'm dating Parker. Once they realize we're not together, it will all die down.

That's what I tell myself, at least.

When I confirm things are done with Parker, Gwen looks sad for the first time since I've known her. "So, none of it was real?"

I take a sip of my latte. Warmth spreads through my hollow chest. "Of course it was," I say. "But what does that have to do with it?"

WHEN WE COME BACK FROM BRUNCH, ONE PAPARAZZO HAS TURNED into two. My friends help me pack a suitcase. Gwen takes it down. I leave separately, with Taryn, to stay in her apartment.

Being in a new place helps a little. I've let my phone die and have thrown any ounce of focus I can muster into my screenplay. It's still due in three weeks, no matter what I'm going through.

Taryn's away at work during the day, but at night we talk, eat dinner, and watch TV. One night, we go to eat in SoHo and pass a street stand selling scripts. "Any of yours?" Taryn asks.

"A few."

Penelope comes over most nights and tells us about her crush on Luke (she, apparently, broke it off with the hot doctor a day after arriving here, because of the distance). And, also, how Parker knocks on the door every day without fail.

I go on walks, trying not to think of him, but the city is full of our memories. He's right. I painted it over. But now, it's all in his shade. I can't escape him.

"Don't read the articles," Penelope tells me, and I wonder if it's because they're awful.

Taryn puts me out of my misery by saying, "Not the worst. Just, you know, typical misogyny." I guess fans of some of the franchises I've written for assumed I was a guy and are deeply disappointed.

I avoid the internet as much as possible and find, with some distance, Penelope is right when she says, "The internet isn't real." What's real is us, on the floor of Taryn's apartment, playing board games none of us know the rules to and can't, between our four degrees (two for Taryn), understand, even when we try. Real is Gwen giving me a haircut in Taryn's bathroom, because she says they always help, and she's been giving them to herself for years. It's just a few inches, a few layers, but she's right. I feel lighter.

Real is my sister calling Penelope (whose number she's had memorized since she was a teenager), demanding to be passed to me, and saying, "Why didn't you tell me?"

Guilt stabs me in the stomach. "I'm sorry, I—"

"I can't believe you're dating Parker Warren!"

That guilt turns into a sudden urge to throw the phone through a window. I take that moment to tell Cali about my career. Apparently, she didn't actually read the article.

She asks questions, says, "I love that movie!" Then: "I had no idea you could be funny."

I frown. "Cali, that's not even a comedy."

"Oh."

After a few days, I hesitantly open a webpage. Then I start clearing out my inbox, deleting all the media inquiries. I click through them quickly, grateful that they seem to get scarcer as the days go by. Then I see something that makes me pause.

It's from a woman named Elena. She's not a journalist; she's a freshman at a college in Texas.

"When I was a teenager, I got mono. Not from anything as exciting as kissing, but because I had a bad habit of sharing cups in the cafeteria. I was bedridden for weeks, at my grandma's house. She kept the TV on one channel, and your movies always played. I was a captive audience, you might say, but I was hooked, after the second one. You became my favorite screenwriter," she wrote. "Your movies would repeat, but I didn't mind. I always found something different to love, each time it was on. I started to think about the structure. I started to write movies in my head. It was all for fun, though. I never thought I could actually do it, until a few days ago. Learning it was you, a woman in her twenties, writing my favorite movies makes me feel like maybe I can make it too. I'm adding a creative writing major, and I've started my first script. I want you to know that your words have helped me through the darkest periods of my life. I watched your last one with my grandma, when she had just been diagnosed with Alzheimer's. We didn't agree on much, but we both loved that movie. We would quote it all the time. It was like a language, or bridge, between us. I tattooed our favorite line after she passed. It's on my arm. Thank you for that gift. The gift of connection. My only hope is I can one day give that to someone else."

I don't even realize I'm crying until the tears fall onto the keyboard. My face is pulled toward the screen, rereading each line.

No one has ever told me that my words have impacted them. I've never given them a chance to.

No one has ever told me I've inspired them. Because they didn't even know who I was.

The last line I read over and over, because it reminds me of my mom. She hated the hospital. She hated the fact that she was too weak, in the end, to put on anything but lipstick. *I despise this place,* she used to say, so movies were her escape. Every time I visited, I brought a new one, a new favorite. We would watch it, and she would hold my hand and say, *I can't wait to watch your movie. I'm going to be there, at the premiere. I promise.*

She didn't live long enough to see me sell my first script.

I didn't even attend the premiere.

I close my laptop. *It's already worth it,* I think. *If one person has taken something good from this, then any bad is erased.* Elena's words are like armor around me. This is why I do what I do. This is why I wanted to become a writer in the first place.

The news starts to settle. Less than a week later, Penelope needs to get back to LA, and it's time for me to go home.

"Thank you for taking me in," I tell Taryn.

"What are friends for?" she replies, and another previously hollow place feels full and warm.

The paparazzi are gone. They're already on to the next story.

I walk up to my unit and am about to knock, when the door opens. A six-four man comes walking out. His smile strains as he sees me.

"Luke?" I say, bewildered. It's nine in the morning. On a Saturday.

"Oh, hey, Elle," he says, and then he practically runs to the elevator.

Penelope is in the doorway. She's wearing scraps of silk as pajamas, and her hair is messy.

"Oh my god," I say. "Did you have sex with my contractor?"

Penelope tilts her head. "Well, he's not really your contractor, he's your sister's. And he's not really your sister's, because he ended work yesterday. But yes. Yes, I did. Several times."

I squint. "On my bed?"

"Well—"

"You know what I mean!"

"No," she says, and my entire being melts in relief. "It was more of a clothes-still-half-on, against-the-wall situation. The first time, at least. Then we were on the floor. And the kitchen counter. And—"

"Do you think they make those exterminator tents, but for Purell? Like, for all over the apartment?"

She laughs as I step inside. I catch her glancing over at me as I put my bags down. "You look good."

I look at myself in the closest mirror. I look exactly like a person who has spent most of the week oscillating between crying and furiously writing a screenplay.

"'Better' is maybe a more accurate word," she says.

I sigh. I do feel better. I show Penelope the email from Elena, and she looks close to tears herself by the time she hands my laptop back.

"You know, I think this can be a good thing," she says. "After you get past, like, the trauma."

I give her a look.

"Now you can do the stuff you never could. You can mentor other writers. You can do interviews about your process. You can brag to the members of your high school class on Facebook."

That makes me laugh.

She gently hits my arm with hers. "You know what I mean."

I do. Being anonymous has kept me from having to grow. I might have wanted to reveal myself on my own terms, on my own timeline, but now that it's happened . . . it doesn't all have to be bad. I know that now.

We spend the day out in the city, going to the places we miss from our college days. We marvel at which stores have closed, which are exactly the same. I take her to some of my new favorites.

"I don't know how I spent this summer without you," I tell her, as we're falling asleep, sharing a bed, the way we did in college, when the other one was going through something.

"Me neither," she says. "But I'm glad you went outside. I'm glad you stopped being an island."

"Me too," I say. And, even though it brought me pain, I mean it.

25

PENELOPE'S ON A PLANE BACK TO LA. SITTING IN MY KITCHEN, WITH 90 PERcent of my screenplay printed out, I get the courage to turn my phone on. I'm bombarded by notifications. Dozens of calls from numbers I don't recognize, texts from long-lost acquaintances.

Then, strangely, it starts to ring.

It's Paola.

I look on the call log. She's called four times in the last hour, each one going straight to voicemail.

"Is she okay?" I say, because Paola has never willingly called me in my life.

"She's going into labor!" Paola says. "We've been calling you for hours!"

The unknown numbers. I thought it'd all been reporters but—

"What do you mean, she's going into labor?" My voice is a scream. No—she's due the third week of September. It's way too early. I had planned to fly from LA, weeks after my screenplay was due.

I drop my script all over the floor. I knock a piece of art on the wall down as I clutch against it for stability. It crashes against the hardwood.

There's banging on my door. "Elle. Elle, are you okay?" I don't say anything, I can't, I'm breathing too quickly. I couldn't move if I wanted to. "I'm coming in," he says, and the door slams open.

Parker's in front of me in an instant.

"You need to get here now," Paola says. "She won't stop asking for you." She gives me the address for the hospital and hangs up.

My hands are shaking as I race through my phone. Parker is on his knees, picking up my screenplay, page by page.

Tears blur my vision. "No. *No.*"

He kneels in front of me. "Elle, what's wrong?" he says, his voice the only steady thing around me.

"My sister is in labor. She needs me. I—I have to be there for her. But it's the middle of the night, the next flight gets there in twelve hours, and then I'll have to take a connection, and I'll be too late! It's all too late, and I—"

"My jet can be here in an hour," Parker says.

I blink. "You have a jet?"

He nods.

I shake my head. "Jets—jets are horrible for the environment."

"I'll buy double the carbon credits. I always do," he says.

"No, that doesn't make it better," I say. I lean my head against the wall. I shouldn't have turned my phone off, I should have been there for her. *What am I going to do?* If only I hadn't—

"I'll sell it," he says, completely serious. "This will be its last trip. I'll never ride in a jet again. I'll buy the carbon credits, and I'll sell it as soon as we land. Or I'll give it to a charitable organization to use. Whatever you want."

What? I shake my head. "No, Parker," I say. "I don't want you to do that just because you think I want you to."

"I'm not," he says. "I'm doing it because it's the right thing to do." He's kneeling in front of me. "Please, Elle. Let me help you." He offers his hand.

And I take it.

PARKER'S JET IS ENORMOUS.

The entire trip, I'm facing the window, trying not to think about whether I'll be too late and how badly my sister needs me.

I remember big brown eyes . . . looking for me. Cali, searching for me at the school pickup line. Cali, awake before I was, asking if I could make her French toast because it was Saturday. Cali, begging me not to tell Mom that she had left her textbooks in her locker. Me, driving to her middle school in Mom's car late at night, to go get them.

Cali didn't talk to me for a week after I told her I was moving across the country for college. *But you're supposed to stay with me. Always.* Mom didn't understand her. Without me as a buffer, they fought more. Isabella Leon had high standards and didn't understand how Cali could skip school to go to the beach. How she didn't seem to care about her grades.

I promised to visit, but the flights were expensive. As she entered high school, she became more distant. Colder. Soon, instead of calling me every night, I was the one trying—and failing—to reach her.

When Mom got sick, Cali barely talked to me about it. After the funeral, she went on vacation after vacation, as if she could outrun her grief.

We fought. Disagreed. Went weeks without speaking.

I should have had more empathy for her. I should have called her more, even if she didn't answer. I should have tried to understand her, even if I didn't understand her choices.

Now, she's alone . . . asking for me. And I'm not there.

"Try to get some rest," Parker says gently. He offers me the bedroom. I refuse, and so does he.

We just sit in silence until we land.

The moment we touch down in Palermo, Parker tells the attendant and pilots, "This was the last trip. Park it until further instructions, please, and I'll have your tickets home sent to you." Then he helps me down the stairs without a second look back at his jet.

The car is moving too slowly, I think, gripping the seat rest, looking down at the time. It's only been seven hours since Paola called me. Even if there had been a flight available, I never could have made it here this quickly, I know that. I think maybe I should thank Parker for helping me, for flying all this way with me, but I'll do that later. All I can think about is my sister.

We race into the hospital, and it's a blur. Getting into sterile clothing. Big brown eyes . . . widening when they see me. Standing by her side for hours as she pushes and pushes, contractions making her scream. Her nails digging into my arm. Her face reddening with effort.

Then a sound I'll never forget for my entire life, a cry that changes everything.

And a baby.

Cali's smiling as the baby is placed against her chest. Pierre is there, looking so happy and in love with my sister that I decide, from this moment forward, I have no choice but to like him.

When the baby is passed to me, I hardly breathe. It's a girl.

Her name is Isabella.

I don't mean to cry. I've cried entirely too much already. But I do. I'm so full of happiness, I don't know how it can fit inside of me.

Parker is in the waiting room. He stands as soon as he sees me and visibly slumps with relief at the smile on my face.

"Do you want to meet her?" I ask. He does.

And it does entirely too much to me to see him holding a baby, a baby I now love more than anything else in this world. Isabella is so small in his arms, but he's careful. He rocks her back and forth, until she falls asleep.

We go back into the waiting room, to let my sister rest. Pierre and Paola begin to pack up their stuff.

"Thank you," I tell Parker. "I—I'm really glad I didn't miss that. Also, thanks for hacking into the door in the apartment?"

I realize he could have done that the night I got locked out. He seems to read my thoughts, because he says, "I learned after that night. In case it ever happened again."

"Well, thank you," I say, meaning it.

"It was the least I could do, Elle," he says. He doesn't say anything else, and I'm grateful.

Paola, despite her deep dislike of me and all my phone calls, is incredible at her job. She has a house rented and full of everything for the baby by the time we're out of the hospital. The next days are a blur of happiness, baby cries, and way too much feeding.

I haven't spent this much time with my sister in years. I'm by her side most of the time, taking the baby when she needs rest, helping her change diapers when Pierre is out getting more supplies.

Parker cooks us all food. He goes to local markets, and we sit together for dinner. Pierre tries to talk to Parker about crypto and machine learning, and he's surprisingly patient.

"You don't have to stay," I tell Parker. "I know you're busy."

"Do you want me to leave?"

I answer honestly. "No."

"Let me know if that changes."

We sleep in separate rooms, but every morning, he knocks on my door with a fresh latte. Italian cappuccinos don't have enough milk in them for me, so he bought a machine, carried it home, and learned to make them himself. "I FaceTimed Jeremy from the coffee shop," he says, "and watched tutorials online."

He holds Isabella when my arms start to hurt and my sister and Pierre are asleep.

"Do you want kids?" he asks me one night.

I try not to melt at the sight of him holding Isabella gently against his chest. "I do," I say. "But not for a few years. I'm too selfish right now. I want a few more years of being selfish." I glance at him. "Do you?"

"I do. In a few years . . . I do."

I'm helping my sister put Isabella to bed and study her as we slowly leave the room.

"You're happy," I say. "I've never seen you so happy."

She nods. "I am. I'm not like you, Elle," she says, when we settle in the family room. Pierre and Parker are out getting groceries. Paola is off planning their next leg of travel. "My big dream wasn't a career . . . it was this. Having a family."

I don't want to break this, I think. This moment with my sister. But I can't help but say, "Cali, you wanted to be a curator."

She shrugs a shoulder. "I guess. It was my dream career, but not my *dream,* if that makes sense."

It doesn't, to me. For me, my career *is* my dream.

"Dad told me he saw you," she says, looking at me quickly, before studying her nails.

Suddenly, I regret even having this conversation. "I did. I wish I hadn't."

Cali nods. "Are you ever going to forgive him?"

Forgive him. As if it were one mistake, one thing to *forgive,* and not years of abandoning his kids and then trying to control them.

"No," I say honestly. "And I don't know how you have, after—after everything he did to Mom."

"I didn't," she bites back, her eyes more intense than I've seen in years. "But I chose not to be an orphan. I chose to want to have at least one parent."

I laugh without humor. "You chose *money,* Cali. You chose an easy life, where you get handed apartments, and your existence gets to be some endless vacation."

Cali just studies me. I expected her to be more offended or outraged, but she just looks sad. "You know, Mom refused child support. We *needed* that money. She refused, out of her own pride, and it made our lives harder. She wasn't perfect."

I remember our life during the toughest years, the one-bedroom apartment with all of us piled in together, the school trips we missed, the shoes that hurt because they were two sizes too small. It only lasted a couple of years, and then Mom got a better job. Eventually, we moved into a house. She was able to give us everything we needed.

"How can you say that? She was trying to protect us."

Cali nods. "I know. She did everything for us. But she made mistakes too."

I don't want to hear this about my mother. It's disrespectful, it's horrible. I turn away, eyes burning.

"I knew," she says, out of nowhere, like the words have stumbled out of her.

I look at her. "Knew what?"

For a few moments, there's just silence. Then, "She got sick right after you left for college, Elle. A year before she ever told you."

I blink. Shake my head. "No. It was—it was sudden." It's part of why I hate change. The day I got the phone call, my life was turned over. Her sickness was too far gone, there was barely anything at that point to be done.

"It wasn't. I found the medical bills, so she was forced to tell me. And she made me swear not to tell you."

I think about how suddenly my sister became distant. "You . . . you stopped answering the phone."

Tears slowly sweep down her face. She brushes them away with her shoulder. "It was impossible to talk to you, without having it all spill out. I—I felt so guilty hiding it. But Mom didn't want you distracted from school. She didn't want you taking a gap year." She laughs without humor. "It didn't—it didn't seem to matter that *I* was dealing with all of it alone. All she ever cared about was you."

I remember Thanksgiving that year. How Cali had left the dinner table early and marched up to her room. How my mom had stared at my sister's full plate and said, "She's going through a phase."

My throat feels too tight. I don't know what to think, but my eyes prickle, thinking about my sister, at fifteen years old, having to deal with all of this herself.

"I'm sorry," I say as I wrap my arms around her shoulders. A moment later, her arms slowly inch around me.

"It's okay. You didn't know. I'm glad you didn't know." We stay like that for a while, so silent, I can hear the ticking of the wall clock. Then, she sighs. Drops her arms. We sit on the couch, both drained, both rubbing our knuckles across our eyes.

"I know you don't agree with my choices, Elle," she says. "But I made them. I knew the warnings, I knew the price, and I made them." She shrugs. "I'm happy. Isn't that enough?"

I don't know. I don't agree with her. I would never in a million years make the same choices.

But it's not my life, I realize. I can't control Cali . . . and I wouldn't want to.

"I'm happy you're happy," I finally say, because it's the truth, and I don't want to lose my sister again. I don't want to become yet another thing that she disposes of and forgets because it causes her stress and is *bad for the baby.*

"I'm happy you're happy too," Cali says. Her eyes slide to the part of the house Parker is staying in. "*He* makes you happy, doesn't he?"

"He does," I say, because it's the truth. But happiness is complicated. People are complicated.

I hug my sister again, breathe her in, and remember when it was just us, playing Barbies, finger-painting at the kitchen counter, watching movies on a quilt.

Life might be complicated, but love isn't. It's pretty straightforward. It's a lance through plans, and morals, and pride. It cuts right through everything. It doesn't care about the mess it makes. It *hurts,* and we let it.

"I love you, Cali," I say into her shoulder. "Always."

"I love you too, Elle. And I'm glad you're here. I'm glad you made it. Thank you."

I hug her harder.

HOURS LATER, IN THE MIDDLE OF THE NIGHT, I CAN'T SLEEP. I GET some water and retreat to the terrace overlooking the coast. It's quiet. Beautiful.

I jump as the door closes lightly behind me.

It's Parker.

The open button-down shirt I'm wearing over a tank top and pajama shorts whips wildly in the wind. It reminds me of what I wore that day at the Yankee game.

Everything reminds me of him.

He haunts me, and I hate it.

I turn around, back toward the water.

"Elle," he says, his tone serious. We've avoided speaking about anything between us for days. I should have known the conversation would come eventually."You don't have to talk to me. I understand that you've moved on. I just—I need you to know that I'm sorry. I never meant for any of this to happen. I wish I could—"

"It's okay," I say, still facing the water. "It's not your fault." Then I frown, turning toward him. "What do you mean, you know I've moved on?"

Something like pain, or maybe anger, flashes across Parker's face. He meets me at the railing, bracing his hands against it. He doesn't look at me as he says, "I heard you with him, Elle. I saw him go into your apartment, and I heard you . . ."

What? "Heard me with who?"

"Luke."

I almost choke on my water, remembering what Penelope told me they did *several times. He thought it was me?* "Parker," I say slowly, "Luke literally thinks I'm a serial killer."

He gives me a bewildered look. "What?"

"Never mind. It just—it was Penelope who you heard. Not me. I moved out for a week."

I don't think I've ever seen Parker look so relieved. Almost all the tension seems to leave his body. "Oh."

I tilt my head at him. "You thought I had sex with someone else, against our shared wall, a week after we broke things off, and you still took me to Europe for my sister?"

Parker lifts a shoulder. "I told you. It was the least I could do after... everything."

For a few minutes, we just watch the water. "They're leaving tomorrow," I finally say. "They're going to stay with Pierre's family in Switzerland."

"And you?"

"I have to get home. My screenplay is due in a week. I have one scene left. The last one."

He turns to me. "Let's go," he says.

"Go?"

"To the last location," he says. "The last one on the list." The one that was very much not part of our agreement, not that it's relevant anymore.

"Paris?"

The studio has a permit for the Eiffel Tower. I've never been, but I was going to look up videos or something to make up for it.

He nods, suddenly full of conviction. His eyes are blazing. "Summer isn't over, not yet," he says. "Let's go."

I frown. "But it's almost Labor Day weekend. Don't you have that important thing in the Hamptons?"

"Fuck the Hamptons."

We book the flights. We say goodbye to my sister and Isabella and, yes, Pierre, and it's hard, but Cali promises she'll be back in the States soon.

Then we're at the airport, flying to Paris.

26

THE PALACE WE PULL UP TO TAKES UP MOST OF THE BLOCK. IT'S ORNATE AND sprawling, but has a boutique feel.

"Which hotel is this?" I say, looking for a sign.

"It's not a hotel," Parker says. "It's my house."

The men outside aren't porters. They're guards.

"Oh."

The home has arched windows, intricately designed iron balconies, and a pale blue roof. There's a gate, then a courtyard, then steps to the front door.

Inside, we're met by a stunning curved marble staircase with the same iron banister. The ceiling is high, the finishes are gold, the floor is a mosaic of stone.

I turn to Parker. He's watching me.

"Do you like it?" he says.

I love it, but for some reason, I say nothing. I just keep walking through, until I see the first hearth. The room is adorned with elaborate finishes, as if originally crafted in another era, but the furniture is soft, slightly modern. There are round white pillows on the couches that look like giant pearls.

He silently shows me around. The kitchen is modern too and reminds me of the one in his New York apartment. The stairs curve, nestled against a stone wall with a towering arched stained-glass window. Every room is painted a slightly different pastel color. Every bathroom is made entirely of marble, matching that color. Light blue. Light pink. Light purple. The closets are painted a dark variation of the shade.

There are endless terraces, and outside, stretching far and wide, there is a garden. It's overgrown in an intentional way, with pastel flowers and rosebushes.

"I can't believe this is yours. It's so beautiful."

"It was going to be demolished, it wasn't in great shape. My mom always loved Paris and dreamed of being an interior designer, so I bought it, and she designed every room. We made sure the renovations salvaged anything historical."

I turn to face him. "You mean, the mother who bought you the vase?"

"Yes, I just have the one."

He must see the surprise I am trying very hard to mask, because he says, "My mom knows the vases are ugly, Elle. That's the point. She thinks it's important to gift me items that lived in our house when I was growing up. So I don't forget where I came from."

He leads me to a clock that looks completely out of place in the house. It has chipped red paint, and I'm pretty sure a rooster comes out of it.

"We got that at a yard sale when I was twelve," he says. "It's how we got most of our stuff. Either that or thrift stores."

"Does she . . . live here?" I ask, wondering if I should dart into the closest bathroom and try to make myself look presentable.

"No. Not right now anyway. She runs my foundation. It's based in Pennsylvania, out of my hometown."

I blink at him. "You have a foundation?"

He nods. "It holds a large percentage of my company shares."

That certainly never came up in my internet sleuthing of him. He must keep it private. "You never told me that."

"You never asked."

He takes me to the library.

It's like something out of a fairy tale. Books stretch to the ceiling. There are sliding ladders. Comfortable chairs fill the corners of the room. There's a desk in the center of it.

I think, for a moment, that this would be the perfect place to finish my screenplay.

"I don't think I've ever liked a place so much," I say quietly. Gently, so gently, he takes my hand.

"Me too," he says. "But as much as I love this house . . . Paris is outside of it."

I change into a summer dress and shoes comfortable to walk in for hours. The only way I've ever experienced Paris is through movies, and even romanticized, even overly used, the reality is even better than on screen.

The buildings are beautiful, with their blue roofs and simple exteriors. Cafés are everywhere, with round tables, chairs huddled together in pairs, and scalloped umbrellas.

We sit at one called Carette, and I order the best hot chocolate I've ever had in my life. It comes with a separate bowl of whipped cream, and I say, "You have to try this," before handing Parker a spoonful. When some cream remains on his lip, I instinctively brush it away with my thumb. It's a simple touch. I don't expect to feel the jolt down my arm; I don't expect his eyes to darken.

I lower my hand, feeling like my skin has caught aflame under the summer sun.

It's still morning, so we order croissants, cappuccinos, and omelets. We sit side by side, watching people walk by, and I say, "I like this."

"What?"

I shrug. "All of it. Eating outside on a busy street. Drinking hot chocolate without feeling like a child. Sitting on one side of the table instead of across from each other."

At that, Parker curls his arm around me. His fingers make shapes against my side.

We walk down streets lined with bakeries, pharmacies, cheese shops, and clothing stores.

I freeze when I see the Eiffel Tower, poking out between buildings, suddenly completely visible at the end of the street, like a pot of gold at the end of a rainbow. Parker has to pull me back onto the curb to avoid oncoming traffic.

"Now I know why everyone loves it," I say. There are no skyscrapers here to block it, like the new builds that always ruin views of the Empire State Building in New York. No, it's everywhere, and it's like a game, walking around and trying to find it from various vantage points.

I'm impatient to see it up close, and not just for my screenplay. "Should we go now?"

"We'll go tonight," Parker says.

We walk to rue Cler, a street full of markets selling fruits, flowers, chocolate, bread, and cheese. We walk in and out of stores, trying different bites, telling each other "You need to try this" every few seconds. We go to Shakespeare and Company, a bookstore with a line outside and where photography isn't allowed. We get crepes on the street and eat them while we walk around Notre Dame.

"Are we close to the Luxembourg Garden?" I ask. We are.

Green stretches out across the city, framed in colorful flowers, statues, and chairs. People read. Children laugh as they race boats in a fountain.

We go to the Musée Rodin. "This looks like your house," I say as we walk toward it, because it does.

Parker's house is not, decidedly, filled with busts of men long dead. We pass a wall of drawings. There are some pieces in this museum

from other artists, but some of these are attributed to Rodin himself.
"I didn't know Rodin made drawings," I say, mostly knowing him from his sculpture.

"I guess people really only get one thing to be remembered by," Parker says.

I turn to him. "What do you want to be remembered by? Your company?"

He shakes his head. "No," he says thoughtfully. "I hope, one day, my company is the least interesting thing about me."

We go outside to the garden. That's where *The Thinker* lives.

"This is me before every single decision in my life," I say, nodding up at the statue. "I overthink everything." I frown. "Only, usually, I'm inside."

"I don't know, Elle," Parker says. "You've been pretty spontaneous this summer." He motions around. "And we've spent a lot of it outside."

He's right.

A man walks by. My soul almost leaves my body when Parker asks, in perfect French, if he wouldn't mind taking a photo of us. He happily says yes and snaps it. I think I might keel over.

I'm staring at Parker, waiting for him to look at me, so I can remind him of his hatred of all things photograph. Instead, he gently flicks my nose and moves on.

We've walked all day. By the time we get back to Parker's house, I'm exhausted. Intending to *just close my eyes for a minute,* I wake up hours later in total darkness.

Barefoot, I walk into the hallway. It's so quiet. I find Parker in the library. He's staring at the wall, deep in thought, leaning forward.

"Shouldn't you be out in the garden?" I joke.

He looks up at me. Smiles. He rises to his feet the way gentlemen do in Jane Austen adaptations whenever a woman walks into the room.

"What time is it? Did I miss the Eiffel Tower?"

"No. I was just going to knock on your door."

He tells me we're going to dinner. I know there are a few restaurants in the Eiffel Tower, but I don't get my hopes up, because I've heard those need to be booked months in advance. We just decided to come to Paris. Even if Parker tried, it's not like they can pull another table out of thin air.

The streets are quieter than usual. I didn't even check my phone before leaving. "What time is it?" I ask.

"Almost midnight."

Midnight? The jet lag must be getting to me, because I only just started getting hungry. I know Europeans eat late, but I wonder if any of the restaurants are even open.

When we approach the Eiffel Tower, it's blocked off.

I frown. "It's closed."

"Yes," he says. "It is."

Someone comes out to meet us. "This way, Mr. Warren," he says. Was he able to get the restaurant to stay open late?

Parker watches me try to figure it out with faint amusement.

We're the only ones in the elevator. Parker grips my shoulder as we quickly move up one of the tower's legs, up to the sky.

It opens to a restaurant.

It too is empty, save for a single table in the center. Paris is spread all around us, lights everywhere.

I turn to Parker. "You did not rent out the Eiffel Tower." He says nothing. "Say you didn't rent out the Eiffel Tower."

"I can't."

Is that even possible? It's in shock that I move toward the window, marveling at the view. It's unparalleled. Midnight Paris is all below us, spread out like a feast.

Parker pulls my chair out for me. He takes a seat on the other side. A woman comes over and begins pouring wine.

"You said you would stop with the over-the-top stuff," I say, still not sure if any of this is real.

He lifts a shoulder. "This, I did for me."

We have a six-course Michelin-starred meal. Every bite is the best thing I've ever tasted, until the next one. By the end, I'm pleasantly full.

When we're done, I think it's time to go, but we're directed to another elevator. "Where are we going?" I don't know why he would willingly get in another one if he didn't have to.

"You'll see," Parker says.

We travel farther up, through the lattice, Paris getting tinier and tinier beneath us. We keep going, then take a flight of stairs, until we're at the very top of the Eiffel Tower.

And we have it all to ourselves.

Wind blows my hair back. I marvel at the sleeping city below. I turn to Parker. "I thought you were afraid of heights."

He's not looking at the city. He's not looking at the tower. He's looking at me.

"When I'm with you, I'm not scared of anything," he says.

I am, I want to tell him. This *scares me.* It feels like we've been careening toward something all summer. And now—

"Tomorrow's the last day of summer," I say, as he joins me at the edge. He's tense, but his hand is soft against my spine. My voice is barely a whisper as I turn to face him. "It's a shame, that summers always end."

"Maybe this one can be endless," Parker says.

"Nothing in life is endless."

"Love is, Elle," he says.

I laugh. "And what do you know about love?"

"Now?" he says. "Everything."

This, I think. This warmth in my chest, filling every missing piece I didn't know I had, is what summer feels like.

I'm kissing him. My body melts against him, as if in relief, as if saying, *Yes, this is exactly where we're supposed to be.*

I break away, and he looks devastated, before I say, "How quickly can we get back to your house?"

The moment we're through his front doors, I throw my purse down, kick off my heels, and he lifts me into the air. My ankles lock behind his back, and I'm kissing him as he takes us upstairs, not missing a single step.

Before I know it, my back is against the softest sheets I've ever felt in my life, and I'm shrugging out of my dress. He pulls it off me in a flash, and I'm suddenly cold, only in the lingerie I thank myself for bringing with me.

I move to take the rest off, when his hand gently covers both of mine. It pins my wrists above me.

"Let me—let me look at you," he says with a tenderness completely at odds with the pure need in his eyes. He studies every inch of me. "Perfect," he says, so softly I don't think he even knows he said it aloud. "Always so perfect."

I sit up and start unbuttoning his shirt. My hands are shaking, not with nerves, but in anticipation, and he helps me. My fingers move to his pants. He stops me again with a gentle hand.

"Are you sure?" he says.

"Yes," I say, and then his clothes are off, and I've suddenly lost the ability to breathe. He's big. I knew that, but—

"I don't mean to sound ungrateful," I say, swallowing. "But there might be such a thing as too many inches."

He smiles slowly, a bit of that ego coming through. "You won't be saying that in a few seconds." He winks.

Then his hands lock around my ankles, and he's dragging me to the edge of the bed. He's taking my underwear off in one fluid motion. He's kneeling before me.

I sit up, eyes wide, and he looks up at me. The sight of him, between my legs, need clear on his face—

“Is this okay?” he asks.

I nod.

“Good. Now lie back for me, sweetheart,” he says, breath hot against my inner thighs. I do. He hooks one leg over his shoulder. Then the other. At the first press of his tongue against my center, my back arches off the bed.

I curse at the ceiling, bucking as he devours me like he can’t taste enough. At first, the strokes of his tongue are long, slow, taking his time, but then he makes a deep sound of pure want and pulls my hips to his mouth, greedy for even more, and my hands fist his sheets as he licks me like he’s starving, like he’s been waiting months to do this.

I can’t form coherent words or thoughts, just cries that sound like they couldn’t possibly have come from me, and when he slips two fingers inside of me, I collapse, clenching around him, riding his tongue as I chase this pleasure, until I melt back onto the bed.

I lift up onto my arms, wrung out, body boneless, only to see Parker rise to his feet, looking entirely too pleased with himself.

“Come here,” I say, and he does, slowly. His mouth traces the inside of my thigh, my hip bone, up my ribs, until he reaches my chest, peaked through the lace. The bra is gone in an instant and is replaced with his hands. His thumbs drag over my nipples, pulling, pinching, and I clench around nothing. I need him. I need everything.

A condom is unrolled, and I’m glad Parker is prepared. As he puts it on, I’m still trying to figure out how this is going to work.

His arms bracket around my head, holding himself up. He reaches down between us. “You’re sure?”

I nod.

He begins to push in, and I gasp at the sheer size of him. He stops immediately. Waits for me to nod again.

Slowly, he inches in, and in, and in, stretching, then filling, and at first there’s a flash of pain, but then it’s replaced by a searing pleasure, and he's dragging through me, against a place that makes me gasp, and I dig my nails into his shoulders to keep from screaming.

Finally, he bottoms out, and we groan together. I'm so full of him, so full of want, and need, and this relentless ache.

Then, eyes locked, he begins to move.

I'm panting in his face. One hand smooths down my side, gripping my waist, and when he drags against that place inside me again, my head tilts back and I cry out, the pleasure so sharp, so saturated. He presses his forehead to mine. He goes harder and faster, and we're looking at each other the way we have dozens of times before, the wordless language we've developed in the last few weeks, like *This is better than I thought it would be,* like *I think I could do this for my entire life.*

He says my name as he slams in one final time, his eyes widening as he finishes, and I gasp as I come again around him.

"I CAN'T BELIEVE WE'RE DOING THIS," I GASP.

"I can't believe it took this long."

He has me against the wall. I'm sliding against the marble. My nipples are dragging against his chest as I move furiously, desperate for every inch of him. He's gripping my hips and moving me on him, helping me ride him.

It's been like this for hours. Finally, after we're done with the wall, I pull on one of his shirts and find a pair of my sweatpants, and we make it downstairs, to get some water. I'm sitting on the kitchen counter, overheated and oversatiated, when he stalks toward me.

My chest is peaked against his shirt again. He takes my hair in a gentle fist, then moves it behind my head. "You drove me out of my mind that night, when you were locked out," he says. "I was so hard, I couldn't sleep." I swallow, and he ducks to trace his lips down my throat. "This is what I wanted to do that night," he says against my collarbones.

My nipples are tight beneath him. Eyes still on mine, he leans down and takes one between his teeth. I gasp, and he licks across the hurt, sucking my chest right through the fabric, making a mess of me. His hand comes up to pinch the other one.

My legs widen, needy, and his hand slips beneath the waist of the sweatpants. He growls at my need. "Always so ready for me," he says.

It's true.

I can't take it anymore. "Let's go back," I say, and he helps me off the counter. I rush out of the kitchen. He's right behind me.

We don't even make it to the bedroom.

On the stairs, Parker pulls my sweatpants down and takes me against the steps. My shirt has been discarded somewhere. My knees drag against the cold marble; his hand reaches around to play with my center.

My cries echo through the tower of the stairway as I shatter, but he keeps going, pulling me up against him, rolling my nipples between his fingers.

"You can go again," he growls into my ear, and I can, I can. I ride him like this, pushing back toward him, deliciously stretched, and he pinches my center.

I come again, my body flush against his so he feels every tremor. He pumps one final time, then finds his release, before sighing against my neck.

"We don't ever have to leave," he says. "We can stay right here."

And I wish, truly, that this night could be endless.

27

WE DON'T LEAVE THE HOUSE FOR DAYS. IT'S LIKE WE'VE DISCOVERED A NEW language that we can't get enough of. Parker once said he wanted to bend me over every piece of furniture in his home, and we get close.

He takes a break to deal with a business call, and I carry my laptop to the office. That is where I sit and write my scene that takes place in the Eiffel Tower.

Two hours later, Parker kisses my neck, interrupting me, and we put good use to that sliding ladder. Then, with our clothes all over the library, I hand Parker a stack of freshly printed pages. "I want you—I want you to read it," I say.

"It's done?"

"Almost," I say. "I'm just finishing up the ending."

I don't tell him I've never let anyone read my unfinished work before. I think he can tell, by the way he gingerly takes the pages, like I've given him an unimaginable gift. Like this stack of paper is worth more than this block-long house.

"Thank you," he says.

He reads it in bed, and I watch him write little notes in the margins, the same way I did when we watched the movie together. At first, I think he's giving me critique, but then I sneak a look over his shoulder and see that his notes say, *Love this,* or *Funny.* The little words make something inside me sing.

The next morning, he wakes me up with a latte and the script, well worn and full of notes.

"You're done already?"

He joins me in bed, the mattress dipping. He steals a sip of my latte, then hands it back. "I couldn't stop. I stayed up reading it." His eyes are mischievous. "You've kept me up for several nights, do you know that?"

Heat drops through my stomach.

"I loved it," he says, before I can ask. "And I loved being able to see you, in the words. The way your mind works." He kisses my forehead, and I think I might melt right through the covers.

"It means a lot that you read it," I tell him, as I burrow myself in his side. "I'll read some of your code, to make up for it, or your acquisition contract."

He barks out a laugh. Then he sighs. "Speaking of that."

"We have to go, don't we?"

We both do. My script is due in just a few days. I need to polish it, then send it off to Sarah.

"We have a little bit of time, though," he tells me. "Our flight is in the afternoon." He puts my latte on the nightstand and I laugh as he lifts me out of bed and carries me to the shower.

I USED TO WONDER HOW FIRST-CLASS INTERNATIONAL FLIGHTS could justify being so expensive. The fact that the price was so much more than business class didn't make sense.

Until now.

We have our own lounge. There's a hotel room inside of it, waiting for us, which we make quick use of. There's a restaurant with a menu without any prices. All of it is included with the price of our ticket. We have the tasting menu.

There are hundreds of seats on this flight, but there are only twelve in the first-class cabin. There's so much space in each of our pods that we're able to sit across from each other when we eat dinner, a table between us, and a seat, complete with a seat belt, on the other side. That begins our next tasting menu.

Airplane food is supposed to be disgusting, but this is as good as any nice restaurant. We have soup. A salad. Seafood. There's a cheese plate in between courses. Nice wine is brought out and served in real wineglasses. Filet mignon. We're given pajamas to change into and full duvets. I have one of the best sleeps of my life, Parker's hand reaching for mine across the space between us.

AS MUCH AS I LOVED PARIS, I MISSED NEW YORK.

The skyline twinkles as we rush toward it in our Uber. The new doorman helps Parker with our luggage. In the elevator, I sit atop my suitcase, wondering what happens now. Seeming to read my thoughts, he says, "I have a few meetings, but can I make you dinner tonight?"

We kiss goodbye, and then I'm back in the apartment again. So much has changed in just a few days.

Sarah texts me. A studio head wants to meet me in person next week. She says it's for an exciting opportunity.

Nerves swirl in my stomach. I'm not used to taking these meetings. But I find that I'm more excited than afraid.

The piece of art that I knocked down in my shock is still on the ground. I put it back on its hook. Then, slowly, I start to walk around the apartment. The renovations are done. Luke and his firm did a good job, I have to admit.

My Frankenstein's monster plot is still on the floor. I don't need it anymore. Slowly, one by one, I start peeling the notes off the floor.

I get an alert on my phone, reminding me that my flight home is in four days. I see if I can change it, just in case. I can't.

It's fine, I think. I have the meeting anyway. I've been gone too long already.

It's raining outside, water slipping down the glass, storm clouds blocking the view, as I sink to the floor and begin to pack. It's better to do it over a few days, I reason, to make sure I don't forget anything.

Just like the city, almost every piece of clothing I fold seems to have a memory attached to it. The dress from the nightclub. The skirt and scratchy shirt I wore to dinner and karaoke with Taryn, Emily, and Gwen. The overalls I wore to volunteer.

I don't want to go, I realize.

But this isn't my home.

It never was. I was just house-sitting.

Parker cooks me all his favorite foods, at my request. I want to know what he likes. I mill around the kitchen, trying to be helpful, but instead, I get called *distracting,* which might be because I keep touching him. I can't help it. Seeing his arms and back flex in a T-shirt, as he's chopping vegetables, does strange things to me.

I set the table, adding candles, trying to make it nice, and help him serve the plates. He's made us chicken Parmesan, spicy pasta, and grilled mushrooms.

"I thought you ate healthily," I say, before groaning after my first bite.

"I do. But you asked for my favorite foods." He looks up at me. "And stop making that sound. I'd hate to ruin the lovely table you set by bending you over it."

Want curls through my bones, but I comply, eating all his food, marveling at how it's even better than a restaurant.

"It's so good," I say. "I'm really going to miss your cooking."

His fork goes still against his plate. Slowly, he looks up at me. "Why would you miss it?" he asks.

We stare at each other across the table. "My flight is in four days."

"Cancel it."

"I can't."

Parker drags his eyes back to his meal. For a few minutes, there's just silence, us eating separately, and I feel a gap opening between us, until he says, so gently I barely hear him, "I thought you would stay."

I put my cutlery down. "Where? That apartment's not mine. I live in LA. My entire life is back in LA." I say that as if I couldn't write anywhere. I say that as if anyone but Penelope is keeping me in California. I shake my head. "You're leaving too. Once the acquisition goes through, right? You'll be in San Francisco."

Parker frowns. Hurt flashes in his eyes for just a moment. "So that's it?" he says. "It's just . . . goodbye?"

"I don't know. I don't want it to be . . . but this was only ever meant to last the summer."

We have completely different lives, different careers.

He doesn't have time for a relationship. Especially now, when he's about to become the CEO of Virion.

We don't fight the rest of the night, but we don't talk much either. There's silence, instead of our typical talking.

And that's even worse.

28

I BARELY SEE HIM THE NEXT FEW DAYS, EXCEPT FOR IN THE NEWS LINKS PENELOPE sends to me, a leak announcing Parker's soon-to-be ascent to the CEO of Virion. It looks like the acquisition is finally about to close. Virion's stock rises immediately.

Taryn, Emily, and Gwen take me to dinner to say goodbye. This time, we do tacos at Tacombi and talk about our autumns over margaritas and guac.

"You'll have to visit!" Gwen says. "Winter in the city is so much fun, there's the holiday markets and ice-skating and the tree."

"She knows," Taryn says. "She went to Columbia, remember?"

"Oh," Gwen says, frowning.

I smile at her. "I would love to." If Cali decides to finally move into her apartment, it would be nice to spend the holidays with Isabella.

I wonder . . . I wonder what Parker will be doing for the holidays this year. I smile, remembering the tiny Christmas tree from the botanical garden.

"We lost her," Emily says. "You're thinking about him, aren't you?"

I was basically forced into (yeah right, I loved it) telling them all about Paris, in detail—*On the stairs?!*—and they're convinced it's possible for us to do long-distance between LA and San Francisco.

"Of course she is," Taryn says, sipping her drink. "You don't just have sex on the stairs and not think about a person."

I nearly choke on my chip. "Remind me to never tell any of you anything again."

THE NEXT MORNING, THERE'S A KNOCK ON MY DOOR. I'M STILL IN MY pajamas. I open it, only to find Parker there, ready for a run.

"It's six in the morning," I say. We usually run at seven. We haven't in days, while he's been busy. Or, perhaps more accurately, avoiding me.

"We have a long day ahead of us," he says.

I blink. "We do?"

He hands me a latte. It has his coffee shop's sleeve. I frown. "It's not open this early."

"I know. I went in and made it myself."

I take a long sip and sigh. "This is the best latte I've ever had," I say, meaning it. "Don't tell Jeremy."

He smiles, but it doesn't reach his eyes. Something is off, but I'm not sure what.

"I thought you were busy," I say.

"I am," he admits. "But we said we would do this before the end of the summer. We're already a little late."

Do what? Then, suddenly, I remember. I blink. "Parker. You can't be serious."

All he looks is serious.

I don't know what compels me to get changed into yoga pants, a T-shirt, and my sneakers, but maybe it's because I'm tired of him avoiding me. I'm leaving tomorrow. If he's willing to give me all of today . . . I'll take it.

"I can't believe we're doing this," I say as we ride the train all the way to the very northern tip of Manhattan.

I didn't mean to quote myself, but he turns to me and says, "I can't believe it took this long," and my cheeks heat.

"NOW ENTERING MANHATTAN" THE PLAQUE ON THE GROUND SAYS on both sides, with two drawings of leaves.

"Ready?" Parker says.

"Ready."

I'm grateful it's so early, because I move in a haze, part of me still asleep. Ten minutes in, we reach the 215th Street steps, rising like a choppy rogue wave. It looks like there are a million of them.

"How much would someone have to give you to run up and down those steps right now?" I ask Parker. He's tired. I can see he's tired, though he's a lot more awake than I am right now.

"There isn't enough money in the world."

The sun is already out, but the streets are decently empty. At the hour mark, we reach the George Washington Bridge and market. We walk in comfortable quietness, as we both fully wake up, along with the world around us. As the hours tick by, there are more people outside. Shop signs are turned around. Doors are propped open.

"First coffee is almost coming up," Parker says. I glance at him. "I found places for you to get coffee beforehand. Every few hours."

I must look surprised or touched, because he just raises a shoulder.

"It seemed like cruel and unusual punishment not to."

We're at Seventy-Second Street. There are benches and a little coffee truck. I order an iced coffee, and Parker gets us water bottles.

A little later, I take a fistful of Parker's shirt, surprise making me still. "Look!" I say. There's a bookstore called Shakespeare & Co. It's not the same, but it reminds me of the bookstore in Paris.

Parker looks at me, like he's remembering Paris too.

We reach the edge of Central Park at Columbus Circle. There's a hot dog cart on the corner, along the roundabout, and clusters of pedicabs. A shining gold statue atop a pillar reflects the morning sunlight.

Four hours into our walk, we start to see billboards advertising Broadway shows and theaters painted to look like their plays. There's an Applebee's sign with a giant apple outside of it, and I say, "I wonder how many people unironically post a photo in front of it." We pass a massive Olive Garden.

Then we're in the heart of Times Square, in the land of selfie sticks, mascots, and aggressive signage. Every store has flashing lights on its facade, from bars to bakeries.

Billboards ripple around us, flashing from ad to ad, featuring cars, movies, music, makeup, clothes, and even phone plans. We stand side by side and watch the screens, willingly being fed commercials. It's weirdly beautiful, I think. We drink water while sitting on the red steps.

"How are you doing?"

"My feet are about to go on strike," I say. "Yours?"

"Same."

It's almost ten. "Do your plans include brunch?"

Of course they do.

Twenty minutes later, in NoMad, we stop at the Smith to eat. I have a plate with scrambled eggs, bacon, and avocado, and Parker has a salad.

"Hydrate," I say, and we both drink water, eyes locked. "I don't mean to alarm you, but I think if I try to get out of this booth, my legs will just fall off."

Parker nods. "I'm feeling a similar sort of way."

We use the bathroom and continue down Broadway, right to the Flatiron Building. We stand, admiring it.

"It looks like a nose," Parker says.

It really does.

We take a turn onto Fifth for just a couple of blocks for, in Parker's words, "Elle coffee stop number two." I've been here before. Ralph's Coffee has green chairs outside and circular tables that remind me of Paris. We wait in line, and I order an iced mocha. Parker gets an iced tea with a slice of lemon. While we wait, I turn around and see a massive mirror on the wall.

Then I regret ever looking at all.

I look exactly like someone who was awoken at six in the morning and has been walking for the better part of the day. I take my hair out of its ponytail and start to frantically comb its top with my fingers. "Why didn't you tell me I looked like this?" I say, cursing the fact that I clearly was too busy washing my hands in the restaurant bathroom to notice.

Parker pulls me to his side. "You look perfect," he says, and then he takes a picture of me. I snatch the phone from his hand and take a photo of both of us in the mirror. Parker is scowling, in clear opposition to the influencer mirror photo.

We grab our drinks, then head back down Broadway. We pass a movie theater and ABC Carpet & Home, a high-end furniture store that also, strangely, has three really good restaurant offshoots. Our path takes us directly through Union Square.

It's hot outside, the sun blazing down, so, at my insistence, we duck into the four-floor Barnes & Noble to get some much-needed air-conditioning. We walk around—me pointing out which books I've read, Parker increasingly puzzled by the book covers. He flips through a few pages of some.

"Do all books have maps?" he asks.

"No," I say. "Only the best ones."

We stop in front of a romance table. Parker picks a book up and reads the back. Frowns. Picks up another. Does the same thing.

"None of them doing it for you?" I ask.

He puts the third one down. "No. Because none of them sound like us."

"I guess someone will have to write it, then."

Adequately cooled down, we walk across the street into the greenmarket. Stands are selling lavender, honey, pretzels, bread, flowers. We stop and buy a pastry, which we split, passing it back and forth, until our hands are sticky. We paper towel them off and keep walking, passing the Strand, another famous bookstore.

"More air-conditioning?" Parker asks, as we step inside.

"No," I say. "More books." I'm not an author, but I love being around stories. There's something peaceful about walking around a bookstore, knowing endless worlds are waiting to be discovered. Knowing there's always an escape, if we need it.

"Everyone has merch," Parker says, and buys us Strand pins as a reminder of the day. Then we head back outside. Buildings start to sport purple NYU banners. We enter NoHo. There's another good coffee shop, La Colombe, but I shake my head. I'd rather power through than have to continue to find bathrooms.

SoHo is packed, and we walk by a mixture of designer stores and brands we've seen several times already.

"I think that's the fifth Sephora today," I muse, and Parker doesn't even know what I'm talking about.

The Jenga Building is in the distance now, and we use it as a guiding star, until we reach the Financial District. By then, I'm only making it because Parker keeps saying "We're so close."

We pass city hall. A few blocks up, there's a line of people waiting to take photos in front of the bronze *Charging Bull.*

Then, finally, mercifully, we reach Battery Park.

The Staten Island Ferry building is our sign we've made it.

"If I collapsed, would you catch me before I hit the ground?" I ask.

"Of course," he says.

But I don't collapse. Instead, with a surge of energy, I jump up and hug him. He spins me around. "We did it," I say.

"You didn't even die."

"I know, it was great!"

I grab his phone and take a photo of us. "Send that to me," I say, and then I remember we don't have each other's numbers.

We look at each other. Neither of us makes a move to exchange them.

Maybe it's better this way, I think. *If I leave, and he never calls me, best if it's because he can't.*

29

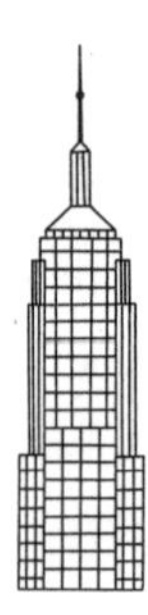

I'M SOAKING IN THE BATHTUB WHEN THERE'S A KNOCK ON THE DOOR. I GRAB a towel, dry my feet, and open it.

Parker's standing there. He looks freshly showered and clean-shaven, and his hair is still slightly damp.

His gaze drops to my towel. It's about the smallest one I could have grabbed.

"Sorry to interrupt," he says. "I can leave if—"

"No," I say. "Don't."

The door clicks closed behind him. My towel drops to the floor. He stalks toward me, and I keep walking backward, until my bare back hits the floor-to-ceiling windows.

"Tell me what you want," he says, his voice more tortured than I expected.

"Everything, Parker," I say. "I want everything."

He sinks to his knees. He hooks one of my legs over his shoulder, then the other, and I gasp, only my upper back leaning against the glass. His hands curl around my thighs, keeping me steady. Then he begins to devour me.

His tongue parts me, and I'm instantly melting, struggling to keep myself upright. He lightly runs his teeth across my center, and I cry out, then shamelessly ride his face until I shatter, nearly bucking off the wall, Parker pressing a hand against my hip. Slowly, he brings one leg back down, then the other.

I lead him to my bedroom and don't make a move to turn the lamp on. All we have are the city lights, glittering below us. In the dark, I take my time, taking his shirt off, running my hands down his arms and chest like I'm committing every part of him to memory. Because I am.

When I sink to take his pants off, I stay on my knees, and Parker says, "You don't have to."

"I know," I say, looking up at him. "I want to." And then my lips are around him. He curses, then braces his hand against the closest wall. I'm not good at this, I don't have a lot of practice, but he tells me how good it feels, and lightly wraps my damp hair around his wrist and fist to keep it out of the way.

When I think he might almost be there, he leads me back to my feet and says, in a voice of pure need, "Get on your hands and knees."

I do, my back arched, anticipation making me breathless, and he gets the condom he says he started carrying around in his wallet after Paris. He slips it on and then slips in and in and in, and I inadvertently clench around him, making him curse against my spine. When I'm used to him, he slowly inches out and then buries himself inside me in a smooth motion, with a blinding flash of pleasure.

He pulls my hips back, higher, and I pant against my pillow as he drives into me harder, faster, until I can't think beyond the sparks barreling up my spine. Just when I think I can't take it anymore, he pulls out and gently flips me onto my back.

"I want to look at you," he says, as he leans over me. "One last time."

I want to look at him too. This time, when he slips inside of me, it's nothing like it was before. He's slow. His forehead presses against mine. His hand cups my cheek.

Our gaze doesn't break as he drives into me, as I meet him stroke for stroke. I reach up and touch his face, *one last time*.

His lips find mine, and the kiss is punishing. The pace of his hips increases, and his tongue follows it, tasting me, running across the top of my mouth, my teeth, branding me, until I'm moaning, until I'm writhing against his length with need, like he wants me to remember, he doesn't want me to ever forget this moment.

His hand curls around my ass, he lifts my hips, and then I'm breaking. I gasp, clenching around him, this pleasure like the tide, drowning me, only to be ripped away again, and he releases my mouth to watch me.

"Parker," I say, and his hand travels to my back, to pull me to his chest as he buries himself deep inside me as he finishes, pulsing, grip tightening. He holds me like that for a few seconds, our hearts speaking Morse code to each other.

Then he sets me down, and we just look. We just look and look, committing each other to memory.

We both know what this is, without saying the words. That's always been our superpower. This is the last time for this, before I leave and our lives diverge again.

What a gift that they converged at all, if only just for the summer.

30

THE NEWS BREAKS THIS MORNING: "AFTER THREATENING TO WALK AWAY, Virion Now Buying Atomic for $15 Billion."

That must have been all those meetings, I think. Negotiating the price even higher. That's why he's been so distant.

Of course his company's acquisition would be more important than spending my last few days in the city together. It makes sense. Still, the flower in my chest that had bloomed throughout this summer feels like it's withering.

I'm all packed up when there's a knock on my door.

It's him. He's dressed far too nicely, like he's about to be on television or something. Is he going to do an interview for the acquisition? It doesn't matter. I'll be gone soon.

I look at him expectantly, but he doesn't say anything. He doesn't make a move to step inside. He looks so serious. This is it, isn't it? The awkward goodbye before we go our separate ways and pretend this summer never existed?

"You must be happy," I tell Parker, trying and failing to summon a smile. "About the acquisition."

Parker doesn't look happy at all. No, he looks tired. Irritated. He eyes my luggage like he wants to burn it.

"Before you leave," he says, "I—I wanted to show you something."

I look around. "I don't know . . . I still have to clean up, and I don't like being late to flights."

The words spill out of him. "Please. It won't take long."

"Okay," I say, because even though I can feel the walls that he broke down being built back up again, like boarding up windows before a storm, I must be a masochist, because I want to spend every remaining moment in New York with him. Even if some of them might hurt.

A car is waiting for us in front of the building. I don't ask where we're going—it doesn't matter. Places never really did. It was all about me and him this summer. That's what I realize as I watch the city pass by in the window behind him.

He was my summer. And now, it's over.

Parker doesn't say anything. He doesn't even look at me. We look so different right now, me in my airport-friendly loungewear, him in a suit that looks like the one he wore for his congressional testimony. It's like a stark reminder that we were never meant to fit together.

My throat is already feeling tight, knowing this is goodbye. Knowing I'll look back at this moment one day and wish I said *something.* But I don't. I turn toward my window and watch office buildings turn into pretty stores that line Fifth Avenue like presents. During the holidays, they're all wrapped in lights, but even now, each facade is perfectly maintained. There's a roadblock ahead. The car stops.

Parker opens the door. I frown. Is there a parade? Are we going to have to walk the rest of the way?

Without missing a beat, Parker helps me out, then leads me past the signs and barricades. "I—I think the road is closed," I say, looking around. I've never seen New York City so empty. We keep walking, and I can see all the way to the park. Nothing is blocking it. There aren't any people elbowing their way past, there aren't any pedicabs charging airline fees for a few blocks, there aren't any earsplitting horns. It's quiet. It's almost like we're on a movie set. Realization hits later than it should have. He did this.

New York City never sleeps, never stops, but it has for Parker Warren.

"You literally stopped traffic," I say, standing in the middle of the street. "Why?"

What could he possibly have needed to rent out Fifth Avenue for? I wait for an answer that never comes, so I turn around for one of my last looks at a city I used to hate. I watch it through an unobstructed view, shadows long across the pavement, sunlight sparkling against metal finishes. The city is beautiful in the summer, gilded, gleaming.

I turn to Parker, expecting him to be taking it in too, but he's just watching me. And he looks far too serious. "What's wrong?"

"Don't leave."

I swallow. This is what I wanted to hear, isn't it? But no. It doesn't make sense. As much as I don't want this summer to end, reality is like gravity, teasing reason apart from feeling. "Parker, you said it yourself. You don't have time for a relationship. And I'm no good in them, I—"

"I'm not taking the Virion deal," he says.

What? I frown. "They're giving you billions more dollars," I say, like maybe he might have missed that part.

"In June, I might have taken it. But now . . . I can't."

"Why not?"

"They insist on selling our customers' data. I negotiated some limitations on it, and they eventually accepted and raised the price, but I—I just can't. I *care,* I guess. And everyone needs something to care about." He's repeating my own words back to me. Something in my chest tightens. He remembers everything, I think. Like every word that comes out of my mouth is a script to be pored over and annotated.

"Doesn't that mean you won't get the money? You won't have an exit?"

He nods. "I'll go back to running it. It will be far less money in my pocket, but at least I'll have the freedom to do what I think is right."

"You'll still be busy," I say. Maybe not as busy as he would be if he became the CEO of Virion, but he'll continue to be the CEO of Atomic.

That was what he said, why this couldn't work. He was too busy for a relationship.

"I will be," he says. "But I'll never be too busy for you."

I swallow. I want that to be true. I want our lives to fit together like a puzzle, but we're both corner pieces.

"You said your company comes first. That it always will."

"Elle, for you, I'll move the company here, to New York. For you, I'll hire another CEO. For you, I'll give all my money away. I don't care. None of it matters. Not the way you do."

He can't mean that. Besides, I don't *want* that. "I don't want you to resent me. I don't want you to do anything just because you think I want you to. I don't want you to give up all these things you've always wanted."

"I don't do anything I don't want to do," he says. "And, Elle, just so we're clear: I've never wanted anything like I've wanted you."

I'm not sure I'm breathing. My eyes are burning.

He steps toward me, in the middle of the empty street. His green eyes are pinning me in place. "I love you, Elle."

"No," I say, shaking my head. "No, you don't."

"I do," he says, voice so earnest it makes my heart break.

"No." I take a step back. "You don't understand. You don't know me. I'm horrible. If I have an appointment, I can't do anything else that day. It's pathetic. I get way too happy when the barista remembers my name. I have to give myself a pep talk for fifteen minutes before calling the doctor's office." I can't stop talking, words are just spilling out, because if I stop, he'll say something else, and I'm afraid of how it might make me feel. "And, speaking of that, how is everyone else so . . . responsible? How do they just, like . . . go to the post office? Or do their taxes on time? I'm such a mess, it's unbelievable. Trust me."

The corner of his mouth crooks up. "Elle, are you trying to convince me not to love you?"

"Yes!" I say. "Yes, exactly."

"Too late," he says. "And yes, Elle, I know you. I know you, and I love you."

He's right in front of me now. His thumb brushes across my cheek, and that's when I realize I'm crying. Why am I crying?

It's because I know. I know he's telling the truth. This summer, I let him in, I let him see me, I let him *know* me. And he loves me.

It's scary. To love me is to know my scars, and I'm the only one who's ever seen all of them.

But I want him to see. I want to shed my bristles, let him learn every piece of me, and love me wholly.

"I know you, and I love you too," I say, before I can help myself. Then I choke on a sob. It's true. I've loved him for a while. No use in denying it now, even though I'm about to get on a plane back home. I shake my head. Tears are running freely now, and I want them to stop, but they won't. "God, feelings are so embarrassing," I say. "That's why I just write them down. Make someone else say them."

That's when Parker slowly, eyes never leaving mine, gets down on one knee.

My body stills. The city is quiet around us, like it's holding its breath.

"What are you doing?" I say, panic closing in, realization settling in my bones. "You don't want to get married," I remind him. "You said it was the world's stupidest contract."

He's smiling now. "If you marry me, Elle, it will be the best contract I ever sign."

There's no ring. I don't care. All I see is him, and my feelings are everywhere now. Every emotion I've pressed down this summer is rising to the surface, and *I want this*. I don't want this summer to end. I don't want to leave. I don't want to be apart from him again.

"Marry me, Elle," he says. "We can figure the rest out later. Together."

"Yes," I say, before I can think about all the reasons not to. His smile widens, eyes crinkling. I've never seen him happier.

Then he kisses me.

He kisses me, and I can see it. A future. A life. An endless summer.

"There's one more thing," he says, and he takes my hand. Walks me to the closest store. Its door looks like an arched gate, like something from a fairytale; there is greenery framing the windows.

Harry Winston. It's empty inside, just like the street. The cases are all open.

I swallow. I've seen this movie. "Do I . . . you know . . . *pick one*?" I say.

Parker frowns, like he doesn't get the reference at all. Like he has no idea what I'm talking about. "No. They're all yours."

I blink. "Parker, I don't need—"

"There are ninety-four. One for every day we've spent together this summer. I picked out all of them." Sensing my reluctance, or maybe horror, he says, "Sell them. Give them to charity. I don't care. They're yours."

He reaches into his suit pocket. "And there's something else."

He pulls out a piece of paper and hands it to me. It's a deed. My eyes narrow, not understanding, until I see the address.

I know it better than my own. I've searched it multiple times, in my worst of writing slumps. I have the listing printed out and glued to the manifestation board Penelope made me make three New Years ago. It's my dream house.

Somewhere behind my ribs, my heart breaks.

"It's yours."

No. Slowly, everything good turns bitter. I blink too many times, hoping, wishing, this isn't what I think it is.

When I look up at Parker, he must sense my horror, because his smile slowly disappears. "Elle—"

But I've stepped away. I shake my head, like maybe my emotions will fall back into place, maybe this will make sense, maybe the last few moments can be eaten up and there won't be this seed of betrayal growing roots in my stomach.

"You didn't, Parker. Tell me you didn't."

He's confused. Panicked. He doesn't know what he did wrong, and that's the worst part.

He points to a place on the document. "This is a transfer document. Once you sign, it will be in your name. It's yours. I'll have no control over it. It—"

"You don't get it, Parker," I say, my voice breaking. "It's not just about control. It's about *pride,* it's about *me*. I wanted to buy it with my *own work,* on my *own terms*. You took that from me. You—you don't even *understand* why that means something to me."

My world starts spinning.

It's him, in the stairwell, implying that he could buy my affection. It's my father paying my student loans right out from under me.

This was *my dream*. The one I've saved for. The one I've had since I was eighteen.

And he's just taken it away from me.

I hear my mother in my head. What am I doing? How could I think this would work?

"Elle," he says, reaching toward me, "what's wrong?"

Everything. Absolutely everything.

I take a step back, just out of grasp. "I can't do this," I say. "I'm sorry. I just—I can't." I turn to leave.

He gently grabs on to my wrist. His eyes are wide—I've never seen him so afraid. Not in front of Congress, not when his acquisition wasn't going through. He was always collected. Uncaring. Now, his eyes are glistening. "Please, Elle. Let me fix this."

But there's no fixing this. There never was. I knew from the very beginning this relationship wouldn't work. I should have listened to myself. I should have known one summer wasn't long enough to change anyone.

I can buy anything I want.

Is that what he thinks? That he could buy me? Buy my dreams? Buy my love? I was wrong. He doesn't know me. He doesn't understand me.

How could he?

"Elle," he calls, as I curl my hand around the door handle, "don't do this."

But I have to.

I leave the jewelry shop. I can feel him follow me. I can hear him calling out my name.

The street is closed, there aren't any taxis. Tears are blurring my vision. I just start walking as fast as I can, then I'm running, then I'm *sobbing,* because I really thought this was it. I thought I had finally found someone who understands the unique and complicated shade of me.

I was wrong.

Streets go by, and finally there are cars, it feels like the city has finally released its breath. There are people on the sidewalks, elbowing past me, who don't care that my chest feels like it's locking up for good.

I wave my hand frantically, until finally a taxi takes pity on me.

It's a blur. Getting my luggage. Leaving the apartment I've spent the summer in. Leaving the building. Saying goodbye to the city.

And then taking another taxi out of it.

31

MOVIES HAVE A FORMULA. A THREE-ACT STRUCTURE. A RESOLUTION. LIFE ISN'T like that. Life doesn't fit into pretty boxes, it doesn't look like an outline, it doesn't work that way.

Life would make a terrible movie.

Awful.

Box office trash.

No bonuses.

None.

The summer is over. My screenplay is finished. And I'm on my way back to LA. This was what was supposed to happen, I tell myself. This was the best-case scenario.

So why do I feel like I've lost everything?

Penelope picks me up at the airport. In the car, I tell her everything. She pulls into a parking lot, and I collapse into her, gasping, sobbing.

"I loved him," I tell her, in between sobs. I say it in the past tense, like I won't love him for the rest of my life. "I really loved him."

"I know," she says, smoothing my hair down. "I know you did."

The studio executives offer me a three-movie deal. They love my script. Filming begins in the fall. "They'll use CGI to make it look like summer," Sarah assures me. I'm invited on set. I refuse. Going back to each of those locations, going back to the city, would be too painful.

I throw myself into writing. Pain produces script after script. Cali puts her apartment on the market.

The city is bad for the baby.

I spend the holidays with her, little Isabella, and Pierre in Switzerland, before they leave to spend time with our father.

Gwen is getting her MBA at the London School of Economics and invites us all to visit her. We do. Penelope has a brief and predictable fling with a thirty-something professor there.

Every few months, there's a new headline.

"Atomic Drops Virion Deal—Parker Warren to Remain as CEO of the Growing Tech Company."

Then: "Atomic Goes Public," accompanied by a photo of Parker ringing the bell. He's smiling, but it doesn't reach his eyes. They don't crinkle at all.

Finally: "Billionaire Bachelor No Longer Billionaire: Tech Genius Gives Most of His Wealth to Charity."

Penelope slaps that newspaper on my desk.

I look up at her. "So?"

"So? That man literally gave all his money away for you."

I roll my eyes. "He has plenty of money left." With interest rates, honestly, he'll probably have to fight *not* to be a billionaire on a regular basis, if it's that important to him. "And he didn't do it for me. He did it because he thinks it's the right thing to do."

Penelope looks exasperated. "I don't understand. You're miserable, Elle. You love him."

"He's the CEO of a massive tech company with thousands of employees. He'll always have more money, more power. He'll diminish me. Next to him, I'll always be no one. Everyone will think I'm some trophy wife, none of my accomplishments will ever matter."

"I don't think that's true, Elle, I—"

"My mom would hate him."

Penelope frowns. "Elle, your mom would want you to be happy," she says.

"I am happy," I say, a little too defensively.

She looks unconvinced. "I don't get you. Why are you so obsessed with money?"

I rear back. "Obsessed with money? If anyone is obsessed, it's him."

She shakes her head. "You are more obsessed with money than anyone I've ever met. And you are letting the love of your life get away because of it."

My eyes sting.

She's right.

But I don't know how to fix it.

32

EIGHTEEN MONTHS LATER

"IT'S A GOOD HEADLINE," SARAH SAYS.

"Meet Elle Leon: The Brains Behind the Summer's Biggest Blockbuster."

It's a great one. And it's the first interview I've ever given.

The movie premiered to rave reviews. I didn't read any of them. When it blew past the box office projections, I didn't even look at the numbers.

In the interview, the journalist asked me, "Where is home for you? Where are you happiest?"

My answer was generic. I wasn't about to turn an interview into my therapy session.

But inside, I knew the truth.

LA didn't feel like home when I returned. It hasn't ever since. Home was across the country in a city I hadn't had the courage to return to.

As for where I was happiest—I wouldn't know the answer to

that. Because, just like Penelope had said, I haven't been happy in a while.

In the last days of my mom's life, she wanted to be at home. She had to remain at the hospital, and she hated it.

Don't remember me here, in this room, she said. *Remember me happy. Remember me with you, in the kitchen, making arepas. Remember us dancing on our tiptoes and painting with our fingers.* I cried and held her hand and promised. I would only remember her happy.

Penelope was right. She would want me happy too.

I drive two hours down to the storage unit where my best and worst memories are kept. I haven't visited it since she passed.

The aftermath was a mess. *I* was a mess. I moved back home for a few weeks, to handle everything. Though, it didn't seem like home, when it was empty.

No, not completely empty. The house was filled with plants, my mother's most prized possessions, exotic varieties she had collected over time. Each of them had names. She *talked* to them. When I asked her why, she said they listened. She said it made them grow stronger. I had to admit, it worked. She would tell them how pretty they looked, and they would bloom. They were bright, colorful, saturated, and always turned toward the sun. She had tried to teach me how to water them, but I hadn't really listened.

I tried. In those weeks, I tried, but they all died, one by one, and I sat there, in the middle of the room, sobbing, *screaming,* because they were just like my mom. So vibrant, so alive, then so suddenly fading. So suddenly *gone.*

Life didn't care about grief. Neither did the bank. Bills had to be figured out. The house had to be cleared, so it could be sold, to pay off all the debts. I had to find this storage unit and put all our moments in it. Closing the door behind it felt like another burial. The only thing I kept was the necklace. I touch it now, as someone from the facility cuts the lock.

I sit on the floor like an anthropologist, puzzling our past back together. Smiling faintly at all the horrible art projects my mom insisted on keeping: Cali's painting that she made from makeup because she forgot to bring home the right materials, the macaroni-framed photos we both made in second grade, our toothless grins filling the centers.

I make discoveries, like the only evidence that my mom had a life before her children—dusty textbooks in Spanish, from university before she dropped out. She saved them. I wish I could ask her why. I wish I could ask her if she would go back and make the same choices again, knowing where they ended.

I wish I could ask her if her hatred ever got her anywhere. If sticking by the rules she made for her life ever made living any easier.

I wish I could ask her about breaking them.

My mom always looked at me like I was her mirror. Like I was her past self. Like she might be able to shake my shoulders and warn me off the path she already went down.

Penelope says my mom would have wanted me happy, but why didn't she choose happiness for herself?

In the last box, I find stuff from the hospital. I almost don't go through it, but then I sigh and find my courage. Slowly, I unpack it. The last magazines she paged through. The last cards work colleagues and friends sent.

At the bottom sit stacks and stacks of paper. No, not just paper. Screenplays. The ones my mom insisted I print for her.

"Let me read what you're most proud of," she said.

I left them in her room, but she was weak at the end, barely awake, and they were untouched by the time she passed.

Or so I thought.

Now, flipping through, I see something that makes me go still. Notes in the margins. Possibly the last words she ever wrote.

Fingers shaking, I flip through them.

They're critical, and spot-on. She crosses out entire swaths of dialogue. Tells me the conflict isn't strong enough.

She tells me which parts she loves. Which characters she sees me in. Which lines she liked enough to underline three times.

On the very last page, there's a paragraph, written hastily, like she wanted to make sure she got all the words out:

"Elle. My little lion. Don't be one of those writers who saves all the best lines for their characters. Say them yourself. Don't save the best stories for your screenplays. Live them. Life isn't a movie. There's never just one start or ending. There's always the chance to begin again. My biggest regret is not giving myself new beginnings. Don't make the same mistakes I did. Begin again and again and again. The promise of a new tomorrow is the best part of living. I love you and your sister more than anything. Take care of each other."

I cry, holding the page to my chest, like I can imprint the words onto my soul. Like I can hold my mom for one last time.

How foolish we are, caring, knowing everything we love will one day be lost.

It's the ultimate rule of life. Everything always ends . . . and still, we begin again.

That's how I end up on a plane back to New York, the last place I lived a life better than one of my movies.

The ghost of him is everywhere, touching everything, like the sun. The city is heavy with memories. There's no hiding from them, so I don't. I go to the same places, but they feel different, like they've been robbed of their souls.

I have the money for the town house now. I stand in front of it, and don't see a For Sale sign. The exterior is painted a new color. Parker would have sold it after I left. I wonder who owns it now.

After several emails, the real estate agent says the owner has agreed to let me see it off-market. She has large hair and walks exceedingly fast in heels. She makes her way up the stairs in a flash, then puts the key into the lock.

The door creaks open.

It doesn't look anything like it did when I used to tutor here. No, it's clearly undergone an extensive renovation. I remember seeing the builders go in and out. The sitting room has been turned into a library, with shelves from the bottom of the wall to the top. There's a window seat for reading. The kitchen is white with a waterfall marble island and a countertop overflowing with coffee machines. The fireplace has been redone in stone. When I get closer, I see it's been made into a floral pattern.

"I'll let you explore," the real estate agent says, and I'm grateful. "It's quite an unusual property," she adds. "Very . . . specific." She laughs. "The bottom floor is, if you can believe it, a basketball court."

Strange.

I walk up the stairs. The second floor is a guest bedroom and an office. The desk is against the window. There's a printer right next to it. There are frames on the walls, but I don't pay too much attention to them. It's not like they'll be staying if my offer is accepted. The third floor has a movie theater, complete with a popcorn machine and projector. Also, another bedroom.

I walk up to the top floor. It's the master bedroom with the skylight. That's when I freeze.

The walls—they're covered in photographs.

Of New York.

Of me.

Of *us.*

Every single photo Parker took, and some I didn't even notice, are hanging there, framed like works of art.

No, that can't be right. I assumed Parker sold it shortly after I left. Why would he keep the town house?

I mindlessly open the door, out to the terrace.

It's covered in flowers. *Roses.* Butter colored, cherry colored, ballerina pink; some are striped like candy.

I rush down the stairs, to the office. The frames on the walls—they are surrounding my scripts. Every single one I've ever sold is hanging on the wall, proudly displayed.

My body is boneless beneath me as I make my way back down to the kitchen. "Who's the seller?"

"Some tech CEO," she says. "He's never lived here, but it's well maintained. A team comes in every week to keep it in top condition."

"And when was it purchased? When was it renovated?"

She looks down at the papers in front of her. "Purchased the end of June, two summers ago. Renovated shortly after."

If that's true . . . then he started renovating it while we were falling in love. This house . . .

It's a love letter to us. A love letter to our summer.

Or, at least, it was.

I think I'm going to be sick.

The real estate agent sighs. "I've had multiple offers for the property, but he refused to sell, until now, until I shared your letter with him." I had written one, to convince the seller to let me see it, since it wasn't on the market. "You must have really made an impression. He says you're the only person he would ever sell it to."

Parker read my letter. He knows I'm looking at the town house. My chest starts to constrict. Suddenly, I'm back on that empty Manhattan block, running away from him, from our future.

I swallow. "How much did he pay for it?"

She tells me.

"That's my offer," I say.

The real estate agent types. Sends. Her phone dings.

It's accepted.

THE ELEVATOR DOORS SWING OPEN, AND I'M MET BY A TEACUP poodle.

Then another one.

And another one.

They're all identical.

"We like to get them all together, once in a while," a voice says, strong as ever.

Edith Adelaide.

She's one of the main donors for the organization I'm involved with, to raise money for arts programs. When I received the invitation to the cocktail party a few days ago, I almost threw it away. I knew being in this place would unearth all types of memories. Still, I came. Part of me wanted to remember, maybe.

I'm one of the first to arrive. Crates are leaning against the walls. Staff comes in and out.

"In the process of selling it all," Edith says. "Approaching your nineties, there's simply no certainty. I decided I don't trust some distant relative not to contest my will once I'm gone. I'm slowly giving it all away, while I'm still breathing."

The studio has given me free rein on my next project. I think about Edith and her story. She interests me for several reasons. There's a question I've been wanting to ask her for a while. It seems rude, but she's an up-front person. It spills out of me. "How do you deal with it?"

"With what, darling?"

"With people always assuming your husband was the one who made the fortune. With people assuming you have all of this"—I motion around the apartment—"because of an inheritance, and not because you were one of the first people to invest in internet companies?"

She tilts her head a bit. "I don't," she says. "It drives me mad." She shrugs. "But I don't live my life for other people. I live it for me. The chatter doesn't really matter." She looks pensive. "Someone close to me once told me that, at the end of the day, the only important thing in life is who you love—and who loves you."

The elevator dings. She smiles at me. "Excuse me, dear."

There are famous poets, authors, screenwriters, and artists in attendance, along with other supporters of the arts. We talk about upcoming school programs. We set dates for different initiatives. It's nice, catching up with people I've seen at the other gatherings I've attended.

I'm at the food spread, considering a line of cheeses and wondering if it would be rude to just take the board as my plate, when a voice sounds behind me.

"Elle Leon?" I turn around, only to see a stylish woman standing there. Her gray hair is tied into a bun, and she's wearing heels I would kill to both have and be able to stand so comfortably in. "It is you! I'm such a big fan."

I smile. This isn't the first time this has happened since my identity was revealed, but it never gets less surprising. Not only that someone has seen a movie I've done, or that my words have been made into movies at all, but also that she knows it was me who wrote them.

It's rewarding to meet viewers. It reminds me who I'm writing for: The girl just like me as a teenager, watching for an escape. The mother and daughter watching to try to understand each other. This fashionable woman in front of me, who tells me that my latest movie helped her through a recent breakup.

"Dating at my age is a challenge," she admits. "But I've never given up on love."

"You shouldn't," I say, even though I did a long time ago.

She's looking at me intently. She smiles. "I feel like I know you," she says, eyes crinkling, and it's not something I haven't heard before. I think of it as a gift, that I've managed to have written material viewers feel so close to. "And not just because of your movies. I—"

"Mother," someone says. He sounds annoyed, like he wants to leave. "We have to get across town for . . ."

And there he is.

Parker Warren.

No, it can't be him. But it is, even though he looks a little different. More severe. His cheekbones are just a little more pronounced, his hair is a little more unkempt. He's scowling, until he looks up at who his mother is speaking to.

His words trail off. He doesn't even make a move to finish his sentence. All he's doing is staring at me with a disbelief and intensity that I recognize, with green eyes that I've tried to forget.

I should have known there was a chance he would be here, but no. He lives in San Francisco. And this is a meeting for a charity benefiting the *arts*.

My heart is hammering. I can't do this. I can't smile and talk to him and pretend, and it's the rudest thing I've ever done, but I say, "Excuse me," to the lovely woman I was in the middle of talking to, and I bolt.

The elevator is taking too long. I press the button a thousand times, but this thing is ancient, and its little bulbs are taking far too long, and we're on the top floor, and I can't really breathe. So, I do the only thing I can.

I take the stairs. I find the right door, and I just start going, faster than I've ever gone in my life. One flight after another.

At some point, I hear the door open. Close.

"Elle."

His voice echoes. I haven't heard him say my name in so long, and that one word makes me go still. *Elle.* In his mouth, my name sounds like someone else. Someone who was happy, someone I'm just barely now starting to remember.

I hesitate long enough for him to make it down three flights of stairs, and then he's right there, right above me.

We just stare at each other.

"You didn't stop running, did you?" he says, his voice just a rasp, his eyes filled with something like hope.

I'm backed up against the wall, bracing it like it might protect me from these raw feelings that are starting to claw through my ribs. "I very clearly just did."

He shakes his head. "No, I mean running regularly. Exercising."

Oh. I wonder if the fact that I'm not folded over my legs and heaving after running down several flights of stairs is his first hint.

He's right. I kept running, even after I left that summer. I run almost every morning now. It's the only thing that clears my head.

It's a part of him I didn't want to end.

There are just ten steps between us. He moves, and then there are just nine.

"You're supposed to be in San Francisco," I tell him accusatorily.

He shakes his head. "I established an office here. I've transferred most of the company's base to New York."

"Why?"

"All my best memories were here," he says simply.

He takes another step. His gaze is gluing me in place. I feel like I'm a specimen trapped beneath a microscope, shifting beneath his unrelenting study.

"Are you happy?" he asks. His voice is sharp, to the point. Another step.

I can't find it within myself to be anything other than honest. "No. Are you?"

"I'm fucking miserable." Another step. "I've been miserable since the day you left me in that jewelry store."

I swallow. His eyes are suddenly on my throat. "I'm sorry," I say, and I mean it. "For . . . the way I just left. I'm sure you hate me. I'm sure you didn't want to see me here, and—"

"I don't hate you, Elle. I could never hate you."

"I would hate me," I say. I *do* sort of hate me, I think. Another step.

Another. He's so close now. Nothing but electricity is filling the space between us, and it scares me how much I want to be near him, even after all this time. I fill it with words instead, the way I always have. "I . . . I saw the town house," I say, even though he obviously knows that, since I just bought it.

Something flashes in his eyes, then. Pain. Another step.

Of course. He didn't just buy the town house . . . he changed it. Renovated it. My voice is just a rasp. "You made it for me."

"I made it for us, Elle."

We're on the same footing now. I crane my neck to look at him. I almost forgot how tall he is.

"Congratulations on your closing." He sounds happy for me, but his eyes haven't lost that intensity, like it is torture for him to stand here and talk to me about the house he made for us and the fact that I'm living there without him. "Are you . . . are you with anyone?"

I shake my head, and his relief is tangible. Me living in that house with *someone else* might have been too much.

"Are you?" I ask, bracing myself, waiting for him to say yes, waiting to hear that he's someone else's summer now.

He shakes his head. "There's no one else, Elle," he says. "There's never been anyone else. Not for me."

Good. I mean, not good, but—

Yes, good.

He's so close, and my body seems to melt beneath me, relaxing like coming back home after a long flight. The day in the jewelry store feels like yesterday. It's so easy, I think, for certain moments to feel more important than entire years.

His breath is warm against my forehead.

A door opens, somewhere. I hear it closing. A few guests are grumbling about the elevator.

This stairwell felt like ours, but the reminder that it's not has shattered the illusion. Parker takes a step back. I straighten.

"It was nice to see you, Parker," I say, outstretching my hand. A handshake. I can do a handshake. If he hugs me, I think I'm going to burst into tears, and I've already been dramatic enough, running down this stairwell.

He takes it.

He doesn't let go as he reaches into his pocket and gets a pen. Without missing a beat, he begins to write something on my wrist, right across my pulse. "My number. You never got it."

And then he's gone.

IT'S MY FIRST NIGHT IN THE TOWN HOUSE.

The movers have just left. I'm surrounded by boxes, or, as I like to call them for this week, my furniture.

I've just taken a shower, and no matter how much I scrubbed, the ink wouldn't come off my wrist. *Stupid expensive pen.* I'm sitting on the floor in my sweatpants, in front of a box/my current coffee table, staring at the numbers, before finally getting the courage to dial them.

It rings only once.

Then: "*Elle.*"

I blink. "How did you know it was me?"

"This is my personal phone. And you're the only person I've given the number to."

I roll my eyes. "You're ridiculous."

"Maybe. What are you doing right now?"

"Sitting on the floor, using a box as a coffee table," I admit.

I hear shuffling, like he's getting up. "Why are you sitting on the floor, Elle?"

"I don't have any furniture yet."

"You bought it furnished," he says. "You didn't like it?" he adds, sounding genuinely concerned.

"No, I did. It just—I just needed something different. So, I donated it. My new stuff comes this week." What I don't say is that the reminder of him was everywhere, and I needed to make this place feel like mine. "What are you doing?"

"I'm at the office."

I frown. It's ten at night. My stomach also chooses that exact moment to growl.

"Hungry?"

"I was moving all day."

"You should have called me," he says. "I would have helped you."

I'm about to say something like I'm sure he has better things to do during the day than to help me move, but I know he would. A moment of silence. Two.

"Can I come over?"

My skin feels like it's on too tight. That's what I wanted, right? No. I should say no. Instead, I say, "I don't know if you heard me when I said I'm sitting on the floor."

"Should I bring food?" he asks, undeterred. "Do you still like pizza? Or do you want something else?"

"Pizza's great."

That's how Parker Warren ends up on my stoop less than twenty minutes later, holding a pizza box. I open the door, take the box, and say, "Thank you, I tipped online," and then slam the door in his face.

When I open it again, he's glaring at me, though it doesn't hold any bite. "Funny, Elle," he says, before stepping past me into the town house.

He looks around appraisingly. "I like what you've done with the place."

It is entirely empty save for three boxes in the living room and two in the kitchen I've stacked to make a barstool.

I nod. "Thank you. I was going for extreme minimalism." I motion toward my box creation. "You take the stool," I say graciously, as I hop up onto the marble counter, next to the pizza box.

The second I do, I feel it. Sparks traveling up my spine. Memories clicking into place. His eyes on me. They're too green, and they've darkened, like he's remembering too. I swallow and move to open the box. We flatten it so we can each use one side as a plate. The crust is still hot. Overflowing cheese sticks to my fingers. It's instinct to look at him as I take the first bite, to nod, to smile, to say in our wordless way how amazing this tastes.

Bite after bite, my stomach sinks. This was a mistake. Everything... everything is coming back, and it's sharper than I thought it would be, it hasn't dulled in the slightest. If anything, it's all gotten stronger.

We eat in silence, and when the pizza box is closed, there is nothing to distract us. There's nothing but a summer of memories between us.

"I'm sorry," Parker finally says.

"For what?"

"For buying the town house. For not understanding. I'm sorry I hurt you." He did hurt me. But I hurt him too. "It took me a while to get it, to understand that it wasn't really the house you wanted but the freedom to buy it. The freedom . . . to do whatever you wanted. The freedom to both dream and achieve that dream, on your own terms. You deserved that feeling of pride. I'm sorry I took that away from you." His voice is serious, sincere.

"Thank you," I say, meaning it. "I'm sorry too. For... for how it all happened."

I was scared that day. Scared that I was choosing love over my career when it had only just started. Afraid that being with someone so successful would diminish me in some way. Terrified that I was letting my mom down.

In the last few years, my career has flourished. I've done better than I ever could have imagined. But none of the deals or screenplays has filled that place in my chest that was full for just a few months. None of that made me as happy as I thought it would.

"Date me, Elle," he says.

"For the summer?" I say, repeating our conversation that feels like forever ago.

He nods. "We're both in New York. We both like spending time with each other. We'll take it slow. We'll go for a run tomorrow morning."

A run. I could do a run.

"Okay."

He helps me off the counter, and his touch is featherlight, but my skin feels electric, like my body has suddenly booted back to life. I haven't wanted anyone in so long. Not like this. Part of me wants to invite him upstairs. Part of me wants to just start where we left off. But I walk him to the front door instead.

This town house came with a key to Gramercy Park, and that's where we run first, before making our way to Madison Square Park. We stop for breakfast tacos at a little truck and eat them sitting on the lawn, surrounded by people lying on mismatched blankets like patches on a quilt, reading books or fast asleep under the pulsing sun.

We run by a furniture store, and I see a mirror I love. He helps me carry it home, both of us fighting to match steps while we get it up the stairs. When my bedroom furniture finally arrives the next day, he helps me build my bed frame. We sit on the floor and count screws and read directions that seem harder than anything either of us studied in college. We finish just minutes before my mattress is delivered, and he helps me carry it up the stairs. He changes the sheets from the washer to the dryer while I'm busy taking in another delivery.

We eat dinner on the floor, off a coffee table that just arrived. He watches me absentmindedly look at the walls, frowning as I chew.

"What is it?" he asks.

I'm staring at the family room. "Nothing."

He gives me a look, and I'm a transparent walkway to him, so there's no use in lying. "I don't like the wall color. But the rest of the furniture comes in tomorrow. I don't have time to change it without making a mess."

That's how we end up at Home Depot at nine o'clock at night. We're standing in front of a swath of endless colors, utterly perplexed at the names. "Ultra Pure White," I say. "Not to be confused with Only Sort Of Pure White."

"Stonehenge Greige," he says. "For when you want your kitchen to remind you of a mysterious cluster of rocks."

I shake my head. "No. Sautéed Mushroom is definitely more fitting for a kitchen."

"But is it sexy?" he says, repeating my words from years before.

I almost choke on nothing. "No," I say, trying to ignore the faint heat I feel spreading across my cheeks. "Whipped Cream definitely gets that distinction."

A sexy kitchen and whipped cream are not the images I meant to summon, but here I am, far too aware of every dip in Parker's gaze as I bend over to look at each color. Finally, I say, "This one." Our hands brush past each other as he reaches for the swatch, and sparks travel down my arm, sinking into the base of my spine. Neither of us looks at the other, though I'm positive he feels this gravity between us, the air stretched taut. These past few days have been almost torturous, spending time in close proximity to someone you're absurdly attracted to without doing anything about it.

"I'll go find some tape," he says.

"Good idea."

PAINTING WALLS IS MUCH HARDER THAN I THOUGHT. SUDDENLY, I understand why so much of the renovation process is shown in time lapse on HGTV.

We lay plastic sheeting down across the floors, covered by a canvas drop cloth. Then we start smoothing the walls. Parker finds the circuit breaker in the basement and shuts off the room's electricity so we can remove the switch covers. We tape the trim.

"This is so much easier on TV," I say, groaning as we begin to pour the paint into trays. "Particularly because while they're painting, I'm sitting on my couch with a latte."

Parker cracks a smile. Then, before I can move, he's flicking paint off the brush, directly onto my loungewear set.

I must look shocked, because Parker starts laughing. I give him a scathing look. "You're laughing now, but I wonder what you'll think when you're scrubbing Fuzzy Unicorn from behind your ears for the next week," I say, making a move toward the closest tray.

Yes. The paint color is really called Fuzzy Unicorn.

He steps in front of the paint tray, becoming an impenetrable wall. He's too quick. I try to fake him out, but his arms end up around my body, and we're laughing, and then, all too suddenly, I'm backing away. We're back to quietly painting.

We're supposed to paint top down. We have brushes, then rollers, and if I had known it would be this much work, I would have kept my mouth shut.

Still . . . painting beside him is fun. *Anything* with him is fun. Even when we're finished with the first coat and literally watching paint dry. I stretch out my body, lying in the center of the floor, on top of the plastic and drop cloth. It's almost like a blanket. From the corner of my vision, I watch Parker flip through the swatch book we grabbed on our way out of Home Depot, in case I wanted to paint any more rooms.

After seeing how much work it is, I'm suddenly very content with the paint colors of the rest of the town house.

"So, do you think there's, like, a college major?" he asks. "Paint namer? Is that a creative writing concentration?"

I snort. "Maybe," I say, eyes on the ceiling. "I think that might be my backup dream job. Naming paint for Benjamin Moore."

I hear a page flip. "Peach Surprise? Really?"

"That actually sounds delicious."

"Milk and Cookies."

"Yum."

"Smokey Wings."

"Okay, this person was clearly ready for lunch."

"So Sublime."

"Nice."

"Pink Prism. Wild Wilderness."

"Clearly, they have an alliteration kink."

"Coffee Beans."

"The paint of my dreams."

"Candlelight Dinner," he says.

"Maybe we should start speaking exclusively in paint tones. There's so much variety."

"Adorable."

"Thank you."

He gives a long-suffering sigh. "Touchable."

"So, we're getting into sexy kitchen territory."

"First Kiss."

I swallow.

"My Sweetheart."

My eyes are fluttering closed. His voice is doing strange things to me.

"Forever Fairytale . . .

"Love at First Sight . . .

"Kiss Good Night . . .

"Heart Breaker."

I can hear him put the booklet down. No more names. For a few moments, he's just silent. When I open my eyes and rise to my elbows, I see him watching the wall, lost in thought.

"What's wrong?" I ask.

"Do you ever regret it? Do you ever wish you never ran out of that jewelry store?"

It wasn't what I was expecting. I would be a liar if I said anything but "Yes."

He closes his eyes, as if that one word has hurt him, or maybe saved him.

"But also no," I say. His eyes open again. "I . . . I had stuff I needed to figure out myself. My career. My own relationship with money. I needed time." Time to see everything I could do alone.

"And now?"

"I don't know," I say honestly. I frown. "When I left . . . I was miserable, but I saw your company flourishing. It seemed . . . it seemed like the universe had righted itself, you know? I thought about trying to reach you sometimes, but you were back in San Francisco, and I—I didn't know if you still cared."

"You didn't think I still cared?" he says slowly. He rises to his feet. I do too. We're standing so close, but it feels like there's a world between us. "Didn't you get my flowers?"

I did. He sent flowers to CAA every single day for an entire year, since he didn't have my address. I had told him I hate when they die, so his solution was to get me new ones each morning. They were always accompanied by handwritten letters. Sarah asked me if I wanted them mailed to my address, but I refused.

"Didn't you see the billboards?"

I sigh. All down Sunset Boulevard, and beyond, the billboards were changed to paintings of my favorite flowers, along with little images only I would understand. Lattes. Baseballs. Cannoli. Some had short phrases, like he was using them as text messages. He must have rented out every billboard in the city at least once.

After a year, they stopped. Everything stopped. And I hoped that was the end of it, even though my feelings never wavered for a moment.

His eyes are burning through me. "I haven't been with anyone since you, Elle."

I swallow. Could that be true? I haven't seen any photographs of him with anyone, but I just assumed he was being more discreet.

"I was busy. And you—*you* seemed busy." It looked like he had thrown himself into his work, and so had I.

He shakes his head, frustrated. "It didn't matter where I was. If you had asked me, I would have gone to LA. I would have walked to you, if you wanted me to."

I'm breathing too heavily now. So is he. His eyes are blazing with intensity. He takes a step toward me.

"There hasn't been a day, an hour, a minute, where I don't think about you, Elle. I've watched all your movies. I know all the words. I've read every script, just to have your voice in my head again. Just to see how you think. I read your interview. I knew you lied about the question about home. I know you came back here to feel a whisper of what our summer was again, to try to find the happiness that hasn't existed since."

"How could you know that?" I demand.

"Because I did too."

He's looking at me like I'm not alone in this regret, this sadness. Like I'm not the only one whose heart and mind were left in another summer. Everything I have of value was trapped there, a snow globe of memories that have now gone still.

"I just want," he says, slowly, taking a step toward me. His eyes are burning, a forest on fire. "A chance to love you beyond that one summer."

My lips crash against his. For a moment, he's still, like he's afraid to move, afraid to break this, and then hands are weaving through my hair, fingers curled around my neck, and he's tilting my head back, and he's tasting me like he might never stop.

My own hands are trailing down his body greedily, like they've been waiting all this time to see if he still feels the same, and he *does,* and I don't want anything between us. I start peeling his paint-splattered clothes off as fast as I can. He starts to undress me too, my shirt is over my head in an instant, his fingers are trailing over the curve of my ass as he drags my sweatpants down. I step out of them and directly into his arms, and then I'm clinging to him. There's nothing tender about this. It is desperate, and wanting, and overdue.

I'm in nothing but my underwear as he sets me down on the kitchen counter, and then that's gone too, and I'm back in his arms again. He makes to carry me toward the stairs, up to my room, but we don't make it that far. Legs locked around him, I start to drag myself down his length, writhing, full of want, and he groans as he presses me against the nearest wall.

I gasp, the wet paint cold against my skin. "Our work—"

"Is just getting started," he says, and then he reaches down to take my breast in his mouth. My back arches off the wall. My nails dig into his shoulders. He drags my nipple through his teeth, biting gently against its sensitive peak, and I'm gasping.

"I need you," I say. Every nerve in my body is on fire. I grind against him, sliding, as if to show him how much, and he curses.

"I'll get a condom?"

"If you want," I say. "But I'm on the pill. And I haven't been with anyone else since you either."

We lock eyes, and I know what we're both thinking. So many days wasted, not doing this. They were necessary, I meant that. But now, with his hand between us, positioning himself, I mourn every moment we weren't together.

We both groan as he pushes in. I dig my nails into his back without meaning to, the stretch nearly painful, and he curses against my shoulder. His hands are gripping my ass as he slowly works me down his length until he finally bottoms out. For a moment, he just stays there, letting me get used to him.

"Please," I say, wriggling, needing to soothe this relentless ache. Then he starts to move, and my nipples drag against his hard chest as he starts to fuck me against the wall.

My head falls back, hair getting smeared in paint, but I don't care, I meet him stroke for stroke, I gasp as he grips my hips. My hands slip as I try to hold the wall, like it might keep me from falling over the edge of this endless pleasure.

We somehow end up on the floor, and I ride him like I've imagined so many times alone, his hands on my waist. He watches me like he's transfixed, and I press my hands against his chest, marking him with the paint as I move shamelessly, desperately. He turns me around, and I groan at the stretch, at the fullness, as he gives me everything I've been missing these last two years.

This is it, I think. This is the best I'm ever going to feel in my entire life.

IT'S ON THE FLOOR, SPENT, CHEST STILL HEAVING, THAT I SEE THE wall we've ruined. My body is very clearly imprinted against it.

"I'm going to have to paint over that a few times," I say, wincing.

Parker's voice is dead serious as he says, "No, you're not. I'm taking it. That's the most beautiful thing I've ever seen. I'm going to hang it in my room."

I turn to face him. "You're ridiculous."

"For you, I am a complete fool, yes," he says.

I stand. The paint on my back is starting to dry. I need to wash it off. Parker stands too. My handprints are against his chest, and I look at them with far too much pride. He follows my gaze and grins. "I wish I could keep these," he says. "I'd tattoo your hands on me, if you wouldn't hate that."

I step closer to him. "We . . . definitely painted over the bad memories. Made new ones. Better ones." I say, remembering his words from before.

"Elle," he says. "There is no such thing as a bad memory with you."

He carries me upstairs, into the shower, and braces my hands against the wall as he gently scrubs the paint off. Then as he pushes into me. I'll never get used to this, to the way my body responds to him, to the way my restless mind goes quiet when we're like this.

When we're done, and the handprints are scrubbed off, he presses my fingers to where they once were and says, "I'm yours, Elle." His lips slip down the water against my throat, down to my collarbones, across my wet shoulder. "I don't want anyone else. I've waited two years for you. I can wait more. Or, forever, if you decide you don't want me." He pulls back to look at me. "I'll be waiting every single day until you're ready."

June turns to July. We decide to take a trip to Upstate New York. We book a cabin that's small enough for us to end up on the floor again, wrapped in blankets in front of a fireplace. We hike in the mornings and make s'mores at night.

Back in the city, we go to Central Park to run. We frequent Parker's coffee shop, which he still owns. They've expanded their scone selection, much to my happiness. I sit and start to write my next screenplay. The words come easier than ever.

When Cali and Pierre come to the city for a wedding, we offer to watch Isabella for the night. I watch Parker play hide-and-seek and blocks and Barbies for the hundredth time, never once looking tired.

Bit by bit, we finish putting our own new touches on the town house. We install new wallpaper in my office. He helps me source rare scripts I want to keep in my new collection. I visit him in his company's headquarters more than once and bring him lunch. He teaches me the beginning of coding, and we marvel at how fast we both can type.

July turns to August. We volunteer at an animal shelter. We fall in love with a dog with a black spot around one eye and wordlessly agree he's coming home with us. We choose his name by going to the paint section of Home Depot. Parker tries and fails to teach Derby to go to the bathroom on a pad, so we take him outside twice every night. Parker usually doesn't wake me, and one night, I feel him slip under the covers, hair slicked with rain, legs tangling back with mine. I feel him press his lips against the top of my head, then, after he turns onto his back again, I hear him say something quiet into the night, something that sounds like "Thank you."

I turn to face him. "What are you doing?" I ask, my question turning into a yawn.

He just looks at me, like it's the most natural thing in the world. "I'm thanking the universe that we got to be here, at the same time."

"Even though I snore?" I ask.

He smiles. "Even then."

"Even though . . . I've changed?" I'm not the same person I was two summers ago. Some parts have gotten better. Others, worse.

"I didn't fall in love with a version of you, Elle," he says. "I fell in love with every you."

My throat goes tight. All he's given me is honesty. He deserves the same. I stare at the ceiling like it's a blank page where I can get the right words out. "I don't even know who I am anymore. I think . . . along the way . . . I lost part of myself." The last eighteen months have been solely about working, not living. "But I know one thing for certain. Our summer, I was me. I was . . . happy." I turn to look at him. "It's not going to be easy, forgetting. Healing. Remembering."

"I know," he says, tracing his lips across my shoulder. Pressing them against my pulse. "I will be there, at every turn. I will be a map to finding your way back to yourself."

Weeks later, we're in Gramercy Park. Derby is staring at a squirrel but not chasing it. Parker is smiling, his eyes crinkling, and I'm just watching him. Something has clicked into place, like a lock I didn't know existed, with a key I didn't realize I was looking for.

"Date me, Parker," I say.

He looks at me. "For the rest of the summer?"

I shrug. "I was going to say forever."

He stills. He seems to know what I mean, but he doesn't move a muscle, like he's afraid he might break something tenuous. But there's nothing fragile about my feelings right now. They are strong and deep-rooted.

"I'm ready," I say steadily. I'm not fixed, I'm not final, but I'm getting there. And I know I don't want to take the journey without him.

Parker smiles then. He walks toward me, Derby not far behind.

"You have no idea how many days I've waited to hear you say that," he says. "Every day for two years, actually." And then he takes a ring out of his pocket. I must look confused, because he says, "It's always been with me, since you left. Just in case you came back."

Before I know it, he's down on one knee. He's offering me the ring. It isn't what I would have ever expected.

Parker Warren bought me the largest diamond in existence. He bought me a chain of coffee shops because they discontinued my favorite scone. He bought me a ring for every day of the summer we spent together. He bought me the ugliest bracelet on the planet because he thought I smiled at it.

Compared with any of that, the ring is modest. It is not meant to be flashy. It is, I realize, tears slipping down my face, meant to be *mine*.

Its diamonds are arranged into the shape of a flower. One that will never die.

I take it from him. Slip it on. And then my lips are on his.

It's the end of August. Summer is almost over.

And this time, I'm ready for it to be endless.

ACKNOWLEDGMENTS

I BEGAN WRITING *SUMMER IN THE CITY* YEARS AGO (DURING AN AUTUMN IN the city), in between writing fantasy books. The rest was written during a summer, winter, and mostly a spring, years later. Every moment spent writing these characters was filled with joy, and I'm so grateful to everyone who made it possible for this story to reach you.

Thank you to Jodi Reamer, my incredible agent, who didn't falter when I said I wanted to publish a contemporary romance. I still don't know how you have time to talk to me every day, but I couldn't be more grateful to have you in my corner. You're Jodi in the City, one of the funniest people I know, and the guiding star that has changed everything. Thank you for finding this book an incredible home.

I am so grateful to everyone at HarperCollins and William Morrow for making this such a magical publishing experience. Thank you to May Chen, my amazing editor, for believing in this book from the very first page, and for your editorial guidance. I smile every time I see your name in my inbox. Thank you to Liate Stehlik, for your fierce championing of me and this book. Thank you to Jen Hart, for your incredible ideas and instincts. Thank you to Kelsey Manning, Jes Lyons, Kaitlin Harri, Danielle Bartlett, and Sam Fox for making it possible for readers to find this book—it is such a joy to work with all of you. Thank you also to Hope Ellis, Jessica Rozler, Andrew DiCecco, and Alessandra Roche, for all you do to get this story ready to be printed and bound.

Thank you to my incredible film/TV agents at CAA, Berni Vann and Michelle Weiner, for making all my wildest dreams come true. Thank you also to Eric Greenspan, for your continued support, since the very beginning. And thank you to Denisse Montfort and Allison Elbl, for all that you do. Thank you also to the rest of the team at Writers House, for all your support and guidance. Thank you to Anqi Xu, for always being so organized when I am not, and for reading everything. Thank you to Maja Nikolic for making it possible for *Summer in the City* to be translated across the world, and to Peggy Boulos Smith for finding its home in the UK.

Thank you to Darcy and the rest of the team at my UK publisher, Bloomsbury. I feel so honored to work with all of you and can't wait to visit the UK soon.

Thank you to my friends and family for your love and understanding when I disappear for months at a time into my writing cave. You know who you are, and I am so lucky to have you in my life.

Thank you to my love for your support for a decade by the time this book comes out. You make the real world better than a fictional one. I am so grateful I get to spend every day with you. I love you.

Finally, I want to say the biggest thank you of all to you, the reader. Everything I write is for you. Thank you for support. It means absolutely everything to me.